PRAISE FOR NEW YORK TIMES BESTSELLER CJ LYONS:

"Everything a great thriller should be—action packed, authentic, and intense."
~ *#1 New York Times bestselling author Lee Child*

"A compelling new voice in thriller writing...I love how the characters come alive on every page."
~ *New York Times bestselling author Jeffery Deaver*

"Top Pick! A fascinating and intense thriller."
~ *RT Book Reviews*

"An intense, emotional thriller...(that) climbs to the edge of intensity."
~ *National Examiner*

"A perfect blend of romance and suspense. My kind of read."
~ *#1 New York Times Bestselling author Sandra Brown*

"Highly engaging characters, heart-stopping scenes...one great rollercoaster ride that will not be stopping anytime soon."
~ *Bookreporter.com*

"Adrenalin pumping."
~ *The Mystery Gazette*

"Riveting."
~ *Publishers Weekly Beyond Her Book*

Lyons "is a master within the genre."
~ *Pittsburgh Magazine*

D1519425

"Will leave you breathless and begging for more."
~ *Romance Novel TV*

"A great fast-paced read....Not to be missed."
~ *Book Addict*

"Breathtakingly fast-paced."
~ *Publishers Weekly*

"Simply superb...riveting drama...a perfect ten."
~ *Romance Reviews Today*

"Characters with beating hearts and three dimensions."
~ *Newsday*

"A pulse-pounding adrenalin rush!"
~ *Lisa Gardner*

"Packed with adrenalin."
~ *David Morrell*

"...Harrowing, emotional, action-packed and brilliantly realized."
~ *Susan Wiggs*

"Explodes on the page...I absolutely could not put it down."
~ *Romance Readers' Connection*

CHASING
SHADOWS

A Shadow Ops Novel

CJ Lyons

This book is a work of fiction. Any references to historical events, real people, or real locales are used fictitiously. Other names, characters, places, and incidents are the product of the author's imagination, and any resemblance to actual events or locales or persons, living or dead, is entirely coincidental and not intended by the author.

Library of Congress Case # 1-273031561

ISBN-13: 978-1496132680
ISBN-10: 1496132688

Published in the United States of America

Want more of CJ's Thrillers with Heart?
Check out her complete list of books:

Lucy Guardino FBI Thrillers:
SNAKE SKIN
BLOOD STAINED
KILL ZONE

Caitlyn Tierney FBI Thrillers:
BLIND FAITH (coming soon)
BLACK SHEEP (coming soon)

Hart and Drake Romantic Suspense Series:
NERVES OF STEEL
SLEIGHT OF HAND
FACE TO FACE

Shadow Ops, Romantic Thrillers:
CHASING SHADOWS
LOST IN SHADOWS
EDGE OF SHADOWS (coming soon)

AJ Palladino Suspense Series
(co-written with Erin Brockovich):
ROCK BOTTOM
HOT WATER

BORROWED TIME, a Romantic Thriller
LUCIDITY, a Ghost of a Love Story

Angels of Mercy, Medical Suspense Series:
LIFELINES
WARNING SIGNS
URGENT CARE
CRITICAL CONDITION

CHASING
SHADOWS

PROLOGUE

MARINE STAFF SERGEANT CHASE Westin lay in his bunk, eyes closed and breathing stilled as the intruder drew close.

Vague disappointment coursed through his veins. Bruno Gianotti needed to hire a better class of hit man—this guy made more noise than a drunken frat boy stumbling to the john.

Cicadas serenaded Chase through the open window beside his bunk. A soft, North Carolina breeze, heavy with July humidity, drifted lazily into the room. As he lay there, debating his options, the most frightening thing was not the possibility of facing death.

What scared the hell out of Chase was that he was hard pressed to find a good reason to make any effort to do something about it.

Had he fallen so far that he couldn't trust in the possibility that tomorrow might have something better to offer? A floorboard creaked, interrupting Chase's existential debate.

The intruder froze.

Chase remained motionless, exhaling a raspy snore to placate any itchy trigger fingers.

What did tomorrow have to offer except the arrival of his

official notification of separation? The medical board had made their final ruling, no more appeals, no going back. Only the dreary prospect of returning to a nowhere town in nowhere Pennsylvania to find a nowhere job. As far away from the real world as Chase could imagine. The closest thing to hell for a Recon Marine.

Make that soon-to-be-former Recon Marine.

The shuffling sound of a muted footfall announced his visitor's arrival at his bedside. All right, maybe the guy wasn't strictly amateur-hour. He had made it from the doorway to the nightstand without crashing into anything. But he sure as hell was no snake-eater. If this was the best Bruno had to send after a Recon Team leader, well, hell. That was just downright insulting.

Now it was a matter of pride. No way he was going to let some Tony Soprano wannabe take him in his bed.

He slid his fingers around the hilt of the K-bar cradled beneath his pillow. Seven inches of carbon steel would be all the weapon he needed against this yahoo.

His eyes still closed, body relaxed as if asleep, he sniffed the air, following his prey's approach. The scent of stale beer, a woman's perfume and a designer's signature aftershave registered.

This guy wasn't one of Bruno's hit men. Adrenalin flooded his veins, jump starting Chase's heart. This was worse. Because they both could be killed if his visitor said the wrong thing.

Chase shot his free hand out into the dark. He found his target, capturing the other man's larynx between clawed fingers and tugging him onto the bed, rolling over on top of him. His visitor sputtered and tried to break Chase's grip. The whites of his eyes glistened in the dim light, reflecting his surprise.

"Hold still and you won't get hurt." Chase's whisper was a mere breath in the wind, inaudible to anyone—or anything—except his intruder.

The other man complied, relaxing his body, signaling his surrender. Chase took no chances, patting him down, removing a Glock from a hip holster, a fully loaded .40 caliber from the heft of it.

"I told you not to contact me, Harriman. I'm done talking."

Chase found no other weapons on the Navy lieutenant and sat back on his heels, allowing Harriman to finally draw a deep breath. Lt. Dwight David Harriman, Hollywood to his friends—a group Chase once upon a time was a part of—said nothing as he massaged his bruised neck.

"Things have changed," Hollywood whispered.

Chase held a finger up in the universal gesture for silence. He couldn't trust that Bruno hadn't bugged his room.

"I don't care," Chase breathed into Hollywood's ear. "I told you everything I know. The rest is up to your boys at NCIS."

Hollywood shook his head. "Come with me. My boss wants to meet you." Chase was silent. "It's important."

If it had been anyone but Hollywood. But they'd been friends too long—Harriman had stuck by Chase longer than most of his old friends once he'd returned from A-ghan. Chase slid off the bed and reached for his BDU's. He was fully dressed and armed with his K-bar and Beretta M9 before Hollywood even made it upright.

Barefoot, Chase padded to the window, carrying his boots. As soon as he'd secured these quarters, he'd loosened the screen and oiled it, allowing him to come and go at will.

Always have an exit strategy. First thing he taught his team members. Once upon a time when his team was still alive.

He slid the screen free from its track and climbed through the window, landing silently on the ground seven feet below. The impact triggered a twang of pain ricocheting through his back, but it wasn't anything Chase wasn't used to. He ignored it the same way he ignored the gnats and mosquitoes swarming around him as he stepped silently into the kudzu-laden bushes. By the time Hollywood plopped down beside him, Chase had his boots laced and tied.

"Where to?" Chase asked.

"Woods beside the obstacle course."

Chase allowed the NCIS man to lead, trying not to wince at the noise he made. To a snake-eater like Chase it sounded like a stampeding herd of elephants. What could he expect? Hollywood wasn't even Marine, just a squid with a fancy uniform and office to go with it. Tonight Harriman wore street clothes, jeans with a black t-shirt, designer hiking boots.

They followed the deserted path to the obstacle course then Hollywood veered off into the thick woods populated by pin oaks and loblolly pine. The faint sound of a live ammo exercise being held beyond the fence in Lejeune's special ops area drifted past them.

Chase's gut tightened as he envisioned the training op running less than a mile away. One that he should have been a part of—would have been a part of if the damned medics weren't such self-righteous, arrogant SOB's that they wouldn't give a guy a second chance. Hollywood stopped, waved Chase to a halt.

They stood in a clearing. The only sounds were Hollywood's stifled breathing and the love-sick cicadas. Chase peered around. There was no one else here, yet he felt an itching along the scars that ran over top his spine. An itching that would not be denied...

He turned, trying to focus his sense of unease. When he pivoted back to Hollywood, she was there.

Just like that. Chase's heart revved into overdrive and he reached for his Beretta. Where the hell? How the hell?

The woman merely smiled at him, the crooked smile of a

magician. Or better yet, a witch.

Chase relaxed a little. Enough to smile back. Damn, she was good. Good enough to be a snake-eater herself.

"Thanks for coming, Sergeant Westin." Her voice barely carried over the raucous calls of the mating insects.

She was 5-3, maybe 110 soaking wet, with long, dark hair frizzled by the humidity and curled around her high cheek bones and above her almond-shaped dark eyes. He couldn't make out much more in the faint light, but she carried herself with the confidence of command.

"Who are you?" The words escaped despite his determination to stand silent, not wanting to reveal he actually gave a damn.

Hollywood stepped to her side. "This is my new boss," he explained. "Rose Prospero."

Chase eyed the woman. She obviously had real world experience, unlike Hollywood and his fellow investigators. It was hard to tell her age, but he would guess she was in her mid to late thirties. That was about as old as the Ancient Mariner in the world of covert ops. Chase himself was only twenty-eight, although these days between the aches and twinges from assorted wounds, scars and surgeries, he felt one hundred and eight. "You're not Navy."

Her smile widened. "Neither is Hollywood, at least not since he's come to work for me."

Hollywood shuffled his feet and looked down. Chase didn't think it was embarrassment at her use of his nickname—the one he'd earned with his Brad Pitt good looks and his lengthy score sheet of sexual conquests. He leveled a stare at Harriman and waited.

Finally, the other man shrugged. "I couldn't tell anyone—not even you." He looked up, met Chase's gaze, his eyes bright with excitement. "But now that you're on the team, you're gonna love it. Rose has put together the best of the best from every branch of the alphabet soup, including a few that I never heard of outside of whispered rumors in the back alleys of the Pentagon."

"Team?" Chase asked cautiously. He didn't do Teams—not anymore, not after losing his men six months ago. The echo of gunfire—M16's peppered with AK-47's—vibrated through the night, blurring in his mind with the memory of automatic weapon fire during the longest night of his life.

The night he'd trusted the wrong person and lost everything. Everything except his life.

"The official name is the Special Threats Response Team," Prospero answered. "No one but a few select members of Congress, the President, National Security Advisor, and Head of Intelligent Services even knows that. We're the last resort, tasked to track down terrorist threats the other agencies can't or won't handle."

Chase straightened. Maybe this was the chance he'd been looking for. "If that means you want to send me back to the sandbox, I'm your man."

"Sorry to disappoint, Sergeant Westin. I'm not planning to send you back to Afghanistan." She paused, her dark eyes scrutinizing him as if searching for hidden flaws.

Chase met her gaze, not really caring what she saw, or thought she saw in him. If she wasn't going to get him back with the troops, boots on the ground where it counted, where he could do some good, then to hell with her. "I already gave you your man. What more do you want?"

"Hollywood told me how you spotted Bruno Gianotti in a bar in Jacksonville, overheard him negotiate with two Marines as they planned to steal weapons for him."

"Right. I did my part. Now you guys go and arrest him."

She shook her head. "We need more. We want more. Gianotti is the major supplier of illegal arms to every gangbanger, drug dealer, and militia fanatic on the East Coast, even has some international connections. We want him and his buyers. To do that we need you."

"Why me?" he asked, although he already knew the answer. Damn it, why'd Bruno have to pick Lejeune of all places? Bad enough the man's business had sent Bruno's own brother to an early grave, now he had to go and mess up Chase's life too? Not that Chase was doing so hot on his own.

Prospero shot him a glance that said she knew he was stalling. "Gee, I don't know, Sergeant. Maybe because you grew up in the same town Gianotti calls home? Maybe because you were best friends with his youngest brother, Nicky, even a pallbearer at his funeral? Maybe because your friendly neighborhood arms dealer has your entire hometown bought and sold and never uses strangers to do his sensitive work, so we haven't been able to get a man inside his operation? Or," she paused, her dark eyes boring into his, "maybe it's because we traced a shipment of Gianotti's stolen C-4 to Deh Rawood, Afghanistan where it was bought by a chieftain named Rahman."

Chase stepped toward her, his throat tightening, hands fisting at the sound of Rahman's name. The bastard. Traitor who'd sold Chase and his men out, not to mention the relief workers they were escorting. "You on the level? Or is this just a scam to get my attention?"

She shook her head solemnly but didn't deign to answer. Hollywood spoke up. "No scam, Chase. I've seen the files myself. Apparently Rahman found Eastern Bloc Semtex too unreliable and wanted better quality merchandise. Gianotti was happy to supply it to him."

Chase's jaws ground together. If Bruno Gianotti had helped in the massacre of Chase's men and the civilians they were protecting, then Chase definitely wanted in. But on his own terms.

"All right," he told Prospero. "But two things you need to know up front. I work alone. I don't want to be part of any team. I don't want any partners I have to keep track of or be distracted by. I'll get you what you need, but you have to let me do it my way."

"Alone," she finished for him.

She pursed her lips, scrutinizing him in a way that reminded him of his mother right before she would wet a finger to slick down his cowlick in an attempt to make him look presentable. Rose Prospero wasn't as old as Sally Westin, but she definitely had the same aura, that of a woman who knew what she wanted and wasn't often disappointed. She nodded her approval. "And the second condition?"

"No part of this operation goes anywhere near my hometown. My brother lives there and the last thing I need is Bruno targeting him."

"That may not be possible. Gianotti lives in Coalton, runs his organization from there."

"I don't care. Any active operations on your behalf—surveillance, busts, whatever—they happen as far away from Coalton as possible or I'm out."

She gave him a grudging nod. "I'll do my best."

"So, what's the plan?" He waited a beat, challenging her with his stare. Despite the fact that he stood half a foot taller, she met his gaze as easily as if they were on equal footing.

Rose smiled, not a smile of happiness or one that made it anywhere close to her eyes. This was the smile of someone tossing down a gauntlet. A predator's grin. "The plan? I'm going to throw you in the brig."

CHAPTER 1

6 months later, Christmas Eve, Coalton, Pennsylvania

CHRISTMAS EVE AND HERE she was, stealing a box of condoms. Not just any condoms. Neil had told her that only the "XTC lubricated and ribbed for her pleasure" would do. The ones in the neon pink box with the not-quite-pornographic photo of a surgically enhanced moaning beauty plastered on the front.

KC sidled down the drugstore aisle, avoiding Old Man Sinderson's eagle-eyed gaze. An outrage, that's what it was. She could pull a wallet from a man's inside jacket pocket by the time she was twelve, being forced to resort to lifting a measly box of condoms was nothing less than an insult to her skills.

Even worse, the best thing for her cover would be to get caught and have to run for it. Salt to injury. No wait, the really worse thing was that the damn condoms would never even be used.

Price she paid. She'd lost the bet—not fair or square, though. She'd tossed in her full house despite the fact she knew she had the winning hand, let Neil rake in the pot and set the terms of her redemption. One box of condoms filched from Old Man Sinderson.

She reached out her hand, ready to make the grab then pulled it back as she heard Neil's laughter coming from the next aisle over. Glancing up, she saw him and the Harris twins elbowing each other as they watched her in the overhead security mirror. KC shot them a glare and Neil laughed harder, his face blossoming scarlet, while one of the twins gave her the finger in a good-natured salute.

Boys, not men. They were nineteen going on nine. Old enough to vote, old enough to die for their country, yet they spent their days playing poker and coming up with asinine bets. They should have been "working"—which translated to sitting on their butts doing nothing all day—but Neil's dad, Mr. Gianotti, had given them the day off. Christmas bonus, he'd called it.

Yeah, right. She'd give a kidney to know what Gianotti really had planned for his Christmas.

Losing this bet to Neil might be a step on the way.

"Hey, what're you boys doing down there?" Old man Sinderson's cigarette-rasped growl chased after Neil and the twins. KC used the distraction to deftly slide the condoms into her jacket pocket before meandering down the aisle to the shampoo display.

Now came the hard part. Getting almost caught without appearing too obvious.

That had been the hardest part of this entire gig. It was easy to put on the clothes, dig the music—especially since she actually did like her rock with a head-banging edge to it—drive the car, talk the talk, and walk the walk of a eighteen year old bad girl, condemned to waste her time as a senior in high school.

No, the hard part was in not being too obvious, not showing that she knew too much, not getting too involved in the lives of the kids around her—including Jay Weston, the kid she was here to save.

High school had been hard enough the first time around. The second time was hell.

The guys left the store, Old Man Sinderson giving them his patented heebie-jeebie glare from his position behind the counter. Bells jangled as the door shut again, blocking out the winter chill.

"And you, missy," Old Man Sinderson bellowed in her direction. "What are you buying?"

KC played it cool, shrugging her shoulders so the chains on her leather jacket clanked as she picked up a bottle of shampoo, scrutinized it as if it were the Rosetta Stone, then replaced on the wrong shelf. She shot Sinderson an over-the-shoulder glance as she did so, smirking at him.

"Here, now. If all you're going to do is rearrange my inventory and make more work for me—" he thundered, his body shaking but never leaving his seat.

"More work for you?" she asked, misplacing several more bottles at lightning speed. "You haven't gotten off that stool of yours in a decade, old man."

His face puffed up and turned as red as a baboon's butt. She thought about telling him, making the comparison, but there was no need, he'd already hit his boiling point.

"Out! Now!" He was bouncing so hard on the stool, his finger jabbing into the air in the direction of the door, jaw quivering, she worried she'd pushed him too far and that he'd stroke out. Then what would she do? Save his worthless, tax-paying ass or protect her cover?

KC did a pirouette, purposefully knocking over the end cap pyramid of hair products, sending pastel colored bottles hurtling in every direction.

"I'm calling the cops!"

"Who cares?" She whirled once more, allowing the condom box to spin free.

Her aim was true and it skittered along the floor, landing

between her and the door. Sinderson had the phone in his hand, but hadn't dialed. His voice deteriorated to a sputter of fury. "You no-good little tramp! I'll have your ass thrown in jail. Give me those," he pointed to the nearly-purloined, pretty-in-pink box of condoms. "Give them to me right now."

KC scooped up the condoms, well aware of her audience beyond the glass doors. "Why? Old man like you wouldn't know what to do with them." She leered at him, hands on her hips, her jacket open to flash her body art and pierced navel. "Want me to come show you?"

That did it. He dropped the phone and instead jabbed his finger on the alarm button below the counter. Bells and klaxons and whoops of sirens stampeded over her, echoing through the small store.

Out on the sidewalk, Neil and the twins scattered, racing in opposite directions. KC blew Sinderson a kiss and pranced out of the store. The things she did for her job. She shoved the condoms into her pocket and ran after Neil Gianotti.

She caught up with him at the cemetery across the street, up on the hill where Jay's folks were buried. Jay and Neil hung out here a lot, sitting on the stone bench beside the memorial Jay had put up for his parents who had died last Christmas. She saw fresh flowers, apricot roses on Sally and Hank Westin's graves and a small bunch of violets on Diana's tombstone, the big sister Jay never knew.

Jay wasn't here, but he'd obviously been here earlier. She wondered if he'd ever be able to come back again. Once she finished her job here.

Neil scattered her morbid thoughts with laughter. He was a good kid, kind of rolly-polly and squat compared to Jay's lean height. Frick and Frack, the townspeople called them. Best friends forever. Of course, Neil was friends with everyone in town—given that his old man pretty much owned the town, that was no surprise. What was a surprise was that he genuinely seemed to value every friend he made, savored them as much as the Gummi Bears he constantly snuck while on his perpetual diet.

Bruno Gianotti's one failure in life: his rotund, not so smart, but very personable and softhearted only child. When Jay was held back from graduating in June, Neil had begun classes at Penn State's Altoona's campus. But he was lost without Jay and his other hometown friends. Flunked out his first semester and returned home to "work" for his father, supposedly organizing the inventory of spare parts Gianotti's moving vans needed.

Lately, though, Neil had let drop rumors that his dad was going to give him more responsibility in the family business, toughen him up for some "real" work. KC strongly suspected the poor kid still had absolutely no idea what his father's real work was: supplying weapons to bloodthirsty predators.

She ruffled her fingers through Neil's dark hair, and he laughed harder, blushing from the attention. If she did her job right, Neil would never have the opportunity to witness Bruno Gianotti's work up close and personal like Jay had.

"So who's the lucky girl?" she asked as she handed him the hard-won box of condoms.

He stopped laughing, his blush deepened, and he wouldn't meet her eyes. Instead he took the condoms as if they might bite him, shoving them deep into the pocket of his North Face parka. Then his laughter started up again as he looked past her down the hill to Old Man Sinderson's drug store. "Sure you and Jay don't need them?"

As if. But she played her role and widened her grin as she pulled a handful of condoms from her inside pocket. "Nah. I think this will be enough." His eyes widened and she couldn't resist— that's what acting like a teenager would do to you, it pulled you right back into a mindset where potty-humor was considered sophisticated. "For tonight, at least."

"Er. Right. Lucky Jay."

Could a stand-up guy like Neil be falling for his best friend's gal? He leaned against the grave marker guarding Jay's parents' final resting place and she wondered at that. Jay would be gone tomorrow, maybe she should continue her charade a while longer than initially planned? Neil could give her the inside scoop on his father's organization.

She stretched out lengthwise on the granite bench, her Doc Martens planted firmly on the end of the slab, knees bent, arms wide, letting her jacket flap open. There was no sunlight, there never was in Coalton, the entire town constantly submerged beneath a haze of gray as if the coalmines were still in full action. The frozen stone beneath her bit into her flesh, but KC ignored it, her attention focused on Neil.

She lay there as if basking in the light of an invisible sun. He watched with obvious interest. His gaze roamed from her face to the chameleon tattoo coloring the exposed flesh of her belly. She stretched and the form-fitting leather vest she wore rode higher. Neil's gaze followed, his head bobbing in time with her breathing. Men. Sometimes it was just so damn easy.

"What'cha doing for Christmas?" she asked, letting one arm dangle to the side, grazing the snow piled around the bench. She was freezing her ass off, but she had a feeling it might be worth it.

He hunched his shoulders as if nervous but his face brightened into a smile. "My dad and I. We're going to go to a business meeting he has set up. Together."

Gianotti had a business meeting scheduled for Christmas day? Now that was news. She sat up abruptly, tugging her vest back into place, trying not to shiver in the cold. She wasn't sure if she'd ever feel warm again, not after six weeks suffering through Coalton, Pennyslvania's terminal gray winter.

"That's nice," she said. "What kind of meeting?"

Neil opened his mouth then clamped it shut, shoulders hunching once more. "Doesn't matter. It will be cool just working with my dad."

Silence. The bells on St. Augustine's steeple rang the hour. She was supposed to pick up Jay, drive him to Neil's where the boys were going to have Christmas Eve dinner while she went home to eat with her "father" like a dutiful daughter would.

"What's up with Jay?" she asked, inserting a stammer into her voice.

"What do you mean?"

"I don't know. He's been acting funny lately. Like maybe," she trailed off, eyes cast down, but staring at Neil up through her lashes. "Like maybe he's not too happy with me."

Neil sank down beside her, his expression one of genuine concern. KC felt a quiver of guilt over her manipulation, but quickly squelched it. Cost of doing business. And in this case, her business might just save Neil's life.

He wrapped an arm around her shoulders, hugged her to him. "Of course he's happy with you, KC. You're the best thing that ever happened to him."

A glimmer of a plan began to form. KC forced a few tears, made sure Neil saw them before swiping them away. "If you say so. I'd better go get him or he'll be late for dinner at your place. You know how your dad feels about anyone being late."

At the mention of Bruno Gianotti Neil stood up, hands jammed deep into his pockets, poofing the down parka up around his ears like a turtle skedaddling into its shell. "Yeah, you're right. We'd better get going."

She stood beside him, looking down at the town arrayed below them. The setting sun and surrounding mountains cast the town of Coalton, population 281, into an impenetrable shadow. She hooked her arm through Neil's and pivoted to give him a quick kiss on the cheek. "Thanks, Neil. You're a sweetie."

The blush that fired his face and neck reminded her that she needed to be careful. This wasn't just a job; there were also innocent lives and hearts at risk.

A weight fell on KC's shoulders and it wasn't just from the leather and chains she wore. She peered out at the cold, unfeeling town below her, a town that had harbored a killer, and she narrowed her eyes. Gianotti and Coalton weren't going to get Jay Westin or, if she could help it, Neil—not like they had taken so many other lives.

Not while she was on the job.

CHAPTER 2

HOME FOR THE HOLIDAYS.

Chase grimaced as he pulled his Maxim binoculars from the Harley's saddlebags and focused on a gray-sided ranch house that sat below the abandoned strip mine he and Lucky had chosen for their rendezvous. He hurled a silent curse at the quirk of fate that had brought him full circle, back home to Pennsylvania in time for Christmas.

No, not fate. He couldn't even blame Rose Prospero, who, despite her promise, had saddled him with a partner, a rookie at that.

No, this mess was his own damn fault.

He'd been working Deacon for weeks, finally convinced him Bruno Gianotti could supply all the arms and demolitions he needed for his whacked out militia group. Only Chase never expected Deacon to set up the final exchange here in Coalton—or Bruno to schedule it for Christmas Day.

"No cops around, unless we meet at Denny's." Bruno had laughed when Chase told him that he'd secured Deacon's trust and The Crusade's lucrative contract for more munitions than it would take to overthrow a third world nation. Then Bruno had slapped Chase on the back. "Good job, kid. Glad everything's finally working out for you."

Oh, yeah. Things were working out just dandy.

Chase didn't mind playing his role as disgraced former Marine, not as long as it got him the information he needed to get those weapons off the streets and Bruno behind bars.

For a short while, it had even been fun returning to the hell-raiser he'd been once upon a time. Riding fast bikes, flirting with fast women, closing down bars and knocking heads together if anyone tried to cheat Bruno during a deal. But after six months of living with the constant tension between his shoulder blades, waiting for the bullet he'd never hear, Chase was ready for this job to be finished.

Plus, it was damned hard to keep up the act when your kid brother looked at you like you were pond scum. Like Jay had the one time he'd visited Chase while he was in Leavenworth. Chase had still been in general population then, but had quickly gotten himself transferred to solitary after jumping a fellow inmate. Solitary. He'd thought it would be safer, easier time. How wrong he'd been. Forty-eight days locked up with nothing but memories. Then emerging only to live a life of lies.

Chase inhaled deeply. The wood smoke from the houses below conjured a vision of a Christmas long past: Dad and Jay roasting chestnuts, forgetting them as they got caught up in a John Wayne marathon on the classic movie channel, almost burning the house down.

An electric blue '91 Mustang rumbled up to the curb in front of his childhood home. Chase straightened, instantly on alert, then relaxed. Definitely a kid's car. No threat there.

The Mustang reminded him of the Chevy Malibu he and

Bruno's youngest brother, Nicky, had resurrected from the scrap heap back when they were kids, convinced of their own immortality, too drunk with life to know any better.

"I can't believe you lived here," his partner, Ed "Lucky" Cavanaugh, said as they watched from the hillside across the road from Chase's old house. Lucky shuddered. "All this fresh air and space, it's suffocating."

Chase ignored Lucky's grousing. The ATF agent was a city boy, a demolitions expert with an affinity for anything explosive, things that blew up loud and bright. Growing up in a small town like Coalton would have been a fate worse than death for Lucky.

"Bad luck the meet's here in your hometown." Lucky zipped his leather jacket against the stiff breeze racing along the ridge top.

"Luck had nothing to do with it. Bruno Gianotti lives here. My best friend growing up was his youngest brother."

"He live around here, too?"

Chase shook his head, swallowed hard against the pang of regret. Nicky and Chase were inseparable until Nicky left for college at Temple. "He's dead."

"Oh. Sorry."

They looked out over the neighborhood festooned with bright Christmas lights. The Twelve Days of Christmas display in front of the Wallace's doublewide was unchanged since Chase's youth—except one of the pipers was missing. Next door, Mr. Roldophski had decked out every surface a man on an extension ladder could reach with Technicolor lights that chased each other around the yard in an endless game of tag.

The people of Coalton might be collecting welfare, supplemented by the occasional cash job from Bruno Gianotti, but they spared neither expense nor electricity when it came to holiday cheer. Only Chase's house was barren of decor, a lone dim light visible on its front porch.

A dark-colored cat crossed the road in front of the house below. "I got a bad feeling about this one," Lucky said.

"So you keep saying. I'd be frightened if you had a good feeling about something."

Lucky stroked the rabbit's foot hanging from his jacket zipper. "I'm not joking."

Chase lowered the binoculars for a moment to stare at his partner. Lucky was new to life undercover. He did most of his work from the comfort of an ATF lab, analyzing and reconstructing bombs under much more controlled conditions, had only gotten pulled into this op because Deacon had been looking for a demo man to design bombs for The Crusade. Chase had passed word to Rose Prospero who had hijacked Lucky from his fancy lab in DC and here they were.

Coalton, Pennsylvania. A town so small MapQuest couldn't find it. A town forgotten by everyone once the mines shut down ten years ago. But once a coal town, always a coal town. Every building in Coalton still cowered beneath a soot-colored haze.

The itching between Chase's shoulder blades intensified. Were Lucky's opening night jitters contagious? Or was it something more?

Nothing Chase could do about it now. "We have to find out what The Crusade is planning to do with those weapons." He paused. "And stop them."

Both men were silent. Chase had sacrificed half a year of his life setting up Bruno and his largest customer, the paranoia-driven militia known as The Crusade. Any other man might have been excited by the idea of such a long operation ending, of the prospect of returning to his "real" life.

Too bad Chase didn't have a life to go back to. Every time he thought about a future after the exchange tomorrow all he saw was an impenetrable blackness.

Like maybe there wasn't gonna be any days after tomorrow for him. Like maybe he'd been living on borrowed time ever since Afghanistan.

Chase had the distinct feeling time was running out. Deacon was about to get his hands on some scary stuff. Not just automatic weapons and assault rifles, but also ordinance, C-4 and the mother-lode, fourteen hand-held SAMs.

Something big was coming soon. And Chase was no closer to finding out exactly what than the day he began this charade six months ago.

It had taken Chase two months to get close to Deacon, The Crusade's leader. Now all he had to do was help Lucky deliver the weapons to The Crusade, learn their plans, pass the word to Rose Prospero, nail Bruno, and get him and Lucky out alive again.

It was that last little detail Chase wasn't so certain about. Lucky had every right to have a bad feeling about this. There was a good chance neither of them would be around to see next Christmas.

Movement from the Mustang below distracted him from his morbid thoughts. Raising the Maxims, he watched a slim woman in jeans and a black leather jacket adorned with metal rings and chains slide out of the driver's seat. Her short, spiky hair was dark purple. She leaned against the car, crossing her arms on the roof, her face turned to the house. Her cropped jacket lifted to reveal a belt made of a chain. Dangling from it at the small of her back was a pair of shiny, steel handcuffs, the wrist loops dancing across her ass in a mesmerizing arc Chase could not help but appreciate.

"Where in hell did she come from?"

Lucky's low-pitched wolf-whistle was his only answer.

Chase kept watching, unable to pull his eyes away from the

sight. He was getting that tingle along his spine again. Somehow it wasn't as irritating as usual, more like the slow dance of a woman's fingers instead of the skin-prickling itch he usually felt. Heat surged below his belt as the woman swiveled her hips in time to unheard music. The binoculars threatened to slip from his sweaty grasp.

What could you expect when the closest he'd gotten to a woman in months had been pay-per-view porn and his own right hand?

Or rather, the closest he'd allowed a woman to get to him. No way he was going to pay for sex, and the women who had offered were all connected to either Bruno or the Crusade. Trampling through a nest of vipers be safer than trusting one of them.

A last, stray remnant of the setting sun glinted from the handcuffs dangling over the best ass he'd seen in a long, long time. Aw man, this just wasn't fair, he was on the job here, couldn't be distracted by the images steamrolling through his mind.

Images like laying her spread-eagled against the hood of the Mustang, her body shivering, quivering beneath his hands as he slowly undressed her, the warmth of her soft, silky skin against his calloused fingers, the ripple of her laughter.

He sucked in his breath and forced himself to hand the binocs to Lucky. No way he was going to let himself be distracted by some punk rocker wannabe chick with crazy purple hair and an ass so tight that he could feel how firm it would feel, filling his hands...

He turned his face into the wind, letting the frigid air beat against his eyes until they teared and his vision blurred. All the better not to see her sashaying around the car, those handcuffs swaying in a tantalizing arc.

Focus, Westin. He had Lucky to look after—and even more importantly, Jay.

The cold air helped to quench the blaze growing within. How

long had it been since he'd held a woman in his arms without worrying that she would get him killed?

He risked another glance at the girl below. Looking couldn't hurt. Oh, but what he wouldn't give to be the one trapped by those cuffs, his hands pressed against her painted-on jeans.

"What do you think?" Lucky asked. "Some rock 'n roll groupie took the wrong exit off the highway?"

"Sure as hell isn't from around here."

"Who's the kid?"

Chase tore his gaze away from the girl's ass to see a tall boy with sandy-colored hair, wearing jeans and a denim jacket, emerge from the house. The kid glanced up, and it was like looking in a mirror at a Chase nine years younger. A Chase not toughened by the Corps or the stress his choice of lifestyle and career had brought. A Chase without scars or nightmares.

"My brother. Jay."

Jay crossed the snow-covered yard, his footsteps leaving purple, bruised shadows that matched the girl's hair. She strolled around the front of the car, slipped her hands into her back pockets and waited. Jay's face lit up at the sight of her. Chase wanted to kick himself for his previous fantasies.

"Kid's got good taste," Lucky remarked as Jay gave the girl a quick embrace.

She looked up at Jay, laid a hand on his arm in a concerned fashion, and Chase felt a spasm of envy. No woman had ever looked at him quite that way. Even before his court martial and short stint in Leavenworth.

Jay nodded at whatever the girl said, and she handed him the car keys. He held her door open for her.

"Polite, too," Lucky continued. With a throaty growl, the Mustang's gears grinding, its rear fish-tailing in the slush, the car drove away. "Is he gonna be a problem?"

"No," Chase said, returning the Maxims to his saddlebag. "I'll handle it. You get back to Deacon, tell him the deal's on for tomorrow."

Lucky stood still for a moment. Chase beat him to the punch before he could express more misgivings.

"Relax, everything's going to be over and done with by the day after Christmas."

Lucky shook his head forlornly. "Boxing Day, the English call it. Let's hope it's not us going home in a box."

CHAPTER 3

AS JAY LEFT HIS house and approached KC, he felt excited, worse than a kid waiting for Santa Claus. A little scared, too.

Having KC with him helped a lot. She really cared about what happened to him, about his dreams and making them come true. Thanks to KC, after tomorrow he'd leave this one horse town and never look back.

No regrets, except maybe one. He wanted to see Chase one more time.

Part of him did, at least. The other part wanted to punch his big brother in the face. Knock him down and tell Chase what he really thought of him—dishonoring the memory of their parents with his stupid scheme to rip off the Marines and sell their guns.

Forget about Chase. After tomorrow, he'd never see him or this place again.

Up and down the street, houses were decked out with plastic Santas, snowmen and a rainbow of blinking lights. The twilight of the winter night made Jay's unadorned home seem small, lonely as Charlie Brown's pathetic Christmas tree. He hadn't had the heart to get any of the decorations down from the attic. The last time he'd seen them was last year when he and Chase carefully packed them away after their parents' funeral.

"You all right?" KC asked, sliding one hand down his arm to squeeze his hand.

That was the thing about KC. Yeah, she was hot, with a body that was lean and tight, but she didn't treat him like any of the girls at school did. She didn't look at him with pity because he'd been on his own this past year after his folks died and Chase left to screw up his own life. Didn't think he was a loser because instead of graduating with Neil and his other friends last June, he'd had to repeat most of his senior year and at nineteen was older than a lot of the other kids.

KC didn't mother him. She cared about him, took the time to listen, to find out what he really wanted.

And she was helping to make those dreams come true. No more boring high school classes, no cafeteria nightmares with the cliques and mini-dramas the other kids seemed to think passed for real life. Jay was out of this place with its three bars, two stop lights, and one grocery store, its dreary weather and even drearier future.

"You nervous?" KC asked. She zipped her black leather jacket up tight, the Mustang's heater wasn't the most efficient.

Jay shrugged in answer to her question and cranked the Godsmack on the stereo. KC didn't say anything. Another nice thing about her, she knew when to shut up. Unlike girls his own age. They all seemed like such children compared to KC.

They drove through downtown, taking all of two minutes despite being caught at the red light in front of Coalton Drugs, the town's communication center. Old Man Sinderson had had a field day after the scandal with Chase. Those Westin boys, run wild with no parents to watch over them, knew no good would ever come of them, he proclaimed to anyone who came near his perch behind the counter. The oldest kicked out of the Marines, served time for almost killing a soldier, the youngest almost flunked out of school, even though he's meant to be some kind of genius.

The Mustang passed St. Augustine's and Grace Lutheran churches with their shared Nativity scene. Christmas Day everyone in town would crowd into one or the other, even those not of the religious persuasion, and at noon precisely, the children of Coalton would parade out from the church doors and escort Baby Jesus to his proper place in the Nativity.

Jay would miss that, he'd been a part of the procession when he was young, still felt the sting of tears when he watched with the grownups as the children, faces earnest and joyful, sang "Away in a Manger".

One thing he wouldn't miss was the combined high school and middle school across the street, "Home of the Fighting Miners".

They drove toward the graveyard where his parents were buried. Even Old Man Sinderson wouldn't say that Sally and Hank Westin deserved the fate that befell them Christmas Eve last year. One of the Kleindeist boys, underage and drunk on Everclear, plowed into them going close to ninety miles an hour. He'd emerged, wobbly but unscathed from his car. The Westins never had a chance.

"Want to stop?" KC asked as the field crowded with marble markers came up on their left.

Jay averted his eyes, blinked hard. Earlier today he'd tried to say goodbye to his parents, to Diana, the older sister he'd never known. He'd ended up just sitting there like a zombie, feeling sorry for himself. He didn't like thinking about stuff like death and what lay beyond, but in the last two months he'd been forced to face the very real possibility that one slip and Bruno Gianotti would have him killed.

If there was some kind of life after death or any sort of decent god, then he hoped maybe his parents were still looking out after him from wherever they were. Maybe they were the ones who sent him KC and his chance for a new life.

"S'okay. We're late anyway."

Except for the Korn now blaring from the radio, there was silence until they reached the neighborhood where Neil Gianotti, Jay's best friend since sixth grade, lived. At the end of the street there was one really big house set back from the plain old Cape Cod's and ranches where regular folks lived.

The mansion was Neil's house. Mrs. Gianotti had split years ago. Mr. Gianotti ran a moving and storage company, was on the road a lot—at least that was what Jay had thought until two months ago.

KC's house was next door, she'd only moved in last month, and he parked in the driveway of her Cape Cod. Neil's father didn't like strange cars crowding his drive.

They crunched through the snow and headed to Neil's back door. KC's Doc Martens left deep impressions in the snow despite the fact that she was pretty skinny. Not thin in a bad way like some of the girls at school who acted like they'd explode if they actually finished a meal. KC loved to eat, just she was always moving, as if she'd be too good a target if she sat still too long.

Jay swallowed against a wave of nervousness. He'd have to learn how to live with that feeling of having a constant target on his back. Learn how to not let anyone get too close, not trust anyone with the truth.

No more best friends like Neil. Maybe no more friends, period—how could you call yourself a friend if you couldn't tell the truth? His stomach did a small flip-flop as he thought about leaving

Neil, trying to say goodbye without saying goodbye.

KC had told him a little about what to expect, how to handle it, but they both knew he'd have to find his own way of dealing with the jitters. The loneliness. And the guilt.

KC's way was to box. She'd pound on the heavy bag Chase left behind until sweat dripped from her spiked hair and her muscles shook with fatigue. Jay had never told her, but sometimes when she worked out, he'd watch from across the basement as he lifted weights, and he thought she looked really sexy then, right at the point where she worked up a frenzy, chasing her demons, whupping them good.

As Neil ushered them into the kitchen, Jay wished he and KC could be more than just friends. Everyone in town thought they were serious, sleeping together, but Jay knew it would never happen. Still, he enjoyed thinking about what it would be like, if only—

"Earth to Jay," Neil interrupted his fantasy. "I asked did you want some pop?"

KC wished Jay didn't feel such loyalty to his friend. But then, if Jay and Neil weren't friends and if Neil's father wasn't the largest illegal arms dealer on the East Coast, she wouldn't be here.

Which maybe wouldn't be such a bad thing. Jay could go on with his life, enjoying in innocence all the things most high school seniors looked forward to: Prom, Graduation, going away to school. She looked over at the tall, thin boy, restraining her impulse to run a hand over his unruly hair. Kid was a neat freak about everything except remembering to get a haircut.

Don't let it get personal, she reminded herself. She patted Jay's jacket, ensuring that the phone she'd given him was there.

"Buzz me when you're ready," she said, standing on her tiptoes to give him a quick peck on the cheek.

"Hey, KC, why don't you stay?" Neil said. "There's plenty of food and stuff."

He spread his hands to indicate the well-stocked kitchen. The room was larger than the entire downstairs of the Cape Cod KC lived in next door. Although she knew servants lurked nearby, awaiting any command, the large house felt empty, devoid of life.

Except for the two teens before her. She gave Neil a genuine smile. The kid was one of those people who wanted nothing more than to please everyone who mattered in his life. KC had the feeling that, growing up attended mainly by servants with an often absent dad, Neil was starved for affection. No wonder he followed Jay around like a lost puppy.

It was going to break Neil's heart when Jay disappeared and KC sent Bruno Gianotti to prison.

CHAPTER 4

KC BANGED OPEN THE kitchen door to her house. A gray-haired man appeared, shaking his head at her appearance, then shrugging, a parent surrendering the battle as far as anyone watching from outside could see. He moved back into the kitchen, and she followed.

"What's up, Pop?" she asked, grabbing a slice of pizza from the box on the counter.

"Do you have any idea what time it is?"

KC shrugged, crammed the pizza into her mouth, snatched a second slice and headed downstairs to the family room.

"Don't you walk away from me, young lady," he said, dogging her steps, closing the soundproofed basement door behind him.

As soon as he shut it he sagged against it, his demeanor transformed as he tried hard not to laugh. "Oh yeah, the police called. Something about you were out stealing condoms from Old Man Sinderson?"

Glenn Michaels wasn't as old as he looked, especially not when his smile met his eyes, like now. KC galloped down the steps. Glenn followed.

"Why? You need some?" she threw over her shoulder.

"Woo-hoo, KC, dig the belt," a second man sitting in front of a massive computer console, one ear covered by a headset, said. Carson was a ginger-haired man with a full beard that defied Bureau guidelines. A fact he could care less about, which made him perfect for her operation. "Those regulation?"

KC glanced back at the handcuffs dangling behind her. "No. Came with the belt. They're like tin or something, but they came in handy, drove the guards at school nuts every time I went through the metal detector." She shrugged, jangling the chains and rings adorning her leather jacket. "After the first few times, they gave up and just let me through."

A lot of thought had gone into deciding on the perfect persona to gain her instant notoriety in a town like Coalton. No one here would forget "bad girl" KC who had stolen away with Jay Westin. If she did her job right, few would think twice about Jay's sudden disappearance, chalking it up to a teenager's hormones run amok.

She walked across the expansive room, ignoring the shelves stacked with video and audio monitoring equipment, the weapons rack, and the large-scale map of Coalton and the surrounding area. The basement was the only place in the house clean of Gianotti's bugs.

"Good to see you, Carson. Glad you could make it." She held the slice of pizza up to the FBI communications expert so that he could share a bite while his hands fine-tuned the feed from the omnidirectional microphone planted in Jay's phone.

"Wouldn't miss your grand finale, especially on a hush-hush like this one. I mean, come on, smuggling me in here in the trunk of Glenn's car? What gives, how's come no ATF or backup?"

Glenn joined them, looked to KC as if he also waited for an

answer. KC swallowed her pizza. Glenn Michaels was only in his early forties, but his premature grayness came in handy on operations like this one. Although both men had seniority over her, neither had questioned her leadership until now, when their lives were going to be placed on the line in less than twenty-four hours.

She turned away to shrug free of her jacket, the burden of exactly what she had taken on weighing her down. Rubbing her palms over her bare arms, she felt herself breaking out in a sweat and blamed it on the proximity to the furnace instead of nerves.

"Too many leaks out of Justice," KC told them. "After what happened to Manny, I'm not taking any chances."

Both men nodded solemnly. KC had been on Manny Ramirez's team working an identity theft ring, building a case against the odd assortment of disgruntled white-collar workers, computer geeks, and street hypes banded together with two things in common: a love of money and the methamphetamine it could buy them.

KC still blamed herself for letting Manny go alone to the meet. She'd had a bad feeling. But he was her boss, it was his operation, and she'd trusted him when he had said everything was kosher. He had insisted she stay out of sight in the alley across the street.

Close enough to see the van drive by, the gun aimed out the door, Manny falling to his knees. Too far away to do a damned thing to save his life.

After a moment of silence, Glenn changed the subject. "We still have nothing on the buyer."

"Hells bells, I need to know what we're getting into here. The buy is tomorrow. Neil confirmed it for me." KC didn't have to look to know Carson was rolling his eyes at her. She knew her reputation as a control freak, planning for every contingency in her operations. It was the only way she could ensure everyone went home alive.

Her operations never went south. Trust no one, assume

nothing—that was what she'd learned from Manny. Too bad he hadn't listened to his own advice.

"After you left Gianotti's," Carson said, indicating the recorder, "Neil told Jay his father was taking him into the business, that he had a big surprise for him on Christmas. Is he talking about our meet?"

"Damn it, we don't need another kid to watch over," Glenn complained.

Amen to that. Watching over Jay Westin, using him to get close to the Gianotti family had been a tightrope act KC had no desire to repeat.

Not to mention the several weeks of high school she had to endure to maintain her cover. Senior year was bad enough the first time around, back home in Buffalo. If it wasn't for her grandfather, she doubted she would've made it through. Now that she had the objectivity of a college education and three years with the Bureau under her belt, KC wondered how any kid survived to graduation. Compared to the emotional obstacle course she'd endured at Coalton High, the rigors of Quantico's Hogan's Alley urban combat training seemed as challenging as a game of hopscotch.

"Once we get Jay out and under, I'll press Neil for more details," KC said. "We need to know this buyer."

She couldn't let Neil Gianotti get caught in the crossfire when she went after his father. Kid had it hard enough already. Unfortunately KC was about to make his life a helluva lot worse.

"I thought we're just taking down Gianotti and his suppliers. What's the sudden panic about the mystery buyer?" Carson asked.

"Thanks to KC planting a bug in Gianotti's car," Glenn said, "we finally got wind of what's on the shopping list. Enough automatic weapons, C4, and other goodies to lay siege to Brooklyn. We've got to nail the buyer before he goes shopping somewhere else."

KC thought for a moment, the plan she'd begun formulating while talking with Neil at the cemetery taking shape. "Make sure the Marshals are ready for Jay tomorrow morning, I'll send him in my car."

"You're not going with him?"

"He only has to get to Altoona, for chrissakes. I think my pop," she smiled at Glenn as her plan crystallized, "and I are gonna have a huge fight when he finds out about Jay and me. Has Jay gotten me pregnant?"

She paced the room, considering and rejecting scenarios.

"Yeah, that'll work. I'm preggo, Pops throws me out, Jay takes a powder, and I've nowhere to go except Jay's best friend. I'll convince Neil to stand up his old man in order to help me. Once he's safe on ice, we'll be clear to go tactical on the bust without worrying about civvies in the way."

The two men contributed a few suggestions to the scenario and went with her lead. KC's phone buzzed. She left them planning contingencies and details while she returned to her role of disgruntled teen in love.

The game was heading into sudden death overtime. With KC now responsible for the lives of two civilian kids.

CHAPTER 5

ONE MAN'S LIFE REDUCED to its essential components: thirty-eight ounces of grit and dust.

Rose Prospero cradled the steel box in her lap, wincing at the rattle its contents made. The C-130 bounced against the tarmac of Andrews Air Force Field as it came in for a landing. Rose removed her headphones. She separated herself from the webbing that had held her safely in the confines of the jump seat during the long flight from Hell's Bend, Texas.

The box held the remains of former Navy SEAL Chief Petty Officer Victor Krakov. One of her people, the third Rose had lost in the two years she'd been running the Special Threat Response Team. Her ears buzzed with the vibrations that came from flying two thousand miles in the rear of a cargo plane, but Rose still could make out the distinctive honk of an Audi TTS when the crew opened the hatch.

Damn Price, she'd told him she would catch a cab. It was Christmas Eve; didn't the man have better things to do than play chauffeur?

Billy Price had been adamant that Rose not travel to Hell's Bend to investigate Victor's death herself. She was the Boss, it wasn't her place, he'd argued, insisting that he go instead, but as with most of her arguments with her Number Two, Rose had prevailed.

She needed to know if Victor's death was truly a mere bar fight gone bad or if there was a more sinister plot lurking behind it, something that might threaten others on her Team. Despite her best efforts, she'd returned with more questions than answers. Along with the cremated remains of one good man.

Rose caught her balance as the ladder leading down to the tarmac shuddered in the December wind. Following their orders that they were merely ferrying cargo, the crew of the C-130 studiously ignored her. The furtive glances they gave her and Billy had "spook" written all over them.

Officer and gentleman that he was, Billy sloshed through the snow to open Rose's door for her and handed her into the sports car. The Audi was all-wheel drive, ready to go anywhere and face anything nature threw at it. It was a two-seater with little cargo space, but Billy, an ex-Delta Force man, didn't believe in being weighed down with excess baggage. Like all of Rose's recruits into the Special Threats Response Team, he was unattached.

Sometimes it seemed to Rose that the sports car was the main love of his life. The thought, as always, made her feel melancholy. Of all the men she knew, Billy Price deserved more.

"You look like hell," Billy said as he slid behind the wheel and put the car into first gear. Rose ignored him, leaned back and closed her eyes. "So what gives? Accident or trouble brewing?"

They both knew that too many undercover agents from too many US agencies were ending up dead. Before Victor, a FBI agent who infiltrated The Crusade was murdered six months ago.

"Trouble, but I'm not sure from where. Victor was ambushed, the bar fight staged. My gut tells me The Crusade was involved. Everyone all right back at the ranch?"

"Kids all safe and sound. Three new red flags and one orange, but they can wait until tomorrow."

Rose sighed. She felt older than her thirty-eight years as they sped past suburban homes with their holiday lights and families nestled within.

Her "kids" were the men and women of the Special Threats Response Team, none of whom would be spending Christmas cozy at home. They were all tucked into their assignments, scattered throughout the globe, or working at STR headquarters in a dilapidated warehouse on the outskirts of Fairfax. The bad guys didn't take Christmas off, so neither did they.

"What about Chase Westin's op? Are his and Lucky's covers holding?"

Rose would deny that she had any favorites among the men and women who came from every branch of the military and law enforcement to make up her team. But if forced to pick one man who'd sacrificed more and without complaint it would be Chase Westin.

"Lucky has a bad feeling, but when doesn't he," Billy answered. "Chase has the deal set for tomorrow."

"At least someone gets to spend Christmas at home."

Billy pulled his eyes from the road to glance at the box in her hands. "What about Krakov? Any family?"

Rose shook her head. She'd be spared making that official visit on the holiday. "His will asked that the members of his SEAL team dispose of his remains. They're out on a job. When they get back to Coronado, I'll give them the news."

"I can do it if you like."

"No, thanks."

She was silent for a moment as Billy maneuvered the car through the slick, snow-covered streets. A white Christmas, oh joy. Peace on earth, goodwill to men.

Too bad a very large portion of the world wasn't experiencing any peace. Most of whom wished ill will to the US, intent on obtaining retribution for their own woes and misery. It was up to Rose and her team to stop them.

That was the job, and the job always came first. Victor Krakov knew that. Still. What a waste, he'd only been twenty-seven. He'd died a hero, but only a handful of people would ever know that. No medals or parades for Rose's people. Only the very real possibility of coming home in a tin box.

"Bottle of Glen Morangie in the glove compartment," Billy said.

After two years of working together, Rose had ceased to be amazed by the way he constantly anticipated needs she didn't even know she had.

"Last one at the PX at Quantico. Had to sweet talk the clerk to get it, she said it was reserved for some Admiral. Told her it was for my dear old auntie home for the holidays."

Rose balanced the box in her lap as she reached forward and removed the sixteen-year-old single malt from the glove compartment. "Who's old? You're four years older than I am, Billy."

He cringed. Like many men who spent their youth being tried and tested by covert operations, Billy Price despised the inevitability of growing old. To him age equaled being a has-been, out of touch with the "real world" where only his wits and skills stood between him and death. Worse than redundant: useless.

"To friends absent tonight, but ever present in our hearts," Rose paraphrased a saying her Razgravian grandmother had taught her. She drank from the small bottle and offered it to Billy. He took a swallow.

"Cheers."

Rose returned the bottle of liquid comfort to the glove compartment where she hoped it would wait a long, long time before a similar occasion arose.

"Step on it," she instructed Billy. "We've got work to do. Somehow Deacon's people tripped to Victor. Which means—"

"That it might not be a very merry Christmas for Chase and Lucky."

CHAPTER 6

KC TROMPED THROUGH THE snowy yard that separated her house from the Gianotti mansion. Any other town and Bruno's place would have been surrounded by a ten foot wall topped with razor wire and patrolled by armed guards with dogs, but Bruno Gianotti preferred to think of himself as a man of the people. He treated the entire town of Coalton as his own personal Fiefdom, assumed that every man in it belonged to him and would defend and protect his (and therefore Coalton's) best interests. To the death, if need be.

When KC and Glenn had first arrived in Coalton, the house they lived in was the only house available to rent. They'd quickly discovered why: Gianotti had bugs throughout, vetting any newcomers. From the dust and decay and collection of newspapers and magazines dating back to the last century, KC figured there weren't many newcomers to Coalton. Another reason why her wild-girl personae was a perfect cover.

She zipped and unzipped her jacket, her fingers needing something to do. Told herself it wasn't nerves but rather a way to ensure she could reach her weapon quickly. Yeah, right. And she didn't feel the sudden urge to barf either, as she raised her hand and thumbed the mansion's doorbell.

A lion's den would be much easier to deal with. Lions were predictable creatures, they only attacked if they were hungry or saw you as a threat. Men like Gianotti held to no such logic. They killed because they could, because they enjoyed it.

And because they could get away with it. She remembered Jay's description of the execution he had witnessed. The sound of the doorbell rolled around the interior of the cavernous house, echoing like a death knell.

KC left her jacket unzipped, kept her hands free at her sides. Last time, she told herself. This was the last time she had to come here. She and Jay were going to crash at his place tonight, stage one last scene in her house in the morning for the benefit of Bruno's bugs, and then she'd send him away with the Marshals. Probably wouldn't see him again until the trial.

Just one more night, a little more than twelve hours. She could hold it together that long. She had to.

The door popped open just as she was taking a deep breath, making her choke and sputter as her throat tightened. Instead of the maid she'd been expecting, it was Gianotti himself who stood in the doorway, casting his shadow over her like the plague.

"Merry Christmas, KC," he said, not moving, leering down at her as she shivered in the night. His voice sounded anything but merry. The fine hairs on the back of KC's neck began to twitch. Her entire body quivered with an electric surge of adrenalin as she met Gianotti's knife-edged gaze. This man meant to kill her.

Nonsense. He had no idea who she was or why she was really here. "Is Jay ready? I told him I'd drive him home."

"He and Neil are in the media room, playing a video game. Why don't you come inside?" He pivoted, gestured magnanimously.

Light from the chandelier glittered from polished gold and silver accouterments, even from the marble floor of the foyer. As if all the riches of the world resided in this house.

"No thanks, I can wait out here," she said.

His jaw clenched, lips pulling back to reveal straight, white teeth—the best porcelain veneers money could buy. No one said no to Mr. Gianotti. Not in Coalton. Not and lived to tell the tale.

"I don't want to get mud on your nice floors," she added in a rush.

"Nonsense. Come in out of the cold, young lady. I've been meaning to have a chat with you."

Before she knew it, her reluctant legs dragged her over the threshold and the door slammed shut behind her with a hollow thud. Gianotti led the way without looking back, knowing she would follow.

Glenn and Carson were only a hundred yards away, could hear everything, but the thought didn't comfort her as Gianotti opened the door to his private study and waited for her to pass him before shutting it again. She stood a few feet inside the room, uncertain what to do. The rug beneath her feet cost more than she made in a year and was so thick that it threatened to swallow her Doc Marten's whole. Oil paintings crowded the walls, too many, too close together for anyone to truly appreciate the artistry—which was exactly the point, wasn't it?

Gianotti didn't want people to admire his taste in art, he wanted them to admire his power in collecting it all in one place. He strode past her, going to the bar behind his burl wood antique desk. "Have a seat, KC."

Cover, she had to maintain her cover. She plopped down in a delicate looking Chippendale chair, rocking it with her weight, and slung her legs over one arm. KC the bad girl wasn't scared or intimidated by power and wealth.

"Do you want a drink?" he asked, glancing back to frown at the puddle forming below her boots.

"You know I'm not old enough to drink," she said with a giggle despite the fact that the real KC was in desperate need of a shot of alcohol. No way she'd take any food or drink this man offered. Her pulse stampeded, making it hard to swallow as he simply stared at her.

"We both know that's not true."

She dropped her feet to the ground, sat up straight, one hand edging close to her Glock. Her cheeks burned with cold as if the winter wind had somehow snuck in to ambush her through the closed French doors on the far wall. Those doors were her closest escape route. A dozen scenarios crowded through her mind, but she couldn't leave without Jay. And she couldn't shoot Gianotti, risk alerting his guards.

"What do you mean? You know I'm only eighteen." Faking a yawn, she patted her mouth, then swept her hand through her hair, bringing it closer to her knife hidden in its sheath at the back of her neck.

Gianotti's smile was that of a politician's: polite and condescending. Infuriatingly superior. "Ah, but girls mature faster than boys. I know why you're here. Why you're really here."

Oh shit, here it came. She perched on the edge of her seat, weight on the balls of her feet, ready to propel her body forward across the desk in one blitzkrieg movement. Knife to the throat, send the alarm to Carson and Glenn, then find Jay and get the hell out of Dodge...

"Why I'm really here?" she asked innocently, one hand flicking the metal rings adorning the shoulder of her jacket.

He whirled around. She almost took him out then and there.

Until she saw the neon pink condom box in his hand. He spun it across the expanse of the desk, aiming it at her like a bullet. "Did you think I wouldn't know? About how you're using Jay to get close to my son? Are you really so stupid that you think Sinderson wouldn't tell me?"

His voice thundered through the room as he spoke of his nineteen year old son as if Neil was a virgin whose honor Gianotti needed to protect. Nervous laughter bubbled through KC. She choked it back, no need to infuriate him further, but she couldn't keep the expression of relief and amusement from her face.

"It was just a joke," she said, relaxing her posture once more. "It was Neil's idea—I lost a bet."

"You mean you made my son think it was his idea. Just like you've mesmerized Jay into thinking you care about him."

That brought her to her feet. "I do care about Jay!"

Her outburst seemed to appease him. He gathered himself, face stony once more, and sat down in the high-backed leather chair. "Your father still hasn't found work?"

She hung her head. Their cover was that Glenn was depressed after her "mother" ran out on them. He barely left the house and they had filled the medicine cabinets with prescriptions for Xanax, Prozac and the like.

"He's doing the best he can," she mumbled. "What's my father got to do with anything?"

"You and your father will be leaving Coalton after the holidays," Gianotti continued as if she hadn't spoken. "I found him a job in Ohio, working as a delivery man. I'll pay the cost of relocating you both and in return you will never contact either Jay or my son again."

He stood and walked around the desk, heading for the door without waiting to see if she agreed to his terms or not. KC bristled, despite the fact that he'd just given her the perfect end game to her undercover scenario.

She wasn't sure if it was her real-self or her alter-ego, the teenaged troublemaker, who blurted out, "Who died and made you God, anyway?"

Gianotti whipped around, rings flashing as he backhanded her. Just hard enough to rock her, slam her teeth together and sting like the dickens. She'd taken harder punches in her time, from guys a lot bigger and stronger than he was. But never from a man whose eyes were as dead as Bruno Gianotti's. If it wasn't too much hassle and mess, he would have just as easily killed her.

He shook his hand as if flicking away an unwanted piece of trash and walked out of the room without saying another word. She stood there, palm rubbing her cheek, staring at the door. Jay and Neil wandered in, both chatting and waving their arms around, as they recreated the final battle of their video game.

"You should have seen it, KC," Neil was saying, his face lit up with pride and happiness. "First time I ever whomped Jay's ass at Dragon Vengeance."

"First and last," Jay put in.

KC ignored them, grabbing Jay's arm, wrenching him out into the foyer. "Let's go."

"What's the rush?" Jay asked, his muscles tensing beneath her grip.

"Stay, KC." Neil joined them. "Open your Christmas presents at least."

"Later, Neil," she snapped, opening the front door and shoving Jay through it. "We'll see you later."

Neil's face crashed into a look of confusion and despair. The large vaulted foyer dwarfed him, leaving him cold and alone standing in the chandelier's spotlight. She was tempted to grab his arm and take him with her. Not just to save his life, but also for the chance to see the look on Gianotti's face when she stole his most prized possession: his son.

Instead, KC followed Jay outside and closed the door behind her, leaving Neil locked up in the solitary confinement of his birthright.

CHAPTER 7

CHASE PARKED HIS HARLEY in the carport behind the '78 Chevy Malibu that was rusting out and sitting up on blocks. He stroked a hand across its dusty hood. He and Jay had spent hours on the car that had been Chase's before he joined the Marines, just as Chase and Nicky Gianotti had worked on it before that. Jay had mentioned something about the transmission finally going. Chase guessed the kid never got around to fixing it.

The door to the house was unlocked. No surprise, this was Coalton, after all. No crime because there wasn't anything left to steal. At least anything not already owned by Bruno Gianotti and no one would dare cross him.

Chase felt for the kitchen light and flicked it on, illuminating the black and white linoleum, the avocado green counters and appliances. Spic and span—you'd never guess a teenager lived here alone. Not even an empty take-out box on the counter. Jay had left the place as if he never expected to return.

Chase raided the pantry—slim pickins except for the stale heel of a loaf of bread and some peanut butter—fixed himself a sandwich, and washed it down with a glass of milk. He took a long, satisfying drink. Pennsylvania milk always tasted so much better than city milk.

Chase wiped his mouth on the sleeve of his flannel shirt as he prowled through the house, searching for clues to the man his brother had become in his absence.

The place was spartan, even neater than Jay's anal housekeeping usually had it. He smiled at the box of Trojans in the kid's nightstand—at least one of them was lucky in love. An image of the purple-headed girl he'd seen with Jay seared through him. Damn. What kind of creep got hard for his kid brother's girl?

He distracted himself by continuing to snoop into his brother's life. Jay's grades were still good: straight A's except for a B in calculus, he read from the report card that was in a stack of mail on the desk.

Chase's own room was untouched, crowded with football and baseball trophies, his foot locker from the Corps, photos his mother had framed. A photographic panorama of Charles Thoreau Westin's life from Little League to Afghanistan.

He sank onto his childhood bed. It was dark enough that the glow-in-the-dark constellations pasted to the ceiling were visible. He remembered his father tottering on the stepladder, so engaged in explaining the story of Cassiopeia that he'd almost lost his balance. In the end, he'd finally raised Chase onto his shoulders and they had invented their own version of the Milky Way.

Thank God, Mom and Dad were gone before the Corps kicked Chase out. The disgrace would've killed them for sure—and there was no way Chase could explain it to them. Just as he could never explain to Jay. Not without placing his brother in danger. He'd rather have Jay disappointed than dead.

Chase sighed and climbed back to his feet. He hadn't come here to revel in nostalgia. He came here to find a way to get Jay out of the cross fire before he took Bruno down.

His footsteps echoing on the oak floors, Chase moved to the front of the ranch house and into the living room. The afghan Mom crocheted was folded over the back of a well-used Barcalounger positioned in front of the TV. The over-stuffed sofa looked as if it had just come out of a show room although Chase knew it was over a decade old. Senior year, he'd almost lost his virginity with Kristy Mancuso on that couch. Until his little brother stumbled in on them, irrevocably breaking the mood.

Where were the photos that had once hung on the wall behind it? There'd been pictures of his parents' and both grandparents' weddings; his, Diane's and Jay's baby pictures; a photo of his father and Chase at the John Wayne museum; and the entire family at the Grand Canyon. In their place now hung generic Wal-Mart art deco prints.

Chase frowned and looked around for his missing memories. Most of the photos were gone from the mantle as well, the few remaining spread around as if to camouflage the empty spaces.

He spied the two small suitcases sitting beside the front door. Packed and ready for a quick get-away.

The door opened just as Chase reached for the first suitcase. Jay entered. His brother's eyes, twins to his own blue ones, blazed at him.

"What the hell are you doing here!" Jay said.

The first words Chase had heard from Jay in almost six months. "Merry Christmas to you, too."

Jay was ten when Chase joined the Marines. Chase remembered the pride in his kid brother's face, how he'd said Chase in his uniform looked like John Wayne in the old movies their father was devoted to. Now Jay's eyes were filled with an emotion more

painful than hatred. They looked at him with a mixture of disgust
and disappointment.

"You got some nerve—" Jay snuck under Chase's guard with a
right hook that caught his attention.

While he'd been gone, someone had finally taught the kid how
to hit like he meant it. He blocked the next punch, wrapped Jay in
a bear hug as they grappled for position. Using his greater bulk, he
rolled them both over and pinned Jay beneath him.

"Stop it!" a woman shouted from behind them. "Let him go!"

Damn, he'd forgotten the girl. Chase looked over his shoulder
and saw her standing in a batting stance, ready to let loose with
the cast iron fireplace poker. She didn't look scared. She looked
determined. Fierce, intent on protecting her man.

Chase raised his hands in surrender, rolled off Jay. The girl
didn't take her eyes from him or relax her stance as Jay got to his
feet. Chase almost smiled. Looked like the kid found himself a
winner. Despite her punk rocker purple hair.

She was maybe five-six, thin but not too skinny. Her jacket was
open, and he could see the outline of her small breasts beneath a
form fitting black leather vest that revealed her pierced navel. Swirls
of color from a tattoo danced over the bare flesh of her abdomen.
He made out several round yin/yang symbols and what looked like a
claw. The rest disappeared beneath the waistband of her jeans.

Chase pushed away his surprising swell of desire. She was Jay's
for one thing. Hell, he didn't even know her name.

So why did he feel like he knew her? Really knew her—even
though they'd never met before. He remembered to breathe and
realized it was all just wistful thinking. He'd dreamed of having a
woman look at him, stand with him like that.

But she was Jay's. Off limits. Especially to the disgraced big
brother.

"It's okay, KC," Jay told her, taking the poker from her hand. "He's my brother."

Chase had no idea what to make of the look of astonished confusion that crossed the girl's face in response to Jay's introduction.

KC STARED DOWN AT Charles Westin. This lunatic with the scraggly hair and day-old beard was Jay's brother? She'd read the file, knew Charles' colorful, disreputable background. Jay had assured her Big Bro was out of the picture; that he hadn't spoken to him since his court martial and incarceration at Leavenworth.

She looked from one brother to the other. Two sets of dark blue eyes blazed with anger. Hell's bells—this was gonna throw a monkey in the works. She had to stay in character, couldn't trust this lowlife loser with the truth.

"This is Charles?" she asked, edging closer to Jay and wrapping her arm around his waist as if seeking his protection.

She listened carefully, scanned the hallway. The house appeared empty except for them. At least Big Bro hadn't brought any dipshit, ex-con friends home with him. The guy had picked the worst time in the world to play prodigal son.

Charles rolled to his feet without using his hands, and KC caught a glimpse of the silhouette of a semi-automatic snugged in his waistband at the small of his back. Damn, just what she didn't need. She slid her right hand inside her jacket, hugging herself as if she were cold, the familiar grip of her Glock in its hidden holster comforting.

"Don't worry, I don't bite. And it's Chase, please."

KC said nothing, watched as he hooked his thumbs in the belt loops of his ripped jeans and rocked on the balls of his feet.

"Nice to see you, kid," Chase continued.

Jay tensed, his grip on the poker went white knuckled. "I knew it," he said, his voice sounding tight. "I knew you'd come back to screw up my life. Is this gonna be an annual event? The ghost of Christmas past returning to make my life hell?"

Chase stopped rocking, his face stony as he stared at his brother. "That's not why I came back."

KC heard the regret in his voice and wondered if Jay noticed it as well.

"Fine," Jay said bitterly. "Whatever. I don't really give a damn, 'cause tomorrow we're out of here. Take the house, it's half yours anyway."

"What do you mean you're out of here?" Chase demanded. "What about school? What about going to college—becoming a doctor?"

Jay shook his head in a tight arc. "I'm done with school—as if you cared."

"You can't just drop out—"

"If it's any of your business, I didn't." Jay leaned forward staring intently at Chase's face as if searching for something. "What grade do you think I'm in, Chase?"

KC kept her gaze fixed on Chase Westin's hands, they never moved toward the gun. Instead they clenched into fists so tight that she thought he would tear the belt loops free of their rivets.

"What do I know what grade? You're in high school."

Jay blew his breath out, his mouth tightening in disappointment. "I should have graduated last year, Chase. I lost half a year because of you and the best you can do in return is come back and mess up the rest of my life again?"

That rocked Big Bro. Westin's hands flew out as if warding off an attack and he took a step back. "I'm sorry, I never thought—"

"No, you never did. So just finish the job and leave me alone. I know what I'm doing." Jay turned toward the suitcases.

Westin's gaze drifted from his younger brother to laser in on KC. "No. I won't, I can't. You had dreams, Jay. Are you giving up everything because of her?" He acted as if KC wasn't even there, as if she were nothing. "You can't. Don't toss away your life on account of some girl—"

Jay whirled, raised the poker. Before KC could intervene, Chase swept Jay's legs out from under him and twisted the poker from his hand in a blitzkrieg strike. Jay lay on the floor, catching his breath. KC ran to his side, helped him to his feet, keeping her body between him and his brother's gun.

"Don't you talk about her like that!" Jay said.

KC flinched at the emotion in his voice. Damn it, she'd tried hard to keep the kid from falling for her. No time to think of that now, she had to stop the two brothers from killing each other.

"Jay's old enough to make his own decisions," she said, giving her voice a touch of pouty whine, "and you can't stop us."

She reached for Jay's hand, pulled him close, where she could keep him out of the line of fire if his crazy brother went off again. "No one can. So why don't you just go back where you came from? We don't need you."

"Better yet, you stay—we'll go." Jay's hand squeezed hers. He pulled KC with him as he marched toward the door and reached for his bags. "I can bunk at Neil's."

"Wait, Jay. I didn't come here to fight. Stay. It's Christmas Eve, I'll only be here for a day or two—"

KC glanced over her shoulder at Chase. The poker hung forgotten from his hand, and he looked like a kid who'd found a lump of coal in his stocking. She felt Jay hesitate. Nothing in the report on Chase Westin mentioned any violence toward his brother.

But who knew how a stint in Leavenworth could change a man? The guy was built, his biceps bulged beneath his flannel shirt. He'd been holding back, could have easily pummeled Jay into the ground if he'd wanted.

No matter how screwed up Jay's brother was, KC couldn't bring herself to tear them apart on their last night together. She only hoped she wasn't making a big mistake.

"Stay—talk, fight, whatever. After tomorrow you'll have the rest of your life," she reminded Jay. He frowned then nodded. She felt Chase's eyes on them and so stood on tiptoe to plant a kiss on Jay's lips. To her surprise, Jay's arms pulled her close, and he prolonged the embrace.

The kid wasn't acting. KC hoped he realized she was. She kept her eyes on his, saw Jay's snap open as she pulled back. His face flushed with embarrassment, and he released her.

"I'm sorry," he mumbled.

KC smiled, placed a finger to his lips. "Don't be. I'll see you tomorrow."

She took one last look at the tall former Marine with his scruffy jeans and flannel shirt and too-long, tousled hair. Chase Westin stared at her with hunger in his eyes. She met his gaze, watched in surprise as he broke first, spinning away on his heel.

One thing for sure, KC thought as her footsteps crunched through the snow, Chase Westin was nothing like his little brother. Chase Westin was trouble.

CHAPTER 8

CHASE MOVED TOWARD THE Barcalounger at the same time
Jay did. He stopped short. It wasn't his house anymore.

He sidestepped to the couch instead. Jay slouched in the
recliner, his eyes never leaving Chase's face, as if he were
frightened of his own brother. Or like Chase was a stranger,
unpredictable and therefore dangerous.

How had he allowed it to come to this? He'd purposely stayed
as far from Jay as possible—to protect him, he'd thought. But did he
have to lose Jay in order to keep him safe? What could he do now to
fix it? Short of telling Jay the truth.

"What's going on?" he asked Jay, nodding at the door KC had
just gone through, shiny handcuffs dancing after her, purple hair
gleaming in the porch light. "She's not your type."

No, but judging by the heat raging through his veins and the
tightness gathering beneath his waistband, KC was **exactly Chase's**
type. The memory of that fierce glare as she made **ready to bash his**
brains in, her chest heaving, the leather vest tightening over those
oh-so-sweet breasts...

Chase grimaced and forced his attention back to his brother. Jay's type of girl was much more apple pie and sweater sets. Someone like Mom. Not a leather and chains punker.

"As if you had any idea what my type is," Jay said. "As if you even cared."

"I care about you screwing up the rest of your life. Not for a girl like her, Jay."

"Shut up! You don't know anything about KC."

"I know her type." On one level, in that dark realm of fantasy that underscored every man's encounters with the opposite sex, Chase wished he had the opportunity to get to know KC better. He hoped Jay hadn't noticed Chase's more visceral reaction to his girlfriend. Girl? Hell, KC exuded more sex appeal than women twice her age.

"She's trouble," he said, his words echoing his thoughts. "Where'd she come from?"

"She and her father moved here from Philly last month. She got into some problems there."

"Figures. I'm guessing that she doesn't exactly fit in around here either."

Jay was silent, got to his feet and began pacing. Chase watched him. The kid had always taken his growth spurts early, but now the gawky awkwardness of youth had faded. He could see why a girl like KC would turn to his little brother as her champion. And Jay, poor sap, was one of those kids driven to always do the right thing. Just like their father, famous for his lost causes and crusades.

Chase was nothing like their father. He wasn't patient, philosophical, easy tempered or brilliant. He was just a guy doing a job, trying hard not to make the same mistakes twice.

"Cut her loose," he told his brother.

Jay whirled on him, and Chase braced himself for another

fistfight. Damn, the kid was stubborn. Figured he'd take after Chase in that department.

"Why did you come home?" Jay asked. "Every time you do, something bad happens—" he stopped himself before he said more, but Chase caught the bitterness beneath the words.

He couldn't blame the kid. After last year, Christmas would never be the same, nothing would.

Chase remembered how excited he'd been coming home after spending fourteen months in Afghanistan. He'd waited outside the Altoona train station, amazed the transport gods had actually gotten him home as promised, on time for the holiday. He brought presents for everyone: an antique copy of the Koran for Dad, an embroidered scarf for Mom, and a Pashtun dagger for Jay.

He'd been so happy, more excited by Christmas than since he was a kid. Right until the moment the State Police arrived to tell him that there had been an accident. A fatal accident.

"I didn't come here to fight with you," he told Jay. "But I won't stand by and watch you throw away your future."

"I'm not, can't you see? I'm trying so hard to do the right thing, help a friend in trouble. I thought you'd be proud of me for stepping up like a man." Jay's voice sounded raspy as if he were close to tears.

"Trouble? Yeah, I'll bet. Is she even in school? I'm guessing she's a drop out. How old is she, anyway?"

"She's older than she looks."

"I'm just hoping she's older than she acts." But Jay was right, KC did seem older. Physically, and, once you got past the body art and Hollywood hype fashion, mentally. He remembered the way she had defended Jay, like a mother lion...Oh hell. Why hadn't he seen it before? The girl was pregnant, that explained a lot. Damn her, she was only using Jay. "So KC's in trouble, and you're trying to do the right thing. Are you even sure the baby's yours?"

Jay jerked his head up as if Chase had hit him. "Why do you always assume the worst about people? Why can't you trust me to know what I'm doing?"

"Maybe because you're a kid who's getting ready to throw his whole life away!" Chase rocked onto his feet, squared off against Jay. "You're the smartest person I know, but damn it, Jay you're such a sap. Just like Dad. Always tilting at windmills. Wasting his life away in this shithole of a town."

"As opposed to you? Wasting your life away—where, Chase? Doing what? Or is the reason why you didn't call or write or anything was because you were back in jail?"

The look of disgust on Jay's face cut Chase to the quick. He was half tempted to tell Jay the truth—anything to erase that expression and replace it with the adoring gaze of the little boy who used to follow Chase everywhere. He opened his mouth, closed it again. The safest thing for Jay was to keep living the lie.

Chase ground his jaws together. It might be the safest thing, but it sure as hell wasn't the easiest.

"I wasn't in jail. I was working," he said, staring at the floor and shifting his feet.

"Working? Where?"

Chase didn't meet his brother's gaze. "For Bruno Gianotti. For his moving company, driving his vans."

To his surprise, Jay straightened and the color drained from his face. "You work for Mr. Gianotti?"

"Sure." Chase shrugged. "He came to me when I got out. Took pity on me 'cause of me and Nicky being friends, offered me a job. You know Mr. Gianotti, nobody says no to him."

"Right," Jay echoed in a distant voice. "Nobody says no to Mr. Gianotti." He backed into the hallway. "Well, good for you, I guess. I'm still leaving tomorrow. The house is yours after that."

The slam of Jay's bedroom door rattled the windows. Chase stared after his brother. Teenagers—how did any of them survive?

Why had Jay gotten so uptight when he'd mentioned working for Bruno? Did he know what Bruno's business really was? It was an open secret in a town where Bruno Gianotti controlled the cops, the town council, and the purse strings.

He slid into the recliner, his gaze fixed on the empty hallway. Could Jay's leaving have something to do with Bruno? Maybe he'd been wrong about Jay's girlfriend, KC?

The image of her face, the way she'd stood ready to protect Jay, her look of fierce determination flashed through his mind. As did the memory of the very visceral response he'd had both times he laid eyes on her. Even knowing what he did now, even seeing her kiss Jay, he couldn't stop imagining the brush of her lips against his, those full, lush lips, swollen and hot with desire.

He pounded his fist against his thigh. What kind of pervert fantasized about his kid brother's girl? A flush of shame spread over him. Jeezit, he had to get out of this racket, he was beginning to think like Bruno and his goons.

KC was using Jay, he was certain. That girl was trouble.

Tough enough that Jay had to grow up early and fast, if KC was pregnant, there was no way Chase was going to let him take on the burdens of parenthood at such a young age. Especially not when there was an excellent chance the baby wasn't even his.

Chase hadn't been the best brother to Jay. He should have figured out a way to watch over him, take better care of him. Now there was no telling if Chase would be around past the meeting with the Crusade tomorrow. There was only tonight. Chase had to make the best use of the little time he had left. Do everything he could to stop Jay from ruining the rest of his life.

He grabbed his coat and went out the back way. KC and her family were new in town—one stop at the Stop n Go to fill up with gas and catch up with Shannon behind the counter and he'd find out where she lived. As well as everything else there was to know about her.

CURLED UP IN HER favorite overstuffed chair beside the TV, KC huddled with her laptop and tuned out Peter Billingsley's pleas for a Daisy Brand, Red-Ryder BB gun. She'd spent most of the evening trying to get more information on Jay's troublesome big brother.

And trying to erase the memory of Chase Westin's intense blue eyes. KC rarely noticed eyes in men, not in the "windows to the soul" sense anyway. When she looked into a person's eyes it was to judge their veracity by watching for the muscular contractions that gave away even the most accomplished liars. No romance there, just an undercover operative trying to stay alive.

Why couldn't she get Chase Westin out of her mind? She wasn't in the market for any kind of entanglements. She had a job to do here.

Who was she kidding? KC wasn't in the market for romance even when she was off the job. Not anymore.

True romance involved too much blood, sweat, and tears. The image of Manny's casket being lowered into a dark hole in the ground filled her mind. Especially tears. And pain, don't forget the pain.

KC wanted love, wanted it all, but she wanted it for a lifetime— everything a man could give her. More than stolen moments between assignments during an illicit affair they had to keep secret because of the rules. Manny had been her training officer, her supervisor—the Bureau would have fired them both if anyone ever found out about their relationship.

KC sighed, remembering her grandfather, the way his eyes lit up when he spoke of her grandmother. That was what she wanted: a love to last forever, the real deal.

She forced her attention back to the laptop and Chase Westin's military career. Sure as hell wasn't going to get that kind of love from a disgraced former Marine, no matter how mesmerizing his eyes were. Dishonorable discharge after being caught with a load of automatic weapons and almost killing the MP who stopped him. What a way to end what was up to then a decent career with several commendations, including a silver star.

Once upon a time, Chase Westin was a bonafide hero. Where had things gone so wrong? Eleven months ago, Westin sustained injuries that forced him to leave the rough and tumble life of Recon. Spent ten weeks in a hospital, another month in rehab, then fought the medical board for the next two months, trying to get reinstated back into Recon. The doctors had refused all his requests, recommending a medical discharge or permanent desk duty.

A slap in the face for a guy who'd pounded as many miles in the service of his country as Westin had. But he was only twenty-eight, still had a lot of career options besides resorting to armed robbery, weapons trafficking and attempted murder.

He was lucky the convening authority allowed him to trade the names of the others in the smuggling ring for time served. Still, he'd spent three months in Leavenworth, most of it in solitary confinement until his release in October.

His life since was a cipher. There was no record, criminal or otherwise, since Chase had been expelled from the Marines. No income reported on his behalf, no wants, no warrants. The guy had either been squeaky clean or living under the radar.

Given that he returned home to the same town that Bruno Gianotti lived in, at the same time Gianotti was putting together the biggest deal of his career, KC guessed the second. Which would explain Westin's really lousy timing.

So Chase Westin was most likely working for Gianotti. How could she use that? Surely even a scumbag like Westin wouldn't endanger his kid brother's life for a business deal. Maybe she could turn Westin, barter his and Jay's safety for info on Gianotti's buyer, his future testimony?

No. Better to wait until Jay was safely out of the way before exposing herself to Westin.

She climbed the steps to her bedroom, the questions swirling in her mind. Probably would be easier if Jay hadn't gotten so attached to her. And if his big brother wasn't so damned attractive. She'd always had a weakness for rugged he-man types, despite the fact that every man she'd known like that had left her disappointed in the end.

Just needed to get some sleep, that was all. KC walked into the bedroom and turned on the light.

Less than three feet in front of her, Chase Westin straddled the desk chair, watching her.

CHAPTER 9

LUCKY ALMOST GOT LOST on the dark and twisty roads that led through the snow-covered forests between Coalton and Mill Run, the closest town with a motel. Hadn't these people ever heard of street lights? he wondered as he steered his Suzuki GSX 1400 over the two lane road rutted with pot holes and dark as a coal mine.

He made it down the mountain in one piece, skidded his bike to a stop in front of the Blue Bird Inn, thankful that at least in December he wouldn't have to worry about actually encountering any real birds, and hurried inside to the bar.

Deacon's people had taken over the place. The bartender and a middle-aged waitress with sagging breasts and penciled-on eyebrows were the only locals remaining. Lucky grabbed a pitcher from the nearest table and filled a smudged mug, downed the weak beer in two gulps. The men at the table laughed.

"Hope you're not looking to get drunk on this stuff," Redman said, glancing up from his hand of poker.

"Tastes like tap water someone took a piss in," Lucky agreed. "I can't wait until this deal's done, and we can get back to the city."

"Amen to that, Brother Cavanaugh," Deacon said from behind Lucky.

Lucky's role was as a convert to The Crusade, unlike Chase whose cover was playing the middleman between Gianotti's organization and The Crusade.

After listening to The Crusade's rhetoric for almost two months now, Lucky had to admit there was something compelling about the idea of wiping out the mistakes of the last two hundred years. Abolishing the bureaucracy that was suffocating the government, overhauling the tax system so that everyone shared in the profits of their labor, ending special interest groups and establishing term limits so politicians could concentrate on getting the job done rather than the next election.

Lucky knew little more about Deacon than when he had started. It was difficult to separate the truth from the urban legends that blossomed around the man. Redman had told him Deacon grew up a gang-banger on the streets of LA, killed his first man before he was fourteen. After the bombing of a LA Medi-Cal office, Deacon abandoned the gangsta lifestyle for the role of underground warrior, preparing for the Second Revolution. And The Crusade was born.

For Deacon it was easy: you were either part of The Crusade, or part of the problem. And, from what Lucky had seen so far, Deacon's solution to most problems involved lethal force.

"We all set?" Deacon asked, gesturing Lucky to an empty booth.

"Tomorrow, noon."

Deacon poured Lucky a shot of Jack Daniels, then one for himself. His knuckles still bore tattoos from his days in the Grape Street Crip gang. He had a surprisingly soft voice, one that made you strain to catch each word. "I hate to keep the men working over the holiday."

Lucky looked around at the men playing pool and cards. None of them seemed to be missing the holiday cheer. "We don't mind—as long as the job gets done."

Deacon raised his glass in a toast. "That's the spirit, Brother. Today's your birthday, you don't regret being far from your family?"

Lucky almost choked on his whiskey. Damn, sometimes it freaked him out that these people, men he was trying to put in jail, knew intimate details of his life. Even Chase didn't know it was his birthday today.

"You guys are my family," he said, giving Deacon the party line. The other man nodded in approval.

"Is Westin coming back tonight?"

"Probably not, he has some family business."

Deacon acted as if he was familiar with Chase's family. Lucky never could tell when the guy actually knew the inside scoop and when he was bluffing—guess that was what made Deacon so good at his job.

Lucky was just a demo man. Give him a bomb to build, something to blow up, or a device to disarm, and he could do it in his sleep. This undercover deal was scary, made him feel like a rookie. He could hold his own with the street thugs dealing modified TEC-9's, but these Crusade freaky-deaks were nuts, totally unpredictable.

He took another hit of whiskey and wished he were back in DC. Mean streets he could navigate with ease. Of course with three brothers, a father and two uncles on the Metro Force and his only sister with the Secret Service, he had plenty of trustworthy backup there as well. Here, in the wilds of Pennsylvania, he felt naked.

"We scouted a few meet sites," he told Deacon, stifling his homesick sigh. All part of the job. Some of it had been fun, like designing the devices Deacon wanted. He'd dreamt up a few beauties. Of course, they'd never get built. Not if he and Chase did their jobs right.

"Find a place suited to our needs?"

"High school basketball courts. They're in the back of the building, a service road leads around and if there's any problems, we can move to cover inside the gym."

"There will be church services across the street."

He was right, but Lucky didn't ask how he knew. Obviously Deacon had performed his own recon. It was what Lucky would do if their positions were reversed.

Trust no one, assume nothing—Chase had taught him that as his first lesson in undercover work.

Lucky shrugged. "Guess so, didn't check. Is that a problem?"

"No. In fact it may be a blessing in disguise. The Lord provides in mysterious ways."

The Crusade's message was strictly non-denominational, focusing on economics and social inequities as common ground. But that didn't stop Deacon from quoting the Bible at odd times, such as when drawing to an inside straight.

Deacon finished his drink and pulled a motel key from his shirt pocket. "Good work."

Lucky took the key. Room Thirteen. Deacon laughed at his expression and clapped him on the shoulder as he stood to leave. "Have faith, Brother. It's just a number, it can't hurt you."

So why did Lucky have a bad feeling about this?

As he left the bar, he failed to notice Deacon nodding to Redman who took Lucky's glass from the table, placing it in a plastic bag.

"How long?" Deacon asked.

"Hour, tops."

CHAPTER 10

KC'S HAND MOVED TO where her gun would be if she still had her jacket on. Except her jacket was hanging downstairs in the foyer. She wasn't supposed to need a weapon, not here in her own damned house!

"Close the door, we need to talk," Westin said, his eyes locking onto hers. With his long, straggly hair and fierce expression he looked like the wolf waiting for Red Riding Hood.

Boy, had he ever picked the wrong girl. She put her hand on the doorknob. One good shout and Glenn and Carson would come running. And she had her backup piece in her boot.

Before she could decide, Westin stretched one long leg and kicked the door shut. Pivoting out of the chair, he grabbed her arm, pushed her back against the wall.

That made up her mind for her. KC knew exactly how to handle bullies like Chase Westin.

She glared up at him, showing no fear or apprehension. His grip on her arm was bruising, but if KC wanted to break it, she could have. Told herself she would have, except she wanted to see where he was headed, see if this encounter could help her operation.

Up close he was even more handsome. Tiny lines, the start of crow's feet, made his eyes look deeper, wiser, and there was a hairline scar trailing down from his lower lip to his chin that gave him a slightly crooked smile. She breathed deep and inhaled his scent. Definitely not an Old Spice man.

"I want you to leave Jay alone," he told her.

His voice was smoldering, whiskey on the fire growing within her. Damn it, this was no time for pesky hormones to get in her way. Why did Westin have to be exactly her type, physically at least? It'd been a long time since any man had this kind of effect on her. Not since Manny.

Her breath caught, a small sound that came from deep in the back of her throat. Westin interpreted it as fear, nodded as if they'd made some kind of bargain.

"Find someone else to be your patsy. I know the baby's not Jay's," he continued.

Smart kid. Jay must have told his brother the line they were going to use on Neil. Obviously Jay didn't trust his big brother with the truth. Neither would KC.

What would a teenaged "bad girl" do in this situation? KC grinned. Turn the tables, take control.

One thing about bullies: if you gave them a dose of their own medicine, they invariably tucked tail and ran.

She kept her eyes locked with his, tilted her head back against the door and used her free hand to pull him close, pressing her lips against his.

To her satisfaction, he resisted her bold move. Of course he did. Men like Westin wanted to be in charge, controlling the situation. Too damn bad. Her house, her rules.

KC's grip tightened, holding him fast as she kissed him hard

and deep until she felt his body respond. Now it was his turn to
make a guttural noise as he shifted his hands to her hips, his long
fingers stretching along the bare flesh exposed between her jeans
and vest.

His touch was pure heat as his hands moved beneath the leather.
KC inhaled his intoxicating scent, closed her eyes against the head
rush that came with it, and fought to remember that Chase Westin
was a dangerous man, a man who could get her and her team killed
if she wasn't careful.

CHASE'S BREATH CAUGHT AS KC pulled him into the
embrace. He tried to resist, but this skinny girl had him totally
overwhelmed.

She tasted of pepperoni pizza and Dr. Pepper—sheer heaven.
And the way her body felt against his, they fit together just right,
like this was something meant to be.

His hands seemed to have a mind of their own as they roamed
beneath the supple leather of her vest. He realized she wore nothing
under it. She tugged his shirt from his jeans, her black enameled
nails biting into the flesh along his spine.

This was wrong, so wrong, a voice emerged from the depths of
his mind. She was Jay's girl.

No, he corrected himself as she circled a leg around his, pulling
him against her so that their bodies lined up tighter than the sights
of a sniper's scope, KC was no one's girl—she was a woman who
knew exactly what to do to make a man forget everything he held
dear.

Earlier, he'd lingered outside her house, debating the right
approach to take. Given her tattoo and wardrobe, it was obvious
KC's father had no control over her. And she and Jay were both

adults, at least in the eyes of the law. Finally, Chase had decided to use his reputation as a dangerous criminal capable of anything. After all, what was the good of working his ass off to establish a cover story if he couldn't use it to help free his brother from KC's clutches?

Chase had climbed up to the porch roof and staged an entrance certain to inspire fear and obedience. Or so he had thought.

As KC's lips tangled with his, Chase cursed himself a fool. He'd broken rule number one: never underestimate the enemy. KC wasn't going to scare so easily.

Anger surged as he thought of this vamp enmeshing Jay in her problems, using Jay's own code of honor against him. How could she be making google eyes at Jay one minute, then be melting in Chase's arms the next? What happened to the girl who'd stepped in with the fireplace poker, ready to defend and protect her man?

Obviously KC was a better actress than Chase had given her credit for. Didn't matter. One way or the other, he'd stop her before she ruined his brother's life. No way this teenaged seductress was going to get the best of him.

He stepped back, took a breath of fresh air and immediately missed her scent. But it gave his head time to clear. Reluctantly and with great will power, Chase released her, allowed his hands to slide away from her body. They hung at his sides, empty.

"What's wrong?" she asked. "Spend too much time in jail, forget what to do with a woman?"

"Is that what Jay told you?" Chase asked, hating the sucker punch of pain the reality of how deep he'd fallen in his little brother's esteem brought. It hurt a hell of a lot more than he ever imagined it would.

"Hate to tell you, Big Bro," she said, her gaze dropping from his eyes to his lips in a silent invitation, "but Jay never talks about you at all."

Ouch, that hurt even more. Chase shook his head, tried to focus. Why couldn't he think straight when he was around this girl?

Chase watched in fascination as KC's fingers traced the outline of her tattoo, a green, blue and purple lizard lying on its back, juggling balls with the yin/yang symbol in the air. Most of the lizard's body and tail lay hidden beneath the waistband of her jeans.

She took his hands in hers, placed them on her hips. "Want to see the rest?"

Chase felt a thump in his chest as his heart misfired. She tilted her head to look up at him, long black eyelashes curling out over deep brown, almond-shaped eyes. Chase was lost, drowning in those depths. How could he not have noticed her eyes before? Sure the purple hair distracted him, and those luscious lips, but still—

"What do you say, Big Bro?"

He followed her gaze to the frilly white and gold canopy bed. Exactly the kind of bed his mother would've bought if her baby girl, Diana, had survived. But Sally Westin had only two living children, both of them sons.

Chase jerked his head up as the image of Jay and KC tangled together on the bed filled his mind. He sucked in his breath and stepped back, pulling his hands free of her.

He couldn't do it. As much as his body yearned to capture hers, to expose every one of her secrets, Chase just couldn't.

KC cocked her head and arched an eyebrow as if surprised by his reaction.

"Suit yourself, then." She gestured to the window he'd climbed in through. "Best go out the same way you came."

Chase hated the urge that swept over him at the sight of her standing in front of him, hands on her hips, offering him something he could only dream of. He wanted to take her, take everything she had to give and more, he wanted to drown in her scent, devour every inch of her flesh, wanted—

Chase choked down his impulse and took another step closer to the window and escape. But he could not tear his eyes away from her. Then she made it easy. Her gaze flicked down to the obvious bulge in his jeans, and she smirked.

"Stay away from my brother," Chase warned, opening the window and sliding over the ledge to the porch roof below. The frigid air was bracing, restoring him to his senses as he climbed down to the yard.

He'd been a fool to come here. To let a girl get the better of him so easily. All she'd done was bat her lashes and wiggle her finger, and he'd practically fallen into her lap. Poor Jay, no wonder he couldn't escape KC's power—an innocent kid like him, always seeing the good in everyone, he wouldn't stand a chance against a vixen like her.

KC was strictly poison. Chase would find some way to keep her away from his brother. Without becoming trapped by her venomous claws himself.

CHAPTER 11

KC LOCKED THE WINDOW, turned off the lights and crouched in a corner. She'd almost lost control, almost allowed Chase Westin to get everything he had come for. What was she thinking? She was such an idiot to start down that path.

But something about Westin fascinated her. It was as if two men shared the same skin. One the war hero, the man who'd saved the lives of dozens of his comrades, the eldest of the family who valiantly defended his baby brother's honor.

The other the criminal, disgraced, betrayer of his oath of honor.

If the second was the real Chase Weston, why had he left? Her play-acting kiss had spontaneously combusted into a flash fire she knew Westin had felt. Lord knew, she had. Yet, he'd walked away, concerned only about his brother.

KC slid free the knife sheathed at the neckline of her vest, twirled it between her fingers. Her hands responded to the blade automatically without her having to think or look.

She knew as well as anyone that a knife was useless in a gunfight and no substitute for the two Glocks she carried, but she felt better feeling its slim outline between her shoulder blades, knowing that if anything went wrong she had a backup plan.

Prepare for the worst, hope for the best, that was KC's motto.

Should have been better prepared for Westin. Next time she would be, she vowed. The man wasn't going to overwhelm her defenses, not again, not with his brother's life in her hands.

The blade flew from her fingers, winging through the darkness to impale itself in the exact center of the windowsill, the last place Chase Westin had touched.

"Hey, KC!" Carson bellowed up the steps. "Get down here, now!"

KC jumped to her feet. Damn Carson, he was supposed to stay out of sight. This had better be good, she thought, retrieving her knife before joining him and Glenn downstairs in the surveillance room as she prayed that his voice and Glenn's sounded similar enough to fool anyone listening.

"That's your Westin guy, right?" Carson was pointing to an enhanced digital image on one of his computer screens. It showed Westin's military identification. Amazing how much the man had changed in less than a year since the photo was taken. In the photo, his eyes gleamed with pride, chin jutting forward, ready to lead a charge. Now his face was all edges, eyes hollowed out, hair long past escaping anything close to a military cut, it now curled against his collarbone. Not that she'd been paying attention.

"Yeah, so?" What was all the excitement about?

"I've been playing with the facial recognition software— tweaking it, you know?" Carson said as his fingers raced over the keyboard. Hundreds of photos began to blink across the screen, too fast for the human eye to process. "So I ran Westin's face through our archives of surveillance photos. And look what I found."

A grainy black and white image filled the screen. A large black man was facing the camera, speaking earnestly with someone out of sight. Beside him, half turned away from the camera, was Chase Westin.

"Where's this from? Who's the other guy?" KC asked.

"That's the part you're not gonna like," Glenn spoke up from his seat at the audio monitors. "The black guy is Lester Dinkum—"

"Also known as Deacon," KC finished for him. "Leader of The Crusade. Aw hell. This just keeps getting better and better." She looked at the two men. "If we're dealing with The Crusade, we're going to need more firepower."

"If we're dealing with The Crusade," Carson corrected her with a frown, "we're going to need more body bags."

"Dinkum and his group will target anything to do with the government. They make David Koresh look like a pansy-assed peacenik," Glenn put in, drumming his fingers against the monitor's screen.

"Yeah, isn't Dinkum that whack job who single-handedly tried to take out the LA Medi-Cal office?" Carson asked, swatting Glenn's hand away from his equipment and calling forth an image of a half-burnt government building.

KC nodded. "He blamed them for not saving his baby sister's life. She needed a new heart or liver, I think."

"Where's Westin now?" Glenn asked. "We've got outstanding warrants on Dinkum. If Westin leads us to him, we can end this tonight."

What was KC supposed to do, tell them that she and Westin had been necking in her room upstairs? Damn it, she knew the man was trouble.

"No," she said. "Then we might lose Gianotti. We need to document the exchange, nail them both." She ignored their frowns. "Glenn, call the Staties, tell them we're going to need back-up from their Emergency Response Team tomorrow. Carson, you get me everything you can on Dinkum. I'll take care of Westin."

"KC, it's too risky," Glenn argued. "These guys think killing federal agents is like bowling for dollars. We need to call Holstrom."

Holstrom was the Special Agent in Charge of the Philadelphia office. KC's boss. Who currently thought she and her team were in Reading working a RICO surveillance. Glenn and Carson had no idea how far she'd strayed from the reservation when she agreed to help Jay Westin.

KC shook her head. She didn't trust anyone except her team. Especially not Holstrom. She couldn't prove it, but she was certain Holstrom was dirty. She was sure he had burned Manny, set him up for the fall. Maybe those other agents whose covers had been blown as well. Could she ask Glenn and Carson to risk their lives based on her gut feeling?

"Remember Manny? Or Webster, the agent undercover inside The Crusade last June? They needed DNA to ID his body, he'd been beaten and tortured so bad. Someone is selling us out, someone with a high enough clearance to have access to the undercover database. We can't risk it."

"So we're on our own?" Glenn and Carson exchanged glances.

"Until tomorrow when the Staties come to back us up. You guys have a problem with that?" She met their gazes, each in turn looked away. Both men knew it was her life on the line, not theirs. KC was the one playing a role where the slightest slip might get her killed.

A slip like getting too close to their new principal bad guy.

She crossed her arms against the frisson of fear that swept over her body as she remembered exactly how close Chase Westin had gotten to her, how he'd almost overcome all her defenses.

Wouldn't happen again, she vowed.

CHAPTER 12

IT TOOK ALL OF Chase's skill and concentration to keep his Harley upright as he sped around the switchbacks down Rattlesnake Pike.

KC filled his mind, her taste was in his mouth, not even the frigid air blowing in his face could dispel the memory of her scent. He'd never been obsessed by a woman like this. Especially not a younger one—he preferred his women old enough to enjoy a drink and intelligent conversation—but KC fascinated him.

In the midst of this gray, dreary winter she was spark of color and vitality. A spark that could turn his brother's future into ashes.

He hoped she listened to him, ended things with Jay. Rotten Christmas present for the kid, but better than a life tied down to misery.

He could almost feel her hands on his, leading him to explore the mysteries of her body, pressing them against her taut, flat belly, the tattooed lizard undulating and winking at him. He imagined her breath quickening as he slowly, ever so slowly, peeled those skin-tight jeans away, taking his sweet time, nuzzling her with his mouth, stroking her until she writhed beneath his touch, hot and ready—

The Harley spun on a sheet of black ice. His stomach lurched as he and the bike flew toward the edge of the mountain. Brakes squealing, leaning all his weight to one side, his leg almost grazing the pavement, he finally regained control. Then, instead of slowing down, Chase pushed the bike faster, imminent danger the only thing able to banish the vision of KC's face from his mind.

He leaned into the next turn, the same turn where he and Nicky Gianotti had almost crashed the Malibu when they were seniors in high school, heading over to Altoona to sneak into Palomino's and pick up beer and girls. Good times, it was a miracle they made it to graduation alive.

By then, Nicky's father had already turned the family business over to the eldest son, Bruno, so Nicky was free to do anything he wanted. He'd taken his freedom and turned it into a heroin addiction, dying his sophomore year after binging on Dominican Gold.

Chase remembered Nicky's funeral. Old Man Gianotti had seemed ancient, bent with grief at the loss of his youngest. Bruno Gianotti had ranted and raved about drugs and the police's inability to do anything about them and vowed that his family would never support the narcotics industry.

Bruno had already begun moving the family's interests out of the numbers racket, and although several of the Philly mob families had reached out to him, after Nicky's death he'd focused his attention on the more lucrative arms trade. Why not give the drug dealers the means to kill themselves, Bruno argued one night shortly after Nicky's funeral when he was drunk on rage and whiskey. Let them put each other six feet under instead of innocent kids.

And now here Chase was, back home, working to put Bruno and his customers behind bars. As soon as he found a way to stop

The Crusade.

Nicky would be laughing, he was sure, raising a glass to Chase's crazy schemes. Stop The Crusade, the largest, meanest bunch of psycho-fanatics in the country? Hell, Chase couldn't even stop one skinny, tattooed, purple-haired girl from making a fool of him.

The Harley thundered around the last curve and the Blue Bird Inn came into view. Chase put on his game face and forced all thoughts of teenaged vixens aside. Time to go to work.

He entered the bar, scanning the crowd. Lucky was nowhere to be seen. Deacon sat alone in a rear booth where he could keep an eye on everyone. Chase gave him a nod before heading in that direction. The sound of a woman's laugh grabbed his attention. Chase spun around, certain that KC had followed him, envisioning her rushing toward him, leaping into his arms, wrapping her legs around him.

It was only the waitress flirting with Redman.

"What's wrong, Westin, didn't Santa bring you anything warm and cuddly?" Redman asked, swatting the waitress' fleshy buttocks. "Shirley here can take care of that, she's just oozing Christmas cheer."

Chase frowned and waved off the waitress, ignoring her feigned pout as he moved around the pool table. Damn it, he couldn't be distracted, not now, not with so much at stake. He slid into the booth across from Deacon, accepted the shot of Jack Daniels.

"Lucky fill you in on the meet details?" he asked.

Deacon nodded. "How's your brother? Everything all right?"

"Family. You know how it goes." He took a drink, hating that Deacon knew about Jay's existence much less that he lived nearby. Couldn't be helped, though. "Anything going on I should know about?"

Deacon paused, his dark eyes boring into Chase's in a way most people would find disquieting. Chase merely shrugged it off. He knew Deacon needed to be intimidating to maintain power over his rag-tag group of enforcers, but he'd been working with Deacon for months now, he had no need to prove anything to the man.

The ex-Crip had some surprises of his own. Chase had tailed Deacon a few times, trying to gain insight into the man. Whenever they were in a major city, Deacon would invariably spend most of his free time at the local Children's Hospital, always leaving behind a substantial anonymous donation.

In small towns like Coalton, Deacon prowled the cemeteries. Chase had seen him more than once kneel down and bow his head over what would turn out to be a child's grave.

Strange behavior from a guy who wanted to kill everyone in authority, but hey, Chase figured even the Nazis had their soft spots.

"What's your opinion of Brother Cavanaugh?" Deacon asked in his quiet voice. "How's he working out?"

"What do I care?" Chase kept his face neutral. Maybe there was something to Lucky's bad feeling after all. "You're the one brought him in on this, said you needed an expert to see that Gianotti's not cheating you." He took a drink. "You're not calling the deal off, are you? 'Cause then I would care. It'd be my ass on the line with Gianotti. Not to mention the commission I'd be forfeiting."

Deacon watched him for a long moment. "No, proceed as planned."

Chase tilted his glass back, then set it down. "Is there something hinky with Cavanaugh?" He looked around the bar, counting heads. Everyone except Lucky accounted for. "You still want me to take him to the meet to verify your shipment for you?"

"I wouldn't count on that," Deacon replied, his tone vague. "Don't worry, I'll handle everything."

"All right, then." Chase slid out of the booth, hoping that Lucky was safe in his room, not lying in a ditch somewhere, a bullet in his head.

The image almost brought the cheap whiskey back up. He swallowed hard. "Tomorrow's gonna be a long day," he said, throwing a five on the table. "See ya."

He felt Deacon's stare on his back and kept his stride easy as he left the bar and made his way through the frigid night air to the safety of his room. He couldn't risk going to Lucky's room. Hell, he didn't even know which one the ATF agent was in. But he had to warn him somehow.

Chase eyed the hotel telephone. Deacon was paranoid about electronics—which was how he stayed two steps ahead of the law. No one in his circle was allowed to carry cell phones or computers. He'd have someone monitoring the outgoing calls for certain, but what about room to room? Chase needed to get Lucky out of here, ASAP. He bounced on his feet, mulling over the problem, then saw the ice bucket.

Chase grabbed it and left the room. Lucky's Suzuki wasn't parked out front, so he tried the rear first. He walked through the covered breezeway that connected the front and back of the building and housed the ice machine. The night was quiet except for the beat of Garth Brooks coming from the jukebox in the bar.

He crept down to the other end of the hallway and peered around the corner. Lucky's bike was parked in front of room thirteen.

Deacon's brand of humor, he assumed. Lucky probably didn't appreciate the joke. At least Chase hoped it was only a joke. He took a gamble and approached the room. It was dark and silent, the drapes drawn shut except for a small crack between them. He looked over his shoulder, no one was near, so he bent forward, strained to see inside.

Snowy white sheets puddled on the floor, the bed was empty.
Something shiny lay beside the nightstand, an overturned brass
lamp.

This was bad, very bad. He couldn't tell if anyone waited
inside, ready to spring a trap if he entered. Or would he find Lucky's
body?

Chase pushed the thought aside and focused on the task at hand,
ignoring the prickling between his shoulder blades. He reached for
the doorknob. It was open. He inhaled deeply and turned it. Nothing
stirred on this side of the building. He slipped inside, shut the door
behind him.

Chaos greeted him. The room had been thoroughly searched by
someone who didn't care if anyone noticed.

No sign of Lucky. Chase crouched on the far side of the bed,
the dim light from outside gleaming against the white fur of Lucky's
rabbit foot. He reached for the leather jacket it was attached to.

Worse than bad. Lucky's tracking device and panic button
remained concealed beneath the collar snap. No coat meant no way
to trace Lucky. The fact that Lucky hadn't found some way to grab
it and activate the panic alarm meant there was a very good chance
he was already dead.

Chase stood, let the coat drop back to the floor beside the bed.

What had happened? All he'd done was spend a little time
at home and then more at KC's—had Lucky somehow exposed
himself because Chase was too busy screwing around, because he
hadn't been there to watch his partner's back?

Why was it every time Chase came home all hell broke loose?

CHAPTER 13

KC RAN HER FINGERS through her hair, tugging on the ends as if trying to pull the answers she needed from her brain.

"You'll be bald you keep that up," Glenn said, sinking into the chair beside her. "Bad vibes about tomorrow?"

She stilled her hands. Her foot began tapping. How could she tell him and Carson that they were on their own out here in the middle of nowhere, that no one at the Bureau even knew where they were, much less what they were doing? The image of the agent tortured to death by The Crusade kept intruding itself in her vision. That could be Glenn or Carson if she wasn't careful, if she trusted the wrong person.

She had to trust herself. Her instincts had gotten her this far, the only other option was to abort and slink back to Philly. Where Special Agent in Charge Holstrom would turn her over to the OPR and she'd get her ass booted out of the Bureau. Maybe even thrown in jail if they really wanted to nail her.

"I don't like dealing with The Crusade. Too many unknowns," she finally told Glenn.

"That's just what Carson and I were thinking. We think you should take us with you tomorrow instead of posting us on the rooftop. If we're going to keep you safe, we need to be closer."

She couldn't hide her smile at that. Positioning them on the rooftop was her way of keeping them safe. "Deacon is a paranoid freak. He gets a whiff of anyone sniffing around either the Gianotti or Westin family and he'll declare war on this town. A lot of innocent people could get caught in the crossfire."

She rolled onto her feet, stretched the kinks out of her spine. "No. We go as planned. Just me on the street, you guys and the Staties ready to back me up if I need you."

When she looked up the older man's eyes were creased in worry. "Don't worry, Pops," she said with a short laugh. "If I do my job right not only will we nail Gianotti and Westin but we'll bring down Deacon and his boys as well. They'll give us medals."

"I'd settle for a home-cooked meal and a few days off. Anyone ever tell you you're a lousy cook?"

KC laughed, for real this time, the movement making her fake tattoo dance. She reached down and patted Glenn's arm. "Us bad girls rely on other talents," she said, sashaying toward the steps. "I'm going to get some sleep. You and Carson all right down here?"

He glanced over at the monitors. Carson's head bobbed in time to music coming through one earphone while he scanned their bugs with the other. "Yeah, I'll wake you if anything happens."

"Night." She peered back down over the banister. Glenn and Carson were good men, good friends. She had to do right by them. If anything happened to them because of Chase Westin and his gang of thieves...

Her grandfather had once told her how they took revenge on traitors, back in the old country. It involved barbed wire, sharp knives and a high tree limb. Not a pretty picture but it paled in comparison with what she'd do to Westin if one of her people got hurt.

No one was going to get hurt, she repeated with every step she took. Not on her team. Her ops never went south. Never.

JAY TOSSED AND TURNED, unable to sleep. He'd actually gotten up once to go apologize to Chase, to talk things over and say goodbye, but Chase was gone. Probably out drinking, finding some new way to screw up.

Like going to work for Mr. Gianotti. What had he been thinking? Before their folks died, Chase never in a million years would have thought of doing something like that. It was as if something had broken inside Chase after what happened in Afghanistan. Left him a changed man.

Jay remembered long hours sitting in silence at Chase's bedside at Bethesda. Chase never once acknowledged his presence, the few times he made eye contact, he'd stare right through Jay like Jay was the walking ghost.

He rolled over again, pounding the pillow, trying to find a comfortable position. He wished he could trust Chase with the truth, maybe even convince him to join KC and him tomorrow. Maybe Chase knew something about Mr. Gianotti that KC could use to convince her bosses to offer Chase a deal.

Or maybe Chase would tell Mr. Gianotti about KC, get her killed.

Jay opened his eyes as the sound of a gunshot echoed through his memory. His body tensed now just as it did two months ago, as if it were far removed from the gruesome sight before him. Then came the adrenalin surge of terror as he ran for his life.

That fear hadn't subsided much these past few months—not

until KC came along. Finally he was beginning to feel safe again. Even daring to hope that he had a future to look forward to.

All thanks to KC. He blew out his breath, forced his eyes closed once more. He had to get some rest. Tomorrow was a big day. He wondered what KC was doing, how she was preparing for the completion of her operation. She could handle Mr. Gianotti's men, he was certain. She'd keep Neil safe as well. Maybe he should tell her about Chase?

He wished he could stay and watch her in action, imagined her sending the bad guys flying with spinning kicks and hard hitting punches, then pulling her gun and yelling at them to Freeze! like they did on TV.

Jay sighed. He would be far away, sequestered in some hotel room with two Federal Marshals. Guys like Jay never got to see any of the action.

Since meeting KC he was wondering if medical school was really for him. Instead, he could get his degree, apply to the FBI— maybe even end up working undercover with KC. Or together under the covers, he thought, his mind flashing to an image of her in his arms. The fantasy put a smile on his face, and he finally drifted into sleep.

Until a pair of hands grabbed his shoulders, shaking him from the unconscious realms of his dreams.

"Get up!" Neil shouted at him. "C'mon, we have to hurry!"

Fear jolted through Jay. Was Mr. Gianotti after him? Did he know what Jay had seen? He sat upright, tugged on the jeans Neil threw at him.

"What's wrong?" he asked, pulling a sweatshirt over his head.

"Your brother—he's gone after KC!"

Now Jay was fully awake. He stepped into a pair of sneakers and followed Neil outside, not bothering with his coat. The anger surging through him was protection enough against the cold. "Is she all right?"

"I don't know," Neil said as he started his Firebird. "I saw Chase at her bedroom window. I didn't know what to do. I didn't want to wake her father, he'd kill her for sure, so I came to get you—" The words poured out of him in a rush until he was forced to take a breath.

Jay's vision cleared as the red haze of anger receded. KC could take care of herself. Heck, she probably had Chase in handcuffs and was hauling him off to jail as they spoke. Except she couldn't do that without blowing her cover and placing Jay at risk—how far would she go to protect him? He knew that was her job and all, but he hated that she was in jeopardy because of him.

Damn it, why did Chase have to pick now to come home and ruin his life?

CHAPTER 14

ROSE PROSPERO PACED THE area between her desk and the door, her eyes never leaving the clock. Something was wrong, seriously wrong. She knew field ops had to be flexible, sometimes contacts were missed. Hell, she'd spent over a decade with the CIA crawling through the slums of the world and how many checkpoints had she missed?

Never two in a row. Except for that time in Razgravia and that was because she was busy rotting in the filth of a jail cell, abandoned by the Agency.

When she took command of the Special Threats Team, she'd vowed to give her people the utmost support. They would never endure the same fate she had.

Damn it, if only she could have gotten that worm in Hell's Bend to talk before he died. She'd known the bartender was holding out on her, that he knew who had set up Victor. Unfortunately, Deacon's people were religious about cleaning up any loose ends. When she'd gone back to interview the bartender after hours, she'd found his gutted remains hanging from the set of elk antlers behind his bar.

As if what The Crusade had done to Victor hadn't been warning enough to prevent anyone in Hell's Bend from talking to strangers. She was glad she hadn't told Billy about the two men who had come after her as she was making her escape from the small border town. They'd underestimated her and paid dearly for it—with their lives.

Probably take days before anyone found their bodies in the arroyo where they'd planned to rape and torture Rose.

Her jaws clenched at the thought of the fate the two Crusaders had intended for her. She couldn't help but hope that the buzzards and coyotes took their time with the bodies.

It had been a long time since Rose had killed anyone in close quarters. She'd showered twice since returning to the STR Headquarters, but still the coppery taste of blood and fear etched the back of her throat.

At least Victor's death hadn't gone totally unavenged. She hoped Deacon got the message: she wouldn't rest until she nailed his ass. And she didn't care if she had to break some laws to do it. Not when the fate of her team and a whole population of innocent civilians hung in the balance.

What the hell was Deacon planning with all those weapons? And how in God's name had he broken past their security? Again.

There had to be someone helping him. Someone on the inside of the intelligence community with access to the most secure databases.

She stopped before the large map of the world spread across one wall. Billy Price kept badgering her to upgrade to a computerized version like the one in his office. One of the many things they agreed to disagree on.

Rose cherished tried and true, the elegant simplicity of methods she'd successfully used in a career that helped to bring about the fall of the last of the Soviet regimes and stabilize the chaos that swept over the Baltic region in its wake.

Billy was former Delta Force, had field-tested and helped to design state of the art equipment intended to help military operatives to infiltrate and if necessary, engage the enemy. The man loved his gadgets and thought Rose hopelessly old fashioned. Just one of the many reasons why Billy thought he should have her job.

Her fingers danced over the red, orange, and yellow pins tapped into the corresponding hot spots around the globe. There were already so many to keep track of, the number of threats growing daily. Most of them were being dealt with by more traditional agencies. But she still needed to keep on top of each one, just in case her team was called in.

Her fingers brushed across a handful of white pins. Her people. Almost three dozen in the field right now, thirty-four men and women missing the holiday, risking their lives for their country. She could put a name and face to every one of those pins, also the name of their closest relative that she'd have to contact if something went wrong.

She tapped a cluster of two pins. Chase Westin—only relative was his brother, Jay. She wondered about the reunion of the brothers now that Chase had been forced back to his hometown. She felt partly responsible for their estrangement. But she knew it was for the best.

The Team couldn't function as the multi-agency organization it was, crossing bureaucratic lines, even the occasional law, if its existence became widely known. When any new team member was recruited, they had to break clean from their former colleagues and start a new life. Which was why Rose only accepted volunteers who were unattached, no spouses, no children.

Her finger moved to the second pin. Lucky Cavanaugh. He was a hot shot at the ATF, best demolitions man around, but this was his first long term undercover assignment. How would he do under pressure? An electric shock raced through her finger, jolted into her gut.

The door opened without a knock, and Billy Price strode in.

"Lucky's in trouble," Rose said.

He joined her, pulling a Blackberry from his pocket instead of examining the map. As if Billy didn't know as well as Rose exactly where all their people were.

"I wouldn't worry," he said. "Chase is looking after him."

Rose turned away from the map. She dreaded calling Ralph Cavanaugh, Lucky's father, a retired DC Metro police sergeant.

She looked over at Billy. He had what some would call hard features, chiseled good looks reminiscent of old time movie stars, as opposed to the pretty boys who graced the big screen nowadays. Character, charisma—Billy Price was a born leader. He tended to the needs of their people, kept the mundane, picayune demands of the politicians away from Rose, freeing her to concentrate on more important details.

"His GPS is stationary, coordinates correspond with the motel," Price told her, swiveling the computer screen her way. "Don't worry, he's got a good head on his shoulders."

When Billy Price told her not to worry, Rose worried; when he told her twice, she started draping the mirrors with black crepe.

"We in contact with Chase?" Billy went on.

"He's made all his regular check-ins," Rose said. "But the phone at his brother's house has been disconnected."

Billy raised an eyebrow at the fact that she'd broken protocol and tried to contact Chase via an unsecured line. Rose ignored his look of disapproval. Billy never said it, but she knew he sometimes thought she let things get too personal. Just like a woman, he'd say if he ever dared.

"Anyone crashing here tonight?"

Billy didn't need to consult his computer. "Hollywood. And Marion's just in from LA."

Rose looked up at that. Marion Rockey was one of the few on The Team Billy didn't call by their nickname or surname. Were the two of them involved? The blonde was pretty, vivacious and smart—she'd be a nice match for Billy.

"Wake them. And get EZ in, he can help O'Reilly in ops. I want a diagnostic on every covert op database, starting with the ATF's. We need to be ready to head to Pennsylvania."

"What good would that do? Any action we take may blow Chase's cover."

As her second in command, it was Billy's job to point out anything she might need to take into consideration. His attention to detail helped her focus on the big picture. Still, it was damned irritating at times. Especially as she knew that if she were a man and ex-military instead of former CIA, he would never question her authority.

None of that mattered now. Something bad was happening to one of her people and Rose had to fix it.

"Do it, Billy. Now."

CHAPTER 15

KC SAT IN THE dark, knowing sleep wouldn't come, so instead she reviewed the plan for tomorrow over and over again, searching for any weakness, any potential fatal flaw she should prepared for. She found none, had covered every contingency—except for Chase Westin, damn the man.

Her eyelids drifted shut, only for a second, she promised herself. She could smell Chase's musky scent, felt his hands warming her as they explored her body. His blue eyes blazed down at her, his hunger and need echoing her own as his mouth pressed down over hers.

Chase Westin may be a lowlife scumbag—but damn, he could kiss.

KC remembered the thrill of pleasure that raced through her during their brief encounter. Would she really have had sex with him? Not only was he untrustworthy, could get her and her team killed, but wouldn't that also be like cheating on Jay? She knew the kid had feelings for her, even if she'd done everything she could to discourage them.

She'd like to think she would not have crossed the line, that even if Westin hadn't left when he did, she would have kept control, stopped things before they went further.

Her breath caught as she remembered the heat of his touch, and she knew herself to be a liar.

Damn, she couldn't risk seeing or touching—hell, breathing the same air in the same room as Chase Westin. Maybe she should have him locked up.

No good. That thought brought with it the image of Chase in cuffs, his back to her as she ran her hands over his rock-hard muscles, his flesh simmering beneath her touch. She envisioned him looking back over his shoulder with that maddening, superior smirk on his face, asking, "Was it good for you?"

And then facing her in a claustrophobic interrogation room, where they shared the same tiny space. Her leg would brush against his, accidentally of course. Restrained in his chair, he would be powerless to move away as she lowered her body onto his, straddling him, their faces mere inches apart. Then KC would begin to—

A tapping at her window woke her with a start. She leapt from the bed, settling into a fighting stance, her knife in her hand.

Once her heart stopped pounding so hard it drowned out all sound, she heard Jay's voice. She turned the light on and opened the window for him.

Didn't the Westins ever hear of using the front door? she wondered as he climbed inside. At least Jay was polite enough to knock.

"What are you doing here?" she demanded, her pulse still racing from the adrenalin surge. "I could have killed you!"

She looked past him and saw Neil watching from the curb beside the Firebird—that explained the unorthodox entry method.

Jay stared at the knife in her hand, his eyes wide. "You didn't have to use that on Chase, did you?" he asked with a gulp.

She slid the knife back into its hidden sheath. Good thing she hadn't drawn her Glock, would've given the kid a heart attack for sure.

Even after everything Jay had seen and done, he still acted as if this was happening to someone else, a character on TV or the movies. About time the kid got a taste of reality. This was serious business with real lives on the line.

"Would've served him right if I did."

"He's all right? He didn't hurt you, did he?" Jeez, the kid was really worried. KC wasn't certain if he was more concerned about her safety or his brother's.

"He wanted me to break things off with you. I pretended to flirt with him, it scared him off."

Jay looked surprised at that. "Really? Nothing happened?"

KC shrugged. "Just a kiss, nothing more—"

Jay's face went red with anger. She kept forgetting that as mature and smart as he was, the kid was still only nineteen, more controlled by hormones than brains.

"It was nothing. In fact, I initiated it. Had to stay in character, you know?" He didn't appear convinced. Then again, neither was she. "Anyway, it worked and he left."

"He didn't," he was blushing now, his eyes cutting over to the bed with its rumpled covers, "want to take things further?"

Whenever she and Jay spoke of Chase, it was obvious that Jay had no idea how to feel about his older brother. Yeah, the kid had a lot of resentment and anger, who could blame him? But Jay also still looked up to his brother, despite how far Chase Westin had fallen in the past year.

Jay slumped onto the bed, his hands hanging between his

knees. KC joined him, the mattress sagging under their weight, and wrapped an arm around his shoulders. They didn't cover this kind of thing at Quantico.

What was she supposed to say? Tough luck kid, your brother's a traitor and an asshole, and the only good thing about it is that your parents died before they found out?

"My grandfather, Konstantine, had a saying for everything," she finally said.

He looked up at that. She'd shared a little of her real life history with him, trying to help him feel comfortable around her. The kid loved hearing about her grandfather and his adventures in Razgravia, the last of the totalitarian former Soviet regimes still standing.

"Did he have an older brother who kept messing up his life?" he asked in a mournful tone.

"Worse. His brother, younger though, not older, wanted to kill him. Gregor, his brother, joined up with Stalin and the Soviets, was dedicated to crushing the resistance Konstantine led. Because of Gregor, one of my grandfather's fighters, a gypsy woman named Rosa, was captured.

"Konstantine trusted that, although they were on opposite sides, his brother would still be honorable, so when Gregor proposed a truce to negotiate for Rosa's release, he went. Then he was taken as well."

Jay's eyes went wide, the story from the past seemed to both distract him and help put his own family problems in perspective. "What happened?"

"He and Rosa escaped, but they were separated afterward. Konstantine was wounded, a young girl from a small village tended to him, kept him safe and hidden from his brother, and together they formed a new resistance cell."

"He fell in love with her, didn't he?"

KC nodded. "That was my grandmother, Sophia. When the resistance crumbled and the Soviets took control, they escaped to America. Anyway, my grandfather used to say increde se inseala, trust is treason."

Harsh words, but a mantra the kid needed to learn if he was going to survive after she brought Gianotti to trial. Her grandfather's words had served KC well during her career. Even with Manny, who had taught her so much, gave her so much, she hadn't dared to offer her trust. At times she woke with regret about that, that he never truly knew how she felt about him. But most times she simply barricaded the thought behind the walls she'd built around her heart.

She offered her grandfather's wisdom to Jay, her final lesson to him.

"You mean I shouldn't trust Chase—not with the truth, not with my feelings?" He frowned, gave his head a small shake, denying her words of wisdom. "You don't know him like I do. He's a good guy. At least he was. He saved the lives of a lot of people when he was in the Marines, he was a hero." Jay hung his head.

"I always felt a little jealous," he continued in a low voice. "My dad's hero was John Wayne, and here my brother grew up to be a real live John Wayne. Tough for me to get much recognition for anything I did after that, you know?"

"Jay, your father loved you. Everyone in town talks about how you're just like him. Well, until I came along, that is, and got you in trouble." She elbowed him, flashing one of "bad girl" KC's wicked grins, and he smiled back.

"I know. Dad and I could talk about anything. He was a great guy. But you should've seen the look in his eye whenever Chase came home or called or even sent a letter. He was so proud of

Chase, of the man he'd become. I know I'll never be half the man he is."

KC sprang off the bed to face him. "You're already twice the man your brother is. He may have been a hero once, but look at him now, a total screw-up. And you, you've shown more courage and strength than a platoon of Marines. You kept your wits about you, stayed cool under pressure.

"Agreeing to testify against Gianotti, much less waiting until we could build a good case before leaving here, that takes guts. From what I've seen, more guts than what your brother has. I mean, come on, how much courage does it take to sneak into a girl's room and threaten her to stay away from his brother?"

Her intention had been to instill Jay with some pride; the kid hadn't had much in the way of positive reinforcement since his parents died. Maybe that was why he'd fallen for her so easily. He looked up, and KC saw that she'd gone too far, the fury at his brother had returned.

Jay got to his feet, started toward the window. "Don't worry, he won't bother you again."

KC stopped him with a hand on his arm. "He didn't bother me, not the real me," she said, reminding him of the role she played. "I'm the one in control here, remember? And you—" She ran her fingers through his too long, sleep tousled hair—what was it with the Westin brothers and their thick, shaggy hair that enticed her so? "You have the rest of your life. You can be anything you want, Jay Westin. It was a privilege to meet you."

He looked away in embarrassment. KC stood on tiptoe, the kid was almost as tall as his brother, and gave him a quick peck on the cheek.

"Go home, get some rest, forget about your brother and start planning for your future," she told him. "Goodbye, Jay."

CHASE RETURNED TO THE ice machine, filled his bucket with ice cubes he would never use and headed back to his room, his steps mechanical as he pictured a thousand unpleasant fates for Lucky. None of which he could do anything about except carry on and get the job done.

Only thing he could do was find a way to notify Rose Prospero of Lucky's disappearance and get Jay to safety. Just in case Deacon suspected Chase as well.

He thought over his options. He needed a cover story, something that would ensure him freedom from Deacon's constant surveillance. Chase headed back to the bar, found Redman washing down Buffalo wings with Rolling Rock. Deacon was nowhere to be seen.

"Thought you turned in," Redman said from his perch at the bar.

Chase just shrugged and handed the bartender a twenty. "Bottle of Jack, unopened."

"You sharing?" Redman asked.

"No, it's for my kid brother. We kind of had a fight earlier and I don't have a Christmas present for him, so—"

"You had a fight on fricking Christmas Eve? Jeez, I thought my family was messed up."

"My fault. I screwed up, well," Chase forced a half smile to bolster the lie, "actually I screwed his girlfriend."

"You made it with your lil bro's girlfriend?" He slapped Chase on the arm. "You dog. She must have been a fine young thing, how old?"

"I dunno. Nineteen, twenty-something."

Redman closed his eyes, his tongue darting out to lick his upper lip. "That's a good age on a woman, not too young, not too old, still firm and always wanting to please, know what I mean?"

"Yeah, figured I'd go over, try to make the peace."

"Better not let Deacon see you go. You know how he gets before a deal."

Chase nodded. "It won't take long. Cover for me?"

"Sure thing, man. If you see your teenybopper friend, tell her to stop by here. I'll give her a ride she won't ever forget."

Chase gave the fellow biker a mock salute and took off for Coalton. The wind in his face helped to cool the jealous fury Redman's words about KC had sparked.

He tried to force the fantasy of KC's strong arms wrapping around him out of his mind, but she'd broken past all his barriers, and he was powerless to stop thinking about her. That crazy purple hair, those riveting eyes, her mouth against his, her arousal as his hands explored her body.

Even her lizard tattoo intrigued him. It wasn't an iguana. Some kind of salamander or chameleon maybe? A lizard juggling fate, there had to be a message there somewhere.

He leaned into the bike, squinting into the darkness, but his mind's eye was desperate to see the rest of the hidden image, to have all of KC's body before him to feast upon.

As he thought of her, it wasn't their brief moment of passion he remembered most fondly, stimulating as that had been. The image imprinted on his mind was of KC standing over him, gripping the poker as her only weapon against a man twice her size, her face fierce as she protected Jay.

Damn, a teenaged vixen with ulterior motives was doing a better job of taking care of Jay than Chase was. He remembered the look of disappointment and disgust Jay had turned on him earlier.

The frigid wind beat into his face, forcing tears from his eyes.

Deacon knew where Chase's only family lived.

Chase decided to tell Jay everything. He would get him out of Coalton, send him to Rose Prospero, have her start searching for Lucky. Chase could handle Deacon alone. There was no way he was going to leave now, not when he was so close to nailing both Bruno and Deacon.

No matter the danger to himself, he couldn't allow The Crusade to get hold of Bruno's weapons.

The mission came first, always. He had a job to do here, couldn't be distracted, had to focus. People's lives depended on him finding out what Deacon wanted those explosives for and stopping him before anyone could get hurt.

But now, because of Chase's mission, it was Jay in the line of fire.

Midnight services were just ending. Crowds of smiling people poured onto Main Street, arms entwined, cheeks flushed, as they walked to their homes or cars.

Chase saw Bruno shaking hands with the mayor and averted his eyes from the happy faces filled with Christmas cheer. If these people knew what kind of serpent they'd sheltered in their town all these years what would they say?

Nothing. They would say and do nothing. Best just to keep their silence, who were they to judge anyway? Especially when Bruno Gianotti had single-handedly kept this town afloat the past nine years after the mines closed.

Chase looked around, spying familiar faces in the crowd. How many of them could he count on if he got into trouble? His gaze scoured the freshly scrubbed families wearing their Christmas finery.

Not a single one would stand up to Bruno, he decided. Not to save Chase and not to save Jay.

Whole damn town was living a lie. And Chase was just one more liar. No wonder he fit right in, had found it so easy to betray Jay by almost succumbing to KC's advances.

He gunned the Harley, ignoring the shouts as he scattered churchgoers before him.

Dammit all, once again KC was the only other person willing to fight for his brother. He frowned. If she cared so much for Jay, why had she practically shanghaied Chase into her bed?

Watching his mirrors, he turned onto his street, his house the single dark spot amidst a festival of lights. No sign of any surveillance, good. He pulled the Harley into the carport and went in through the kitchen door.

No more lies, he vowed. Not between Jay and him. Chase would explain everything, even tonight's encounter with KC.

The house was silent, ominously so. He went through it quickly, leaving the lights off. It was empty.

A cold finger of fear began to trace its way down Chase's spine. Jay was gone.

CHAPTER 16

CHASE, WHERE WAS CHASE? Lucky needed to warn him. Lucky's muddled thoughts slowly coalesced as brain and body rejoined. Pain stabbed through his arms and legs, he was shivering uncontrollably while a jackhammer pounded behind his eyes.

It was freezing. Then he realized he was naked except for his boxers. They'd come for him while he slept. He remembered fighting, struggling, the crash of breaking glass, a bright blue jolt of electricity shooting through him. His legs crumbling, then everything had gone black.

Lucky cautiously opened one eye. The pounding in his head increased momentarily, then resumed its previous medium-grade rumble, so he opened the other.

A wave of nausea hit him, and he tried to lean forward but couldn't. He lay on his back, hogtied, arms and legs pinned beneath the weight of his body, duct tape binding them together. He blinked, swallowed back the nausea and sucked in a deep breath to clear his vision.

He was on the dirt floor of some kind of prefab hut. A single dim light bulb hung overhead. Lucky rolled on his side, strained to raise his head enough to look around, search for a weapon, anything that might get him out of here. He had to warn Chase—they would go after him next. And Chase's kid brother.

There was a dust-covered metal desk and chair shoved against one wall, stacks of rolled up blueprints or maps in a rack on the other. Some kind of construction site? Lucky listened for the sound of cars, of any indication of people close by, but there was only absolute silence. He couldn't even hear the wind or any of those other country noises that had kept him awake the first night he'd arrived in Pennsylvania.

His eyes lit on a calendar hanging over the untidy desk in the corner. On it a bikini clad blonde smiled as she adjusted a hard hat with a headlamp on it. The date on the calendar was over a decade old. That fit with what Chase had told him about the mines closing down.

Lucky had the sudden image of dark shafts with deep, deep drops into the bowels of the earth. Great place to dispose of a body.

It wasn't going to get that far, he promised himself. There was always a way out. He just had to be resourceful enough to find it. Only another puzzle to solve.

Voices echoed beyond the office. Damn. He returned to his previous position, feigning unconsciousness as footsteps approached. There was the sound of a padlock being unsnapped from the door, then the door scraped open.

A steel-toed boot nudged his ribs. "Wake up sleeping beauty," came a high-pitched voice that could have belonged to a man or woman. The nudge turned into a bruising kick. "Now!" the voice commanded. "I didn't give you that big of a jolt."

Lucky rolled away from the next kick, this one would have broken a few bones if he'd allowed it to connect, and opened his eyes. Crouched over him was a flinty-eyed man with a large head, long, gangling arms and thick legs connected to a squat trunk. He wasn't a dwarf, but was short and bow-legged, like the deputy in that old TV show, Gunsmoke. Only a hell of a lot uglier.

The man grinned down at Lucky, his breath fetid enough to make Lucky gag. "Hey," he shouted to an unseen accomplice beyond the door, making the crashing in Lucky's head crescendo, "secret agent man is awake!"

He held a small device, dangling it in Lucky's face. The man pressed a button and blue lightning arced between two terminals as he teased Lucky with the stun gun, feinting toward Lucky's naked skin and laughing as Lucky pulled back.

"So you remember my toy?" the man said. "You're gonna see a lot more of it. You must think we're stupid since it took us so long to tumble to you." He shook his head. "Took us a little longer than it used to, after you guys beefed up your security, but we've got friends in high places."

"Who are you?" Lucky asked, maintaining his cover. "What do you want?"

He tried to keep his voice from quivering, but it was hard to do when his body was shivering uncontrollably. All he could think of was the FBI agent The Crusade tortured and murdered six months ago.

"Name's Fergus," the man told him with a laugh. He grinned down at Lucky as Lucky realized the implications that revelation held. "That's right, Agent Cavanaugh, you're not going to be alive long enough to tell anyone who I am. You're only going to stay alive long enough to tell me who you're working with."

The hair on Lucky's head stood at attention as Fergus brought the stun gun closer.

"I don't know what you're talking about." Lucky squirmed

back from the crackling electricity.

"Sure you do," Fergus said, planting the stun gun over Lucky's heart.

A surge of pain shot through his chest and up into his left shoulder. Lucky cried out as his muscles locked into spasm. His heart stuttered for a moment, then began to race. It must have been a lower jolt than they used back at the motel because he didn't black out, although he wished he had.

Fergus took the gun away. Lucky lay there, panting, cold sweat breaking out over his body as the pain slowly subsided. A residual pins and needles sensation continued down his left arm and his hand flopped uselessly behind his back.

"That was only setting four," Fergus said. "Now tell me about your partners. We know there must be others in The Crusade. Who are they? How do you communicate with your superiors?"

They didn't know about Chase. All Lucky had to do was hold out, keep quiet.

"Go to hell," he told Fergus.

"I was hoping you'd say something like that," Fergus said as he lowered the stun gun once more.

CHASE GRABBED THE PHONE but there was no dial tone. Damn. Jay's denim jacket hung from the coat hooks on the back of the door, a small, telltale bulge in the pocket. Cell phone, hooyah.

Chase dialed the number he knew best, the green glow from the phone's face bathing his fingers in a ghostly shimmer. He drew his Heckler Koch nine millimeter, trying to ignore the chill that had enveloped him, and squatted down on the floor, his back to the wall, senses alert for any disruption.

"Standard Communications, how may I direct your call?"

came a chipper sounding woman's voice. Teresa O'Reilley, head
of The Team's communication complex. Figured she'd be working
the holiday. Teresa probably gave the rest of her staff time off and
stayed on to man the complex herself.

"It's Westin, I need Prospero or Price—code red."

"They're both here, Chase. Hang on one sec." There was a beep
followed by a click. "Okay, the line's secure. You're through to
Rose." Another click and Teresa was gone.

"What's your status?" Rose Prospero's clipped tone was a
contrast to Teresa's warmth.

"Lucky's missing, looks like they grabbed him—don't know
if he's dead or alive." Chase quickly outlined the events of the day.
He marveled at how calm and steady his voice remained, despite
the flutter of anxiety trilling through his veins. "Now Jay's missing
too."

"We're already working on Lucky. I'll make some discrete
inquires with the State Police about Jay. Local authorities are
compromised, they'll be no help."

"Excuse me," Teresa's voice broke in. "Chase, whose phone are
you using?"

Chase was startled by the interruption, but knew Teresa must
have a good reason for it. "My brother's cell, why?"

"There's a tracer on the bandwidth, when I tracked it back, the
signal's also being broadcast on a radio frequency—"

"You mean it's bugged?" Chase looked at the phone as if it
were a snake. At least Teresa had already secured the line. "How the
hell did Deacon plant a bug in Jay's phone?"

"Not Deacon, unless he's using classified government
technology. This is a configuration exactly like the ones we use. If
you give me the serial number, I can run it down."

"Why would a government agency be monitoring your teenage

brother?" Rose asked, cutting to the heart of the matter.

"I have no idea," Chase answered after giving Teresa the serial number. Headlights swept across the front windows and stopped. He crept to the dining room, glanced outside.

And was able to take his first deep breath since he'd found the house empty. Jay was sitting in the passenger seat of Neil Gianotti's Firebird, parked right at the front curb.

Chase restrained his desire to run out and pummel his younger brother for scaring the crap out of him. Probably a midnight rendezvous with KC, he thought, hating the wave of jealousy the image brought with it. He re-holstered the HK at the small of his back and tugged his shirt over it once more.

"I'm pulling you out," Rose told him.

"No need. I'm fine, my cover's solid."

"Not if they have your brother—"

"Jay just pulled up in his friend's car. Must have been out carousing somewhere. And Lucky won't give me up." He heard her sigh and knew she was sorely tempted to move him someplace safe, abort the mission.

"Just give me a little time, Rose. Once I make contact with The Crusade, find the rest of their stash, we're golden. This is too important to walk away from." Not to mention the six months of his life he'd sacrificed for this job. And the best way to guarantee Jay's future safety was to end this now. He sweetened the pot. "Besides, Deacon is going to be at the buy tomorrow."

Her intake of breath echoed over the phone. Deacon never got his hands dirty, never. That was why they hadn't been able to nail him yet.

"Dinkum is there, in Coalton?"

"He will be tomorrow. Said he'd see to the delivery personally." Chase dangled the bait, knowing she'd never be able to resist.

"All right," she said. "Stay, but for godsake, get your brother out of there. Send him on a cruise, I don't care, I need you focused on this mission, not babysitting."

"Yes, ma'am."

"The phone belongs to the FBI," Teresa broke in once more. "The case number is assigned to a RICO investigation, the case agent is a Manuelo Ramirez from the White Collar Crime Unit. The man they're investigating is named Dunlap, Albert Dunlap, he lives in Philadelphia."

"Any of this ringing bells for you, Chase?" Rose asked.

Chase frowned, more confused than ever. What the hell had Jay gotten himself mixed up in? Philadelphia? That was where KC was from—had Jay's good for nothing girlfriend stolen Dunlap's phone? Probably gave some FBI agents an earful of phone sex.

"Nothing except Jay's new girlfriend comes from Philly. I'll ask Jay, here he comes now."

"Be discrete, don't risk your cover. We'll take care of Lucky. Chase, be careful." She hung up.

Neil drove off as Jay walked up the front steps. Damn, Chase was gonna kill the kid. He turned the phone off and pocketed it.

Jay opened the door, saw Chase standing there waiting for him and let loose with an uppercut that sent Chase sprawling.

"You bastard! If you ever go near KC again, I'll—"

Chase looked up at his little brother towering over him, sputtering with fury, fists raised. He rubbed his jaw and decided the better part of valor was to remain where he was.

Otherwise someone might get hurt.

Chase raised his hands in surrender, waited until Jay backed off, then rolled to his feet. Good God, couldn't he and Jay just once meet in a civilized fashion? Although, depending on how KC spun the tale to Jay, he could well understand his brother's anger.

Jay looked down at his fist, unclenched it and shook it out as if surprised that a sock to the jaw hurt the socker as much as the sockee. He stumbled back into the Barcalounger and sat down, hands dangling between his knees.

"Nice punch," Chase told him, taking a seat on the sofa. "You must think this girl's something special, huh?"

No surprise there, he did too. What was it about KC that bewitched and bemused the Westin boys so they couldn't see straight?

"She is special," Jay said, looking up, his jaw jutting out, defying Chase to contradict him. "You had no right—"

"I was just trying to look out for my brother. That's the only reason I went there, Jay. Honest."

Jay pursed his lips, considering Chase's statement. "When Neil told me he saw you, I thought," he blushed, "I thought you were trying to take her away or something." Then he smiled as if that was an impossibility and shook his head.

Did Jay think the girl so hopelessly in love with him that she would never betray him? Chase remembered the way she'd thrown herself at him. He needed to tell Jay, but it would probably end with the two of them not speaking, bitter enemies again.

Maybe there was another way to separate the two lovebirds. Chase took out Jay's phone. "Want to tell me why you have a phone that belongs to the FBI?"

Jay jumped out of the chair, grabbed the phone from Chase's hand. "That's mine." He retreated across the room, clutching the phone as if it was a lifeline. Then he frowned. "FBI? How do you know it belongs to the FBI?"

"I was stationed at Quantico, remember?" Chase adlibbed. "Where'd you get the phone, Jay? You can get in big trouble if they catch you with this."

Jay looked from the phone to his brother. Chase was surprised to see an expression of deep consideration cross his face, as if Chase were the one caught with stolen government technology, as if Chase were the one who couldn't be trusted.

"If you tell anyone about this," Jay began in a voice that sounded very serious and older than his years, "it could get me killed."

CHAPTER 17

THIS WAS CRAZY, JAY thought. KC had warned him not to trust anyone, especially his brother. But, even as messed up as Chase was, he would never, ever do anything to hurt Jay. That was the one thing Jay knew.

He couldn't stand having Chase looking at him like he was screwing up his life, worried that he was following in Chase's footsteps.

"Killed?" Chase said, leaning forward, his eyes darting around the empty room as if searching for hidden danger.

Chase got that look a lot. Ever since he came back from Afghanistan. And it seemed to be getting worse. Jay didn't know what kind of trouble his brother was in, but he wished he could do something to take that haunted look away from Chase's eyes.

"What the hell are you talking about?"

"I saw something a few months ago." Jay swallowed hard, the memory of that awful night still made him sick. "I was supposed to meet Neil. He was going to sneak out and we were going over to a party some kids from Bishop Guillfoyle were throwing. I went by his place and I was a little early, he was supposed to meet me behind the garage after he snuck out. I heard these voices, and I ducked into the bushes.

"Mr. Gianotti and another guy were arguing. Something about a shipment that wasn't paid for and the guy was in tears, saying it wasn't his fault the truck got stopped by the cops, and he'd come there in person to show his good faith."

Jay paused, closed his eyes against the memory. That did nothing to block the sounds echoing in his mind. The man weeping, Neil's father saying the reason he was going to die was because he dared to come to the Gianotti house, to violate his sanctuary, threaten his family.

"It was stupid, I know," he went on, "but I wanted to see what was happening, so I got a little closer, looked through the window. They had a plastic sheet on the floor of the garage and Mr. Gianotti had a gun. Two other guys were holding this other man down on his knees, like he was begging or something. He was crying so hard, he wet his pants."

"Jesus, Jay." Chase was off the couch in one swift movement. He crouched beside the recliner, his arm wrapped around Jay's shoulder.

Jay appreciated the support of his big brother. Chase was trained for stuff like this—stuff that Jay had only seen in movies until that awful October night.

"Mr. Gianotti shot him. Right in the face," Jay whispered. "I always thought guns would make more noise than that. It was just a sort of a pop, nothing compared to the blood and—"

His voice trailed off. He realized he was shaking. Jay turned away from Chase. He sucked in a deep breath, tried to pull himself together. He could do this. He had to get used to telling it, in a few months he'd be telling it to a jury.

"No one saw you, did they?" Chase asked, his voice filled with concern. "Mr. Gianotti or Neil don't have any idea that you saw?"

Jay shook his head. "I came home and called Neil, told him I was sick, we'd get together some other time. No one even knew I was there. It was no good going to the local police, Mr. Gianotti is best friends with the Chief, so I took the bus to Philadelphia and went to the FBI office there. That's where I met KC."

"KC? She's not really your girlfriend?"

The thought forced a wry smile from Jay. "I wish. She's like twenty-seven or twenty-eight or something. She moved here to keep an eye on me and help get evidence on Mr. Gianotti. They never found the body of the man I saw him kill, so they didn't have much to go on."

"Why is she pretending to be pregnant?"

"She thought that would give us a reason to run off together without anyone getting suspicious—only I'm on my way to join the witness protection program. After I testify and Mr. Gianotti is in jail, the government has agreed to help with my tuition to college and medical school. But," he looked away, "it means I can never see you again."

"You did the right thing," Chase said. "I'm proud of you, kid."

Jay smiled at the sincerity in his brother's voice. It was almost as good as hearing the same words from his father. "Thanks, Chase. I'm glad you came home for Christmas. Sorry I couldn't tell you before, but KC said not to trust you."

CHASE ROCKED BACK ON his heels, stunned by what his brother had been through and how well he'd managed everything.

Poor kid. He should've been here to protect Jay instead of chasing Bruno and Deacon and a bunch of lousy stolen weapons.

If he'd been here, Jay could have come to him, they would have figured something out.

At least he hoped that was what Jay would have done. He thought back to Nicky Gianotti and their own wild times in high school. They knew Nicky's big brother was involved with illegal gambling and loan sharking, had inherited the family business from his father.

It was kind of a joke—ominous black limos cruising up to the house at strange hours of the night, the tough guys with guns that Bruno Gianotti surrounded himself with, the spending money Nicky was always too happy to share with his buddies. Like having their own version of the Godfather right here in Coalton.

Chase had never seen the Gianottis actually hurt anyone, but if he'd been in Jay's position, at his age, would he have betrayed Nicky and gone to the authorities? Or would he have lived the lie, looked the other way, like the rest of Coalton?

He clapped Jay on the shoulder and stood, pacing the room. His little brother was already a man Chase was proud to know; a man very much like their own father.

Chase stopped at the mantle, stared at a photo of Jay and their dad with Jay's first buck, an eight-pointer. He hated that Jay still thought the worst of him, that Jay wouldn't trust Chase with the truth until Chase forced it from him.

In a few hours, up and down the street, giggling children would be racing to open presents, delighting their parents. While here he and Jay sat, two brothers alone in the darkness, each trying to do the right thing and neither trusting the other enough to share the truth.

Sorry state of affairs. None of this would have ever happened if their parents were still alive. Of course, then Chase's leave wouldn't have been extended and he would have returned to join his unit instead of being delayed. Sally and Hank Westin and five Marines would still be alive if not for the Kleindiest boy and an industrial sized bottle of Everclear.

He looked over at his kid brother—not a kid anymore. Jay had grown up fast, even more so since Chase had seen him last. What would Mom and Dad do if they were here now?

They would protect the family. To hell with Deacon and Bruno and The Crusade and the job. They'd find a way to keep Jay safe. With his parents gone, it fell to Chase.

"When do you have to leave?" he asked Jay.

"Later today. I'm worried about Neil, though."

"He still doesn't have any idea what his father does for a living?"

"No. He'd die just to have his father pay attention to him for a few minutes. He's so excited his father is taking him to some big meeting later today. Said it was the best Christmas present ever."

Chase nodded to the cell phone still clutched in Jay's hand. "Let me talk to KC."

"Why?"

Chase grimaced against Jay's eyes narrowed in distrust. Jay didn't say it, but he knew what his brother was thinking: What are you going to do now to screw up my life? Again.

He took a deep breath. Time to tell Jay everything. "There's something you need to know," he began. "You can't say anything about it to anyone, not even KC."

"Why not?"

"Because I once trusted someone, not only with my life but the lives of my men, and they betrayed me. I'm not risking that ever again."

"You mean that tribal leader in Afghanistan. The one who led your squad into that ambush?"

There was a lot more to the story than that, but Jay had the gist of it. "Yeah. After I got out of the hospital and was sent to Lejeune, I found out some guys on base were smuggling weapons and selling them to Bruno. That's what he does, he finds weapons and buys them and sells them to drug dealers, gang bangers, you name it. These guys had a few MP's working with them, so I went to NCIS and offered my connection with Bruno. I went undercover and we busted the ring, but I purposely kept Bruno's name out of it so we could go after him later. After I got out of Leavenworth, he contacted me to thank me for my 'professional courtesy'."

Chase grimaced at the memory—after the meeting he'd spent an hour in the shower washing the dirty feeling from his skin. And another hour with the heavy bag venting the anger and frustration over letting Bruno go free in order to catch his other customers. "Bruno told me about a group he was working with, The Crusade."

"I've heard of them. We watched one of their webcasts for a school project on current events," Jay said. "It was pretty cool—the way their leader's got a secret identity, no one knows who he really is or anything. They just call him Deacon."

Great, now they were inviting lunatics like Deacon into the schools. Chase wondered how many students went home with a sense of admiration for Deacon, how many were swayed by his rhetoric, felt that he was the path to their gaining what was rightfully theirs. A depressed town like Coalton was ripe pickins for The Crusade.

"What did you think of what he said?" If Deacon could influence a level-headed kid like Jay, then they didn't have a prayer.

"A lot of what he said made sense. Everyone already knows how screwed up the country is. Kids like me, we're gonna be the ones paying the price."

The look he gave Chase lumped Chase in with all of the other "old folks".

"But I didn't like how he was so vague about how he was going to change things. He just said to watch for the signs, and revolution was coming—to be ready to embrace it when it happened. Sounded kind of scary to me."

"You have every right to be scared. Something bad is coming. Bruno has me setting up deals between him and The Crusade. He has a huge shipment of guns and explosives that they're buying."

"But you're going to stop him, aren't you, Chase? You won't let The Crusade get a hold of that stuff!"

Chase hid his smile at Jay's tone of pride and certainty. The kid still thought he was John Wayne. The thought left him feeling invincible, a man of steel.

"Of course not. I'll let them think they have it, just long enough for us to track them down and stop whatever they have planned. But I have to let everyone think that I'm one of the bad guys."

Jay nodded his understanding. "Just like KC."

"Remember, you can't tell her any of this."

Chase was relieved to hear KC and Jay weren't really involved, but hotshot FBI agent or not, he still wasn't trusting her with Jay's life. He held out his hand for the phone once more. "You're going to tell her you're leaving, call off your deal. I'm going to get you out of here before anything more can happen."

"What do you mean more?"

"One of my men has gone missing, I think The Crusade has him."

"Chase, what if they know about you? Maybe you should come with me. KC can take care of everything. I know she can. You can trust her."

Hadn't the kid heard anything he said? You don't trust your team's lives with strangers, even if they were strangers with seemingly good intentions. He thought about Lucky and the undercover FBI agent whose cover was blown last summer and shook his head.

"No, I can't. It's too dangerous. Either you call her or I do."

Jay stood, feet planted, chin jutted in the air. "No. I promised KC I would help her. I won't tell her anything about you, but I'm not backing out."

"I don't have time to argue. Get your things, make the call and let's go."

He tried to stare Jay into submission, but the kid was now at eye level and wasn't going for it. Damn it, why'd he have to be so stubborn?

"What'cha gonna do, Chase?" Jay said, rocking on the balls of his feet in an unconscious imitation of his big brother. "Knock me out, carry me on the back of your bike? What would Mr. Gianotti or your friends in The Crusade think about that?"

Chase was silent. The kid had a point—he just wished he hadn't picked this moment to make it. "When are you due to leave?"

"This afternoon. I'll take KC's car, meet the Marshals in Altoona."

Chase rolled his eyes. The kid was such an amateur.

"Never tell anyone your plans. Not even me," he told Jay. "Always have a plausible lie ready."

"How do you know I'm not lying now?" Jay countered with a raised eyebrow. Chase had to smile. Maybe the kid would make it after all.

"All right," he conceded, hating the idea of allowing anyone else to take charge of his brother's safety. "But don't wait until this afternoon. Stick beside KC until she takes you out of here."

Added bonus was it would also make his job easier, ensure that KC wasn't around to screw up the weapon exchange between Bruno and Deacon.

Jay thought about it and nodded. "Thanks, Chase," he said, extending his hand.

Chase grabbed it, then pulled his brother into a quick embrace. He might never see him again. The thought finally hit home with the power of a mortar round. At least Jay would be out of this town, pursuing his dreams, making something of himself.

"You're going to make a great doctor someday," he said. He grabbed his jacket and turned to leave. "Watch your back, kid."

CHAPTER 18

AS CHASE CROSSED THE carport and approached his Harley, he heard the crunch of snow behind him. He whirled, one hand reaching for the HK. Deacon and his men come for him and Jay? he wondered as he cleared the gun from his holster.

"Jeez, Westin," came the familiar drawl of Addison, one of Bruno's men. "We knew you were a rat bastard who'd sell out his own men. We just never knew you were a pervert. Is that how you get your kicks? Climbing into little girl's bedrooms and showing them your gun?"

Chase looked around the dark carport. Addison leaned against the Malibu, a .357 Magnum trained on Chase. Out of the shadows on either side of Chase emerged two more men, both roughly the size of guerillas. He could take them if need be. He waited, his weapon ready.

"I'll bet that semi is the only thing he could get up," one of the guerrillas said with a laugh. Chase watched him clench and unclench his fists, preparing for a good old-fashioned beat down.

Chase could handle that, but he'd rather talk his way out of it.

"She's no girl," he retorted. "And she didn't get anything she wasn't asking for."

"Not what we heard. You know, Westin, you are one ungrateful sonofabitch. Mr. Gianotti's been keeping an eye on your kid brother ever since your folks died and you ran back to the Army. Kid's practically family to Mr. Gianotti. Now you repay him by messing with the kid's girl?"

Addison shook his head in disapproval and clucked his tongue. He raised his gun at Chase. "You know how strongly Mr. G feels about family. Nobody messes with his family, nobody."

Dammit, now he had to deal with psycho mobsters who thought they were defending the "family" honor? Why couldn't Bruno have just left Chase's family out of it?

"It's between me and Jay," he said. "If Mr. Gianotti wants to talk to Jay about his tramp of a girlfriend, let him. You guys don't have anything to do about it."

"Sorry, Westin. That's not what Mr. G told us. He's who gives the orders around here. Now drop the gun and take your punishment like a good boy."

"How about I just get on my bike and leave, nobody gets hurt."

"You do, and the deal's off. Don't think Deacon would take kindly to that. Might be a good way to get yourself and your brother killed."

Hell, he couldn't risk anything blowing the deal or putting Jay in The Crusade's crosshairs. Oh well, three to one, he'd faced worse odds. Chase gave Addison an elaborate shrug and lowered his gun to the hood of the Malibu. Which put him in the perfect position to brace himself for a side kick to guerrilla Number One's groin.

As soon as Number One hit the ground, Number Two rushed in, trying to grab Chase in a bear hug, wrestle him to the ground.

What did he think this was, the WWF? Chase slipped free,

twisted under the bigger man's guard and came up behind him. He aimed a kick, buckling the would-be wrestler's knees and brought his elbows down on the back of the guy's head, sending him sprawling under the Malibu.

Chase straightened to face Number One and Addison who'd moved in to join the fray. A quick feint with a jab followed by a right hook to the jaw took care of Addison who went down on his ass.

Number One circled warily, keeping out of Chase's reach, looking for an opening. Addison made a sound, and Chase slammed a kick into his abdomen just as Number One rushed forward like a locomotive, plowing into Chase and crashing him into the Malibu.

Before Chase could catch his breath, Number One punched him in the solar plexus. Chase would have shaken that off, except that while he was tangling with Number One, Number Two crawled free of the Malibu and yanked both his legs out from under him. Chase went down with a thud, smacking his head against the concrete floor.

His vision went hazy. He was hauled to his feet, his hands pulled tight behind him.

"C'mon, Westin," Addison said, rubbing his jaw. "Mr. Gianotti wants to talk to you in person. Give you a lesson in family values."

THE TRILL OF HER cell phone jolted KC from her dream. She almost rolled off the sofa where she'd finally crashed. Damn, it was a good dream, too.

Her thoughts were muddled as she reached for the instrument of the devil. Chase Westin and her on a tropical island, far away from Coalton, this dreary winter and any semblance of reality.

"Yeah," she mumbled into the speaker, the memory of Chase's

naked body glistening beneath her still filling her vision.

"KC, I need your help."

Jay Westin's words energized her into full alert mode. She sat up, already reaching for her boots. "What's wrong?"

"Gianotti's men, they took Chase. Neil told his father about his climbing into your room."

Served the idiot right for pulling a stunt like that. A little poetic justice for thinking he could bully a supposedly eighteen year old girl.

"Jay, your brother is a grown man, he can take care of himself." Last thing she needed was to risk her cover or Jay's safety for his loser brother.

"KC, please help him. Mr. Gianotti's men said something about Chase was messing with his family and would have to pay—"

The kid's fear shot through the phone line and she understood. Those were the same words Gianotti used before shooting Moscone, the man Jay saw die in Gianotti's garage.

"I'm on my way, don't worry," she said and hung up.

Off to rescue Prince Not-so-charming, she thought as she shrugged into her jacket. She ran downstairs to where Glenn and Carson were taking shifts monitoring the audio and video feeds. "You guys got anything from Gianotti's garage?"

"I was just coming to get you," Carson said. Glenn was asleep on the battered sofa in the corner. "Three of his guys got there a few minutes ago, sounded like they were getting ready to beat the crap out of some poor slob, but Gianotti told them to wait, he wants his kid to watch." He shook his head. "Guess it's his twisted idea of family entertainment."

"Yeah, he's trying to toughen Neil up, wants him to follow in his father's illustrious footsteps," KC said. "The guy they got is Chase Westin. I'm going to head over and put a stop to it—make them think me and Chase have something going."

"How you gonna do that?"

She flashed him a "bad girl" KC grin and jangled the chains on her jacket. "Don't worry, I've got it covered. Keep an ear out in case things go the wrong way. I'll head to Westin's afterward. Call Jared Wright over at Wit-Sec, let him know we're gonna have to move Jay's pickup ahead of schedule."

"Sure thing, KC."

Damn Chase Westin. She stomped through the snow to Gianotti's estate next door. Because of him everything was getting way too complicated. She couldn't keep risking Jay. She was going to have to get him out of there tonight. But how to keep Chase from suspecting anything?

She muttered a curse under her breath. Everything had been fine until that man showed up. Served him right if he got the tar beat out of him.

Instead of making her slow her pace, the thought of what Gianotti's men might be doing to Chase Westin forced her into a run.

CHAPTER 19

PROBLEM WITH SUMO WRESTLER wannabe's, Chase thought as his knees buckled after another punch to the solar plexus, was they lacked finesse. Sure they had plenty of power—ugh, like in that kick to his kidney—but this was strictly amateur stuff if you really wanted someone to suffer.

Try being blown up by a RPG, thrown thirty feet, unable to hear anything over the thunder in your head, unable to move, to breathe without red hot pokers of pain spiraling through every nerve in your body, and worst of all, unable to do anything as your men are slaughtered around you. That was real pain.

Guerillas One and Two hauled him to his feet as Bruno Gianotti ushered his son into the garage.

"Watch it, there," Bruno said. "He's dripping blood onto the Lexus."

Addison whipped out a bandanna and wiped the offensive body fluids away. He jerked his head to the two guerillas who half carried, half dragged Chase front and center.

"My son here tells me that you've been doing a little breaking and entering in your free time, Chase. Is that true?"

Chase hung his head, gave the appearance of being beaten, and remained silent. Best to see how seriously pissed Bruno was—or was this just a show to impress Neil?

"I am disappointed," Bruno went on. "It's bad enough you betrayed your own brother. But think how humiliating this is for me. After I've I practically took your brother in while you were in prison."

Chase thought hard and fast. Only option to save his mission and his life was to get down and dirty with some serious groveling.

Before he could start, Bruno reached an arm around Neil's shoulders, turned him to face Chase. "What do you want to do to him, Neil? You're a man now. Jay is your friend. It's your call."

Great, Chase thought, now his life was being decided by a nineteen-year-old boy who thought Chase was after his best friend's girl.

"I just don't want him to hurt KC, that's all," Neil muttered, obviously flustered by the responsibility being shoved onto him. "Can't you just make him go away, never come back?"

Bruno took a deep breath as if discouraged that his only son was so naive. "There are a few things to consider, Neil. First, there's business. We could lose a very large amount of money if Chase went missing before the deal he's arranged between myself and The Crusade."

Chase knew that this small fact was the only reason Bruno hadn't just come out and killed him. For all his fancy speech about family values, Bruno always put money first.

"And there's Jay, how would he feel if his brother 'went away'?" Bruno continued his lesson. "Never do something irrevocable until you're certain of all the consequences."

Neil's face went pale as he realized that his father's definition of "going away" was a lot more permanent than the change of address Neil had in mind.

Chase almost felt sorry for the kid. Neil glanced around, taking notice of Addison's gun, held so nonchalantly on Chase, and the blood still dripping from Chase's nose. Wake up and smell the coffee, Chase wanted to yell at the kid, get out now while you still can.

But it was too late for Neil Gianotti. Just as it had been for his uncle, Nicky, who'd drowned his shame about the origins of the family fortune in a heroin addiction.

"Maybe," Bruno said, lips pursed together as if he'd given the matter extensive consideration, "it's KC who should leave town."

"KC?" Neil said, almost jumping away from his father. "No."

Bruno sighed dramatically, spreading his hands wide. "It's all up to you, son. What do you want me to do?"

Before Neil could answer, the outside door opened and a figure in black ran inside. A figure with familiar purple hair.

"Stop, please, Mr. Gianotti," KC yelled as she sprinted across the cavernous garage to where they stood. "Please don't hurt him anymore, he didn't do anything."

Damn it, he was almost free and clear. What the hell was she doing here, ruining things? KC the teenaged vixen had been trouble enough. KC the FBI Special Agent could get him killed.

CHAPTER 20

"MR. GIANOTTI, PLEASE, IT'S not what you think." KC tugged Bruno Gianotti's hand into hers, playing to his delusion of being the next Godfather. She hung her head low, not making eye contact. "Neil misunderstood."

"My son sees his best friend's older brother climb into your bedroom window and he's misunderstood?" Gianotti jabbed a finger under her chin, forced her head up. "Look at me, young lady. What kind of games are you playing?"

Damn, Carson would have heard that. She was going to have some explaining to do for the official record. Later, after she got herself and Westin out of here alive.

KC chewed on her lower lip for a moment before answering. "Chase wasn't there to do anything. He was offering me money to stay away from Jay, to leave town and," she faltered, eyes darting around the room, "give up the baby."

The announcement had the desired effect. Gianotti dropped his hand, stepped back as if she was contaminated. Beside him, Neil made a small sound of surprise. For the first time, KC was wondering if maybe she was in over her head. Too late to back out now. And by twisting the story this way, she should be giving Gianotti just what he wanted: a way to get her out of Neil's life for good.

"I didn't take his money." KC raised her head high now. "I told him he has no right. I threw him out. I'm having Jay's baby, and I'm keeping it. Jay and I have plans, we don't need him." She jerked her head at Chase.

Gianotti turned. "This true, Westin?"

"Look, Mr. Gianotti, my brother's smart, he wants to go to college, be a doctor someday. I have to protect him from girls like her," he cut his eyes at KC with a dismissive glare, "who just want to take advantage of his good nature. You know what I mean, family comes first."

Gianotti nodded, obviously enjoying playing his role as King Solomon. "I see. Let him go. Leave us," he said to his men. He turned back to KC. "Does your father know about this?"

"No, sir. Please don't tell him, he'll kill me for sure."

Gianotti looked over at Neil. "See son, why it's so important to never turn your back on family?"

In response, Neil glared at Chase as if he was to blame for KC's alleged condition.

"KC," Gianotti continued in a gentle voice, taking her arm. "After the holidays your father and I are going to have a long talk. Have you seen a doctor yet?"

KC shook her head, hanging it like a chastised fallen woman. It took all her restraint not to jerk away from Gianotti's patronizing touch.

"We'll set up an appointment for next week. One thing I know for sure, young lady," Gianotti ran a finger over the length of chain that adorned the sleeve of her jacket, "you can't keep running around half naked in this weather. You have to start taking better care of yourself, thinking of your baby."

KC sniffed loudly. Sanctimonious prick. Acted now like he should be nominated father of the year when a few hours ago he was ready to do anything to keep her away from his son. She couldn't wait to get him in custody then he'd see who was really in charge around here.

First, she had to save Chase Westin's sorry but oh-so-cute ass. She risked a quick glance in his direction. He was slouched, leaning against the fender of the Lexus, one arm wrapped around his belly, barely standing. A flutter of panic seized her chest. Was he badly hurt? God, she'd make Gianotti and his goons pay for this.

"Yessir," she mumbled, her eyes locked on the concrete floor as she swallowed her fury. "Can I take Chase home now? I promised Jay—" she let her voice trail off, waiting for him to grant her a royal boon.

"Westin, no more fighting, do I make myself clear? I'll take care of Jay and KC, you've got your own life to attend to."

Chase's head jerked up at Gianotti's imperious tone.

Don't blow it now, KC pleaded silently, locking her gaze with his. How in hell had Chase managed to piss so many people off in a few hours was beyond her—but as long as it didn't interfere with the arms deal today, she didn't care. Finally Chase nodded.

"Yes, sir. Thank you for helping my brother, Mr. Gianotti." The words emerged clipped, as if they were forced under threat of torture, but Gianotti appeared appeased.

"All right, you two get home. It's late and today's a big day." With a wave of his hand, Gianotti dismissed them, ushering Neil back into the house.

KC ran over to where Chase was slumped against the Lexus. "Can you walk?" she asked, wrapping an arm around his waist to help support him. "My car's not far."

It was difficult to contain her temper during the drive to Jay's house. Idiot could have ruined everything. All her time and effort, all almost flushed down the toilet because of one psycho brother who suddenly felt like he had to play Mr. Mom. KC kept her silence, afraid she might blow her cover if she told Chase what she really felt.

Number one on the list of feelings that she wasn't about to reveal to anyone was the fear that had choked her when Gianotti's thugs were whaling on Chase—they could have killed him. She spun around the corner onto Jay's street twenty miles over the speed limit, gearing down when the wheels began to slip into a skid, and screeched to a halt in front of the house.

Should have just driven Chase right over to the police station, get him safely out of the way of her operation and his own idiotic impulses. But then she'd lose her chance to nail Gianotti and Dinkum. Westin was small change, she reminded herself.

Other than to refuse to go to the hospital to get checked, Chase remained silent during the short trip. Didn't even thank her for sacrificing her reputation to save his sorry ass.

KC slammed her car door so hard the Mustang rattled. Why should this ex-con give a shit about her reputation? After all, the only thing they'd shared was a kiss. And she'd been faking it, playing a role, it hadn't really been her that he'd kissed. Not at all.

The memory of her erotic fantasies involving him teased her brain. She shooed them away with her hand. Snow slushed beneath her Doc Martens as she stomped around to the passenger side of the car. Chase had managed to unfasten his seat belt and open the door but still sat in the passenger seat.

She blinked hard at the sight of his battered face. His lip was split, swollen. One eye was already turning black and blue. His eyes were half-closed as if he were too tired to fight his way out of the low-slung sports car. She blew her breath out and with it most of her anger and reached a hand down to help him.

He grabbed her arm, leveraged himself upright. Then, in a sudden move that caught her off balance, he spun her so her back was against the car, his body pressed against hers. His mouth took hers with bruising force, a greedy quenching of his desire.

KC's hunger matched his in intensity. After her initial gasp of surprise, her body surrendered to her need.

She opened her mouth beneath his, inviting him to deepen the kiss as her free hand slid under his jacket, dug into the muscles along his back. A feral noise emerged from his throat. He adjusted his position so that his leg was between hers, his thigh pressing against her in a way that made her pelvis rock.

The kiss was blinding, white hot and searing. Nothing had ever felt so right before to KC. This man who was wrong, so very wrong in every respect, sparked something within her she was helpless to control.

He slid his hand beneath her butt and lifted her onto his hip with one hand, stepping back far enough to swing the door closed. Then he lurched forward, almost slipping in the slush, and propped her on the Mustang's hood. The engine was still ticking as it cooled, its heat radiating into KC.

Chase pinned her legs between his, pressing her back against the hood, his fingers dancing as he unzipped her jacket and peeled it open. A wicked grin played across his face. He kissed her roughly, a quick, tantalizing taste, then ran his palms over her chest.

She struggled, fearful that he'd stray too close to her concealed weapon. "No. Not here, not now."

Her voice surprised her as it emerged a breathless wisp. Like a woman who meant exactly the opposite of what she'd just said.

In response he rested one elbow on the hood beside her, aligning his body against hers, watching her face as he flicked one thumb over her hardened nipple, rubbing it against the leather of her vest.

"Do you want me to stop?" he said, his own voice taut and raspy.

Before she could answer, he slid his hand down, between her legs, stroking her through her jeans. Her hips arched up as heat surged through her, engulfing her. He pulled his body away from hers enough so that he could lower his face to the naked skin exposed above the snap of her jeans.

His tongue found her navel ring, flicking it, taunting and teasing her as she writhed beneath him.

"We can't," she managed to gasp.

He pressed his hips forward, pinning his hand between them and she bit her lip against the wave of pleasure the pressure brought.

"Do you want me to stop?" he repeated.

"I'm," she gulped as his fingers pressed down, "I'm asking you to stop."

"That doesn't answer my question, KC."

He buried her mouth beneath his. She tasted his blood as their teeth and tongues and lips collided. A breathless, brutal, primitive taste of passion made her temples pound and her vision blur.

"Chase—"

"Do you want me to stop?" he insisted.

He ran one callused thumb across her swollen lips, tracing its path with his tongue. His gaze bore into hers as his pelvis ground against hers.

She met his glance. Was he insane? Who in their right mind would ever want this to stop? How long had she been hoping, dreaming, fantasizing about a moment like this?

But not this man, not this moment. Not with the lives of his brother and her team at stake.

She slid her hands up, pressed them flat against his chest. "I'm telling you to stop. Now."

His eyes blazed in the night. For a moment he resisted, leaning his weight onto her, his mouth hovering over hers.

"You want to be in control, KC. But you like it when someone can make you lose control, don't you? Don't you?"

He lowered his lips for one more kiss. It took everything she had not to struggle beneath him, not to give in to the sudden panic that he might be right. The kiss was surprisingly gentle, soft and warm. She opened her mouth beneath his, wanting, demanding more. And he gave it to her. In spades.

Then, just as he stole all conscious thought and will from her, Chase stepped back, abandoning her, leaving her alone in the cold.

"What the hell was that?" she asked, her voice quavering.

"Payback," he said with a grin that mirrored the one she'd given him earlier in her bedroom. "Come into the house. We need to talk. Special Agent."

KC's stomach clenched in fear and surprise at his words. He didn't wait for her answer but turned on his heel and stomped through the snow into the carport.

To hell with having Chase Westin arrested, KC thought, shivering now that his body wasn't next to hers.

She straightened her vest and jacket, slowly stood, her vision spinning until she caught her breath. Her hand rested on the cold comfort of her Glock. Should've shot him when she had the chance. Might still just shoot him.

The man was nothing but trouble.

CHAPTER 21

ROSE LOOKED UP AS Marion Rockey entered the conference room. The California blonde ran her fingers through her long hair, wincing at the bright lights overhead.

"You know, we have this quaint tradition in LA." Marion shuffled over to the coffee machine. "It's called a good night's sleep."

Billy poured coffee for Marion, stirred in two sugars without asking. Hmm. Rose wasn't certain if it was such a good idea for her second to be fraternizing with the troops. Although part of her, that deep, hidden kernel of maternal instinct, was glad Billy might have found someone. He was a good man, deserved to find a woman worthy of him.

Marion Rockey could definitely be a match for Billy Price. The FBI forensic accountant had been working with the Team for almost eighteen months and had helped to track several terrorist cells. As Marion said, show her the money, and she'd follow the trail to the crooks.

"Lucky's been blown," Rose said bluntly as Marion took her

seat beside Hollywood. "We don't know if he's dead or alive."

"And Chase?" Hollywood asked.

"He thinks he's all right. The meet is set for noon today."

"What can we do?" Marion asked.

"I'm not sure if there is much we can do for Lucky. But I'd like to get as much back up for Chase as possible."

"Just one problem," Billy put in from his seat at the computer. "Someone from the FBI is working a case and somehow, we're not sure how, Chase's younger brother, Jay, is involved. His cell phone is FBI issued and being monitored."

"Was being monitored," Rose put in. "We had Teresa block it until we know what's going on. Wouldn't want the wrong people to hear the wrong thing. With Lucky gone, Chase is our only chance to nail Deacon and stop The Crusade. Not to mention Gianotti and a boatload of weapons. I can't let some white collar RICO case get in the way."

"I'll bet that's where I come in," Marion said as she moved to take Billy's place at the computer terminal. Billy stood behind her, looking down over her shoulder as she began to access the FBI database.

"What do you want me to do, boss?" Hollywood asked.

"Get working on satellite imagery from anything that may have passed over that area of Pennsylvania during the time Lucky went missing. Teresa is already downloading the pictures, you can start analyzing them. EZ is on his way in to help as well."

"What about traffic cameras and the like?"

Rose rolled her eyes. "Afraid modern law enforcement technology has yet to make its way to Coalton, PA."

"This is weird," Marion said, her fingers pausing their typing. "The investigation that phone was assigned to ended months ago. And there was never any activity near Coalton." She spun in her chair to face Rose. "The agent of record was murdered when his cover was blown."

Rose exchanged glances with Billy.

He pursed his lips in a frown. "So we either have an under the table investigation going on—"

"Or it's not the FBI who have been monitoring Jay Westin," Rose finished. She pushed off from the wall and began to pace the room. "We know The Crusade has been able to access confidential files of government agents. Every time security thinks they have the problem solved, The Crusade finds a new way in."

"Chase wasn't in those files," Billy said, looking to Hollywood for confirmation.

"That's right," the former Navy man said. "When we realized it was going to be a long term operation, we kept everything out of the record. As far as everyone but maybe half a dozen people know, Chase's arrest and court-martial were legit."

"Maybe Deacon or someone else in The Crusade suspected him anyway," Rose continued. "Deacon is infamous for his paranoia. His hackers must have found a new way into the system."

"Welcome to the computer age," Billy put in.

Rose shot him a glare. Things were a lot simpler without technology—and safer, as Lucky and the other compromised agents could attest to.

"Just because it's new doesn't mean it's better," she retorted. "Anyway, it would be easy for Deacon to find Jay Westin. Maybe he slipped him the phone as a way of monitoring Chase, keeping tabs on Jay in case something threatened the deal and he needed to coerce Chase's cooperation."

"Then who's this girlfriend Chase said gave Jay the phone?" Marion asked. "Does she work for The Crusade?"

"I wish I knew."

CHAPTER 22

CHASE CHECKED ON JAY while he waited for KC to follow him into the house. That expression on her face—shock and surprise and fear all mixed together as if he'd sucker-punched her—that hurt. Almost as bad as when Jay gave him a similar look earlier tonight.

Crap, it was only three am and this was turning into one of the longest nights of his life. A memory of smoke and fire, his head ringing, pain lancing through his body as his men cried out engulfed him.

No, not the longest night, he corrected himself as a whiff of KC's musky scent and the velvet touch of her lips replaced the memories of pain and terror. And most definitely not the worst.

Jay was asleep in the Barcalounger, one hand cradling his cell phone close to his chest. Chase couldn't help but smile. Exchange the TV remote for the phone and add the Sands of Iwo Jima flickering in the background and it could have been **Hank Westin** sleeping there instead of his youngest son.

Chase ran his fingers through the kid's hair, something Jay would have never allowed him to do if he were awake. He couldn't resist the urge to touch him—it reminded him of why he did what he did, of the importance of protecting the future for kids like Jay.

The carport door opened. KC came in, eyes blazing, chains jangling on her jacket.

"Kid's asleep," Chase said before she could say anything.

"Wake him up, we're leaving. Now."

Chase merely shook his head. "Kid gets sleeping that deep, you could fire an M-16 in here and it wouldn't wake him. Let's talk in the kitchen."

He walked past her, half expecting her to draw a weapon and make a stand, glad when she didn't. She cursed softly under her breath then followed him.

"Jay told me everything," he said, leaning against the avocado green counter.

He pulled his feet back as she paced the small space, glaring at him. A lioness protecting her young.

"I should've let Gianotti's thugs beat the crap out of you," she muttered.

"Looks to me like you'd rather do it yourself," he said with a smile, nodding at her fisted hands. She pulled up short, took a deep breath, and spun around to face him.

"All right, Westin. What do you want? You gonna turn me in to Gianotti or your friends at The Crusade?"

So, she'd figured that much out. He knew she was smart. Maybe too smart for his own good. "I want Jay safe. I just haven't decided the best way to get that."

"Your brother's an intelligent man, he's already made up his mind."

"My brother's a kid half in love with you," he shot back.

"Think you can do a better job of protecting him than I can?" Her voice softened, and her gaze dropped to his lips. "Listen,

Westin," she said, moving closer to him. "Why don't you help yourself and Jay? Gianotti's going down. You don't have to go with him. Help me out here, give me Dinkum and The Crusade, I'll get you a deal."

She was close enough that he could feel the heat radiating from her body. One deep breath and he was drowning in her scent, unable to think. His fingers stretched out, desperate to touch her, to pull her close. He felt his mouth go dry but managed to keep control, ignoring the colorful tattooed lizard jeering at him with every breath she took. Fisting his hands, Chase slid sideways, putting a safe distance between them.

"Don't kid a kidder, KC."

She shrugged, leaned against the counter he'd just vacated. "Can't blame a girl for trying."

"You're no girl, and we both know it. You can have Jay, but only if you don't arrest Bruno until after the meet today."

"No deal. I'm taking Gianotti and Dinkum down. If you want, I can arrange for you not to be there."

"How?" he challenged her.

Her chin jutted up, her gaze locking on his. God, those eyes. Deep, dark and beckoning to him like a siren's call. A man could drown in there, never coming up for air—and never regretting it.

"Do what I should have in the beginning. Have you picked up on a weapons charge. You are a convicted felon."

"Nice try, but I'm clean." He smiled, lifted his shirt, revealing the absence of the HK. One good thing had come from the visit from Bruno's goons, the nine millimeter was on the floor of the carport.

Her scowl deepened. He itched to reach across the distance separating them, to smooth the wrinkles away from her brow with a caress. It took everything he had to stifle the urge. Instead, he hooked his thumbs in his belt loops, hanging on as if the denim was a lifeline, a tether of sanity providing a way out of this mess. He wanted so much: to see Jay safe, to stop Deacon, to lock up Bruno, to rescue Lucky, to finish this mission. But suddenly it was hard to remember all that, suddenly he wanted even more: time.

Time alone with KC, to explore, to learn, just…to be.

For so long he'd concentrated solely on the mission facing him here and now, but suddenly he wanted a chance at an unknown tomorrow. The thought rocketed through him, leaving behind a gaping hole of black, searing heartache. Not the same pain as when he'd lost his parents or his men, but close, so close that he couldn't look at KC. Instead, he forced himself to focus on the feel of the counter edge digging into his spine, the rasp of Jay's snores, the odor of Pinesol…details of a normal life, of a life he would never have.

"Why is it so important to you that the meet go through?" KC's voice was soft, as if she might even give a shit about his answer, but the question slapped him back to reality. He was a man on a mission; he could only afford to worry about the next minute, the next hour. Anything beyond that was a luxury forbidden him.

"Because it's my ass on the line if it doesn't. I'm the middleman. Anything goes wrong for either party and—"

"And you're the fall guy." She looked at him appraisingly as if she hadn't expected him to be so highly placed in the criminal hierarchy. Her eyes narrowed, cold-hearted steel replacing the warmth that had been there earlier. "You're thinking you can pocket your money, then make a deal with us so you walk after ratting out your partners."

Pacing again, she moved out of range before he could succumb to any insane impulses. Like reaching for those chains dangling from her jacket and yanking her close to him.

She pivoted, gave him a small nod. "Okay, I can live with that—but I can't take any chance that those weapons make it into the wrong hands. We'll put tracking devices in some of them, wire you for the meet."

Chase shook his head. He needed to get those weapons into Deacon's hands, learn what The Crusade planned to do with them. Besides, if Lucky was still alive and anything went wrong at the meet, they would kill him for sure. "Won't work. They'll spot them."

"Give me a break, Westin, my people are professionals." She stepped forward, her face tilted up to meet his eyes with an earnest look. "Trust me."

God, he wanted to, was desperate to trust someone, to share the burden he'd been carrying for so long. He let out his breath. "I wish I could, KC. But there's too much at stake here."

"I can't help you then." He swore he heard regret in her voice.

Chase knew he should just let things drop, send her on her way and get on with taking care of business. He knew that. But he couldn't let her go so easily.

He needed to see if the feelings she stirred in him, that sense of rightness, of belonging, had only been part of her undercover role. Now that she no longer had anything to hide from him, how would she react?

He settled his hands onto her shoulders, turned her around to face him, pulled her close to him. A look of uncertainty clouded her face for a brief moment, then she stepped into his embrace, raised her face up to meet his. He tangled his fingers in her hair and slowly lowered his lips onto hers.

Their kiss was a long, deep sharing that awakened something buried inside of Chase, feelings he'd never experienced before, was at a loss to describe. More quiet than the animal passion they shared earlier, this was a soothing calmness, as if KC had pulled him down into a warm, safe place outside of time where he could forget all his worries, forget everything except the woman in his arms.

His eyes locked onto hers. Her pupils widened, their black depths reflecting his own face. The face of a stranger—he recognized the scars, the familiar wrinkles etched into his skin over the past year. But the expression was foreign. He was lightheaded, realized he'd forgotten to breathe as he slid his hands down her body, lifting her onto the counter top. His hands roamed over the exposed flesh of her back and abdomen, not caring what he touched, only knowing that he needed to feel her, that somehow she was his anchor, his touchstone.

She laughed when he found a sensitive area and the noise, musical, throaty, was the most sensuous sound he'd ever heard. He tried a different spot at the small of her back and was rewarded with another taste of her laughter. She grabbed his hands in hers.

"This is a bad idea," she said, looking down at their intertwined hands. He closed his fingers around hers, they threatened to swallow hers whole.

"A very bad idea." He leaned forward to taste her again, sliding his mouth down the side of her neck, pausing at her pulse point, feeling a thrill as her heartbeat raced beneath his touch.

"Westin."

Why couldn't she call him Chase? He liked it when she called him Chase.

"I can't do this." The tone in her voice brought him to his senses.

"You're worried about Jay."

"This is so very wrong on so many levels, but yeah, Jay tops the list." She looked down, sighed. "This never happens to me. My operations don't get so—"

"Complicated?" he supplied.

"That's a polite way of putting it. Damn it, Westin, your timing really stinks." Her gaze moved past him out to where Jay slept. "I never meant for Jay to get so involved. We never did anything—the kiss you saw was the first."

"First time I've ever been jealous of my little brother," he admitted. "Also the first time I found myself lusting after a teeny bopper." He enjoyed seeing her flush at that. "So what did you and Jay do during your, uh, dates? 'Cause Old Man Sinderson says—"

"Sinderson repeats what Neil tells him, and Neil tells him what Jay tells him." She was silent for a moment, her eyes still aimed toward the living room, a small smile playing across her face. "We watched movies. I now can boast that I've seen the entire John Wayne collection—most of his war movies twice."

Chase chuckled. "My father was a huge fan, indoctrinated both Jay and I."

"I know—only you grew up to become John Wayne. Jay worships the ground you walk on."

"At least he used to, you mean."

He was silent, his gaze darting out to where his brother slept, wishing things were different, but glad that before Jay left he would at last know the truth about Chase. He had to bite down against the sudden urge to confide in KC as well—loose lips, he reminded himself. Besides, her mission and his were at loggerheads.

KC seemed comfortable with the silence, allowed it to lengthen, then pulled him back to her with a touch of her finger on his hand.

"He still does," she assured him. "Just the knight's shining armor is a little dented and rusty now. He's a good kid, even if he's sorely mistaken about what makes for a good western. He'll die defending the Duke in The Searchers." She shook her head mournfully. "Someday the kid will come to his senses, learn his

166 | CJ LYONS

mistake."

Chase squeezed her hands, appreciating her change of topic. "You mean to tell me there are better westerns than John Wayne's?" he asked in an incredulous voice.

"My grandfather adored movies, any movie as long as it was black and white. Technicolor was the biggest mistake this society ever made, he used to say. It made movies seem too lifelike, removed the barriers between the fantasy world and the audience. Made that dream world too ordinary, seem commonplace."

"I think my father would have liked your grandfather," Chase said. "He could spend hours dissecting a film, tracing it back to its Jungian and mythic archetypes."

"Exactly. Westerns were Konstantine's favorites. Beowulf retold with six shooters."

"Let me guess, your favorite is," he paused, scrutinizing her face, enjoying how ordinary this all felt—as if she wasn't carrying at least one gun and prepared to use it on him, as if he weren't busy hiding the truth from her, "High Noon. Because of Grace Kelly, right?"

That earned him a wide smile. "Most people don't appreciate how feminist that movie was for its time. Gary Cooper isn't really the hero, he never changes, is the same from start to finish. But Grace Kelly, she first stands true to her principles, then forsakes them to defend her man, finally makes the ultimate sacrifice and takes a man's life. She decides her love for her husband is worth sacrificing everything—her honor, her religion, her life. Then in the very last seconds of the film—"

"He hands her the reins to the wagon," Chase finished for her. She looked at him in surprise, obviously pleased with his response. "Because she's chosen him, he chooses to leave his old life, start a new one with her, as equals."

"Partners. That's right."

"Too bad we can't do something like that—just ride off into the sunset, forget who we are, what we are—"

Her gaze shifted away from his once again. "We can't. There's Jay, for one thing."

"You do care about him."

"Not in that way. I'm responsible for his safety. Just as I'm responsible for the safety of all my people." She leaned back, looked at him, this time with a serious expression. "People who could get hurt depending on what you do next."

He stepped away, pulled his hands from her body, wincing as the connection between them was broken.

"You think I'm going to sell you out to Bruno or Deacon."

Of course, she still thought the worst of him, he hadn't given her any reason to trust him. If their positions were reversed, he wouldn't trust her either. Even now, despite the feelings she aroused in him, he couldn't trust her with the truth. Much as he yearned to.

"You know I won't do anything that might get Jay hurt," he said.

"And once I have Jay in protective custody?"

He turned away, hooked his thumbs in his belt loops, bouncing on the balls of his feet as he thought. He could tell her the truth, maybe they could work together—no, even if he trusted her, he couldn't trust any of her coworkers, not after what happened to Lucky. Too many leaks in the Justice Department to risk it. He wanted to tell her everything, but what he wanted wasn't important, the job came first.

"Give me time to think," he pleaded. She looked at him with doubt in her eyes. "I could have said something to Bruno back at his place, but I didn't," he reminded her.

She considered that. "All right," she said, jumping down from the counter. She walked past him then turned back. "You know, Jay has a chance to make something of himself."

"Unlike his big brother, you mean."

To his surprise, instead of moving to the garage door, she went into the dining room.

"Where are you going?" He followed her out into the living room.

"You wanted time. You and Jay have," she pushed back her jacket sleeve, looked at her watch, a large black skull and crossbones with purple numbers, "twenty minutes before we have to leave."

Before he could say anything, she shook Jay's arm. Jay's eyes fluttered, then opened. He raised an arm to swipe at his face as he blinked in confusion.

"Chase, you're okay?" Jay asked, his voice still blurry with sleep.

"I'm fine, just a little sore."

"KC, what are you doing here?"

"Change in plans, Jay. We're leaving in a few minutes. I thought you'd want to say goodbye to your brother." She stood, looked Chase in the eye. "I'll go use the facilities, give you two a little privacy. Jay, keep an eye on your brother for me, all right?"

She didn't bother hiding her smile when Jay immediately whirled on Chase, demanding, "Damn it. What did you do now?"

CHAPTER 23

A WOMAN CALLED LUCKY'S name, rescuing him from the frozen darkness he'd lost himself in. She stood, surrounded by a lush forest of trees, streams of sunlight dancing through the rich canopy of leaves to illuminate her in golden radiance. Long, thick dark hair swirled over her shoulders, but could not camouflage the rich curves of her body. She held out a hand, beckoning for him to join her.

The forest felt primeval, removed from time and space. Lucky stretched his hand, yearning to join the raven-haired beauty. Pain came at him from every direction, but still he tried to reach her. Their fingers touched and joined. She was almost as tall as he was, their hands fit together perfectly, and suddenly the pain was gone. For one blissful moment, she was his entire universe and he felt peace.

Not the calmness of surrender. Rather a deep, certain knowledge that he would survive. He had to, how else would he ever get the chance to meet her? He couldn't give up, not now that he had something to live for, something more than loyalty to a cause or to a friend.

She was his life and he was going to find her again. All Lucky had to do was stay alive.

He choked on his own blood, and her image faded as Lucky coughed himself awake. The shack was empty. Where'd his Lady go?

His thoughts were hazy, and he fought to focus his vision. She was never there, a cruel whisper from the recesses of his mind taunted him as he struggled to sit up. Just a mirage conjured from the Art Survey course he'd taken to impress that sophomore—what was her name?

Juliet—no that was what Lucky had called her. Julie, that was her real name, plain old Julie. He remembered sitting in the dark auditorium, holding her hand while larger than life Raphael and Botticelli paintings floated on the screen before them. Man, those guys had it right—women should be life sized, warm flesh you could get a hand on, not waifs too fragile for a man to touch.

He spit out a mouthful of blood. Bit his tongue during that last session—was it the third, or the fourth? No matter.

Fergus had been joined by another man, a man who was obviously calling the shots. Making him a bigger fish than Deacon, even. Rose Prospero had said there was more going on than a single nutso militia group led by an ex-gangbanger. Looked like she'd been right on the money.

Lucky hadn't said anything, had kept his attention focused on trying to find any distinguishing characteristic he could use to identify The Crusade's true leader. Fergus addressed the man only as Preacher.

Lucky would be the only law enforcement officer alive able to confirm his existence and give a description.

Make that alive for now.

Just a little longer. Sooner or later, Fergus, Preacher's Taser-happy dwarf, would make a mistake and Lucky would take him down. All he needed was a chance.

He ran his tongue over parched lips. His entire left side was tingling with sharp jolts that ran from his heart down to his fingertips. He tried to wiggle his left hand, but it flapped useless in his right.

Lucky blew his breath out, fully awake now. He thought he might have had a seizure after the last electric shock session—or maybe a heart attack. His chest felt like an elephant was sitting on it. Ugly purple marks where the prongs of the stun gun had burnt his skin were grouped over his heart.

Hey, he was still breathing, time to worry about the rest later. In between each session, he'd been busy prying the metal trim free from the base of the desk. The painstaking process had loosened a two-inch by one-inch strip of metal that he had managed to bend out before the last session. Thank God, they hadn't noticed it.

Now or never, Lucky told himself as he inched over across the floor, his arms and legs screaming in agony from their position hogtied behind him. Finally he reached his destination. He hauled himself upright and began the painful process of sawing through the duct tape that bound him.

Within minutes blood was seeping over his wrists and hands, dripping onto the floor. No way to camouflage that, he thought, realizing this was his last chance.

That was all right, he was long past ready to blow this joint. Had a date with a pretty lady to keep—although he suspected that he was more likely to find her in an Art History textbook or hanging in the National Gallery than in flesh and blood. Didn't matter. Life was hope.

He mumbled the words in time with his movements until at

last he was rewarded. The tape began to give. He pushed harder, his breath coming in small grunts that formed ice vapor clouds in the frigid atmosphere of the shack.

Finally he was free. Lucky peeled the tape off, carefully not allowing it to bunch up. He turned to the job of breaking his sharp edged piece of metal trim free from the desk. As a weapon it was puny, laughable—but the only one he had.

He twisted it back and forth until a fissure formed and the metal snapped off in his hand. Wrapping one end, the one less jagged and therefore less lethal, in his hoarded duct tape, he leaned against the desk and stood.

Immediately he regretted it. The movement made his vision go black. When it returned, the small room was spinning. He retched, but there was nothing left in his stomach to throw up. Lucky thanked God for small favors and took some deep breaths, ignoring the pain spiraling through his chest, until his vision cleared. He searched the desk drawers but they were empty except for a few yellowed scraps of paper and rusty paper clips. The door was padlocked from the outside.

Just you and me, he told his trusty homemade shiv, teeth chattering and goose bumps covering his naked body. Good thing his Lady of the forest wasn't here, he wasn't exactly at his best right now.

He got into position and waited.

CHAPTER 24

LET THEM ARGUE, SAY their farewells, KC thought. Short of placing Chase in handcuffs, it seemed the easiest way to make certain he didn't run off. She moved past them into the hallway and the bathroom across from Jay's room.

She held the door open, listened to their voices. Damn the kid, what had he been thinking, telling his brother the truth. What the hell was she going to do to avoid Chase blowing her op? Or was it already too late?

No, Chase wouldn't sell her out until he knew his brother was safe. Then all bets would be off. She could take him into custody, except for the niggling little fact that she had no proof that he'd done anything wrong except come home for the holidays at exactly the wrong time. She leaned over the sink, splashed cold water over her face, tried to clear her mind.

It was her own damn fault. Should've gotten Jay out last night as soon as Chase showed up. Should've never gotten soft, giving them time together—time which Chase had used to sneak in and try to seduce her, she reminded herself.

174 | CJ Lyons

Except it had been the other way around, hadn't it? She'd
jumped him—in her persona of KC, the teenaged bitch, of course.
She remembered the way his touch scorched through her, igniting
her passion instantly. Maybe she wanted him to seduce her.

Her fingers stretched along her abdomen, following the path
Chase's mouth had taken earlier, where her temporary tattoo was.
She'd been surprised when Raymond showed her his sketch of
the body art. It was the most intricate that he'd ever designed for
her. He'd been right, though. Bad girl KC with her cropped tops,
leather and chains, piercings and less than subtle body art, had taken
Coalton by storm. No one would be surprised when Jay Westin
disappeared with her, never to be heard from again.

She looked at the tattoo in the mirror, its bright colors a
Technicolor swirl in the fluorescent light of the bathroom. A
chameleon juggling karma. Pretty much described the life of an
undercover operative. Right now bad karma seemed to be all that
she was getting.

This was what she got for breaking all her rules. Her operation,
her chance to nab Gianotti, Lester Dinkum and take down The
Crusade was now on the verge of falling apart. All because of one
man.

KC looked at the bathtub with longing and sighed. A vision
of her and Chase in there together filled her mind, his large hands
overflowing with soapsuds as he circled them over her body. The
scent of wild, exotic flowers, promising passion, the taste of his
flesh, the feeling of him inside her, rocking her to her core...

She shook her head to clear it. She needed a plan, some way to
keep Chase from blowing things before the meeting at noon.

Why couldn't she bring herself to think of him as a bad guy?
It was more than a mere physical attraction. Something about him
seemed wrong, as if there was a hidden man beneath the surface,

one that only she could bring to light.

Like when he kissed her in the kitchen. Here she was, wearing the same clothes as yesterday, sweaty and, she raised an arm, definitely not smelling shower fresh, yet he treated her as if she was a princess, looked at her as if she were the most precious thing in his world.

Dr. Jekyll. Only problem: she was certain there was also a Mr. Hyde. Chase Westin was most definitely lying to her about his dealings with Gianotti and The Crusade. He was a damned good liar, but not good enough to fool KC. Until he told her the truth, there was no way in hell she could trust him.

She turned the water as cold as it would get and dunked her face in the basin. Faster than a cold shower and it didn't involve getting naked in Chase Westin's bathroom.

Raising her head, she ran her palms over her eyes, whisking the water away. Despite the frigid water, she still felt flushed.

CHASE MOTIONED TO JAY to keep talking as he crept out to the carport and retrieved his HK. Feeling better with its familiar weight at the small of his back, he returned inside.

"Haven't you told her the truth?" Jay muttered when he returned.

Chase pitched his voice below the sound of the water running in the bathroom. "I can't. There's too much at stake."

"Chase—"

"Trust me on this, will ya? I know what I'm doing."

He moved down the hall to where he could see KC in the mirror that hung there. She'd taken her jacket off, was washing her face. Water beaded off her long eyelashes and down her cheekbones. His breath caught with the urge to be in there with her, his hands rubbing soap over her soft skin.

Who could have guessed he'd ever find a woman like her here of all places? She was as out of place as a diamond in a coal mine. Smart, intelligent, quick witted—her fast thinking and superior acting abilities had saved him with Bruno tonight. And the way she was so protective of Jay...

He shook his head, backed up into the living room. This was nuts. A guy like him, leading his kind of life, just wasn't built for long-term commitments. If—big if—he ever did consider settling down, it would be for the kind of relationship his parents had: an enduring, quiet passion that even after thirty years of marriage still charged the air every time they exchanged glances. Soul mates.

Not a chance in hell of finding a woman who could complete him like his mother did his father. At least that was what Chase had always thought. Then KC charged into his life with her sashaying handcuffs and colorful tattoo and purple hair and suddenly everything felt different.

This couldn't be love, could it?

Sure as hell wasn't only lust. He'd never been obsessed by a woman like this, unable to think, to stop touching her when she was near, to take his eyes off her.

This constant knot in his stomach, similar to the anticipation he felt before battle, it jazzed him, gave him energy, but also in a strange way it comforted him, made him feel like, no matter what, everything was going to be all right.

Impossible. He couldn't be falling in love with a woman he just met, a woman whose real name he didn't even know. What would Lucky say about that?

Lucky. Damn, how could he have forgotten? Lucky could be dead, lying in a ditch, a bullet in his head. Or worse.

The autopsy on the FBI agent The Crusade killed last summer

revealed evidence of torture before the poor bastard was put out of his misery. Could Lucky be suffering a similar fate while Chase stood here, mooning over a woman?

Chase shut his eyes on that unpleasant image, wishing there was anything he could do to help his friend. Much as he wanted to tear out of here and start a search for Lucky, he had to leave it to Rose and her people. Best thing for everyone involved was for the meet to go as scheduled, for Chase to maintain his cover and nail Bruno and Deacon, hopefully before Deacon's pals killed Lucky.

If that meant lying to the woman he was beginning to fall in love with, then that was the way it was going to have to be. If KC was half the woman Chase imagined she was, she would understand in the end.

He hoped.

CHAPTER 25

KC HEARD A DOOR slam shut. Damn Westin, he was going to make a run for it.

She grabbed her jacket and rushed back out to the hallway. Standing in the entrance to the living room, blocking her path, was Chase Westin, all six foot of commanding presence and self-confidence, grinning at her like a boy who'd just gotten a Daisy Brand, Red-Ryder BB gun.

"It's all fun and games until someone loses an eye," she muttered, ignoring his smirk and shoving past him into the living room.

Jay came from the kitchen, scraping the bottom of a jar of peanut butter with a spoon.

"And what's your excuse?" she demanded of the younger Westin. "You're supposed to be the smart one, remember?"

Jay flushed and gulped down a mouthful of peanut butter, offering her the spoon.

"Merry Christmas, KC," he said with a tentative smile.

KC rolled her eyes as both idiot brothers stood together.

Although her stomach was growling, she ignored the peanut butter, watching Chase as he took the spoon from Jay and licked it, his tongue stroking it like—

Snap out of it, she commanded herself. You're on the job here.

She took control of the situation, with these two someone with a little common sense had to.

"Jay, get your bags out to the car." Jay nodded and grabbed his coat. She pointed to Chase. "You're driving." She tossed him the car keys, which he snatched from the air with ease.

"Excuse me, Madame Special Agent, but I don't take orders from you," he said, leaning against the wall, licking the last of the peanut butter from the spoon.

KC narrowed her eyes at him, sending him her best Death Star glare. She didn't have time for this crap. "Don't make me cuff and frisk you, Westin."

Chase's grin widened. "Sounds like fun, KC."

There was a smudge of peanut butter on his chin, and she couldn't take her eyes off it. It took all her will power not to go over and lick it herself.

"Does getting your little brother killed sound like fun?" she retorted.

He straightened at her words, tossing the spoon to the dining room table with a clatter.

"How about if I take you into custody for obstruction of justice? Maybe a few days cooling your heels in a holding cell will dampen your libido."

"You can't do that," he said, his voice menacing. He stood so close now that she had to tilt her head up to meet his gaze.

"Just try me, Westin. Right now my priority is keeping your brother alive and to do that I need to be certain that you're not off flapping your lips to your buddies."

"I would never—" he protested.

"I can't trust you farther than I can throw you, so shut up and get in the car. Your choice, either drive or you get to ride handcuffed in the trunk with the spare tire. No difference to me."

The glower he sent her would have made any Marine DI proud, but KC wasn't moved. No one screwed with her operations. It was how she kept control, kept everyone safe. Including Chase Westin, the big, fat idiot.

He turned to grab his jacket. He was carrying again, a semiautomatic holstered at the small of his back. Where the hell had he gotten that from? The cookie jar? Man like him, ex-Marine, probably had a knife somewhere as well.

Fine, so they were basically matched weapon-wise. She'd deal with it after she saw Jay safely in the hands of the Marshals. No time to strip search him now, as much as the prospect of running her hands over Chase Westin's bare skin excited her.

His eyes followed her gaze, and KC was surprised when he lifted his shirt to reveal the Heckler Koch nine millimeter. Mr. Gosh-shucks, I'm as honest as the day is long. She rolled her eyes. Yeah, right.

"There's no permit," he said. "You can arrest me later if you want, but right now we're in this together, KC."

When he spoke her name it sounded intimate, as if he was caressing her.

"I want to keep my brother alive, that's all. Don't get in my way on this. Besides," he finished with a wolfish grin, "if we get into trouble, I'll cover your ass." His gaze dropped down to the handcuffs dangling from her belt.

KC shook her head. As if she would trust a man like Chase Westin to watch her back. No way in hell.

"Get moving," she ordered, following him out to the car where

Jay waited in the back seat.

KC kept one eye on the road and the other on Chase as he drove. Jay leaned forward from the back seat, his fingers drumming against KC's headrest in an irritating rhythm.

"Tell Chase about your grandfather, KC," he said, breaking the silence.

KC cut her eyes at him. No way she wanted Westin to know about her personal life. She never should have told Jay so much about herself. "I doubt he wants to hear about ancient history."

"Sure he does. KC's grandfather was my age when he organized a resistance, fought against Stalin," Jay said, bobbing his face forward between the two front seats. "He was even younger when he fought against the Nazis."

Chase's gaze darted over to KC. "Where was this?"

"Razgravia. It's a small country, between Bulgaria and Romania—"

"I know where it is. Rogue nation, base for terrorists. Your people have a reputation as hell raisers."

"They're not my people, well, they are, but—" She broke off. Damn the man, he was the devil the way he twisted everything she said. "We're not quitters, we fight for what we believe in."

"And right now that happens to be a right wing totalitarian dictator."

How dare he? He knew nothing of Razgravia or the role her family had played in its struggle for freedom. Her cheeks burning with anger, she turned to face him. "My grandfather was safe here in this country, he had a wonderful life. After the fall of the Soviet regime, he sacrificed all that. He returned to lead the revolution to topple Gregor. Thanks to the CIA, he failed. But he died fighting for the freedom of his people."

"Don't mess with KC," Jay put into the awkward silence that

followed her speech. "She knows how to take care of herself."

KC glared at him, willed him to shut up. Jay was a great kid, but he was so naive sometimes. It was her own damn fault for confiding in him in the first place. What had she been thinking?

Chase had switched the radio station to Froggy, the local country station, so she leaned forward to change it back to Qwik-rock and cranked up the volume to drown out any further conversation.

Chase reached out and turned it off just as Metallica was rolling into "King Nothing".

"Driver's choice," he said when she began to turn it back on. "So what did your mom and dad think of your grandfather's going back to the old country? Did they go too?"

KC crossed her arms around herself and settled into the seat, staring out the window at the snow-covered mountains. She was not having this conversation.

"KC doesn't have a father," Jay chimed in from the back. "And her mom died when she was twelve. She lived all by herself in New York City for a year."

"Shut up, Jay," she snapped.

Had she told the kid that? Oh yeah, Thanksgiving when he was mooning over never seeing Chase or Neil again, when the impact of moving into WitSec had hit him. They'd stayed up all night talking, sharing family stories. Damn, the kid had gotten under her skin—he was almost as bad as his big brother.

She looked up to see Chase's eyes on her instead of the road. The expression on his face was one of concern—as if he really cared or something.

"It wasn't a year," she muttered, "only seven months."

Chase gave a small nod, his gaze returning to the empty highway. "Until it got cold?"

"Yeah. There was a nun in a van—anyway, they found my grandfather." She stretched her seatbelt out, it was too tight against her chest, making it hard to breathe. "Ancient history." Time to turn the tables. "Tell me about Lejeune."

His face went stony and his hand shot out to click the radio back on. KC's hand intercepted his.

"My car," she reminded him. To her surprise, it was Jay who answered her question.

"He never should've been there," Jay said in a bitter voice.

"Quit it, Jay," Chase barked—the voice of a Marine giving a command. Jay seemed immune.

"You know what time it was when I got the call, Chase? Three-fourteen in the morning. The phone rings and it's Colonel Hicks. He's sorry to tell me, but you've been injured, they took you to Kabul, if you live long enough, they're going to fly you to someplace in Germany. And, oh yeah, there's not a damn thing I can do about it—don't call them, they'll call me with more information when they get it. Here's the number of the Red Cross if I need anything, have a good night."

KC pivoted in her seat to look at Jay. She'd never seen the kid like this before. She reached back to lay a hand over his, gave it a squeeze. "That couldn't have been easy. After just losing your parents."

Jay sucked in his breath. "After that Christmas, those first couple of days were hard, but Chase and I, we made it through together. We were a team. Then he left and I was on my own and it was only a few weeks later—"

"Jay, we don't need to talk about this," Chase said from the driver's seat. KC could see him looking in the rearview mirror at his brother.

"Maybe you don't need to talk about it, but I do," Jay shot

back. "You never need to talk about anything. When they finally transferred him to Walter Reed for his second and third operations, I would go down on weekends to visit. Take the bus or me and Neil would drive down."

Chase looked up at that. "You took the bus? What was wrong with the Malibu?"

"Dropped the transmission and I didn't have the extra money—mom and dad's insurance hadn't paid yet."

"Why didn't you say something? I could've gotten you—"

"Half the time I didn't even know if you knew I was there! You just lay there, staring out the window like you were a zombie or something. Like I was the one who died, not your squad. Like I didn't even exist anymore."

Silence descended over the car.

"I knew you were there, Jay," Chase's voice was low, but it echoed in the small space. "I knew. I wouldn't have made it without you."

"So why did you chose to go to Lejeune?" Jay demanded. "The doctors were ready to give you a medical discharge right then. I heard you argue with them, convince them to put you on limited duty while you tried to get back into shape. They told you it would never happen. You could have left, come home. Why did you pick the Marines over me? Why'd you go to Lejeune, Chase?"

KC found herself holding her breath, waiting for Chase's answer almost as anxiously as Jay was. Chase fiddled with the defroster, stared out at the empty road before them. When he finally answered, his voice was distant.

"I had to try," he said. "I couldn't let them down again." Then he gave a small, frustrated shake of his head. "Guess I was scared to come back home. You'd be leaving for college and I would—what? Work on the Malibu, collect my disability pension, dwindle away

like the rest of the town? What was I if I wasn't a Marine anymore?
I didn't have the answers and I sure as hell wasn't going to find
them in Coalton."

"Did you find the answers at Lejeune?" KC asked.

Both brothers looked at her. She could swear Jay was getting
ready to say something, but Chase spoke first. "No. There aren't any
answers, you just have to take it one day at a time."

Right, like that had gotten him real far. Stealing weapons,
court-martialed, now working with Bruno and The Crusade. Chase's
future seemed to be headed in the wrong direction—one day at a
time.

"You sure showed those doctors, though," Jay put in with a
touch of pride in his voice. "They kept saying you'd probably never
walk again, but you beat them all, didn't you Chase? I'll bet that's
the only reason they kept you from going back to your unit, you
pissed them off by doing it on your own."

"They don't let you in battle if you can't be trusted to watch
your partner's back, Jay," Chase said in a voice that made KC
wonder if he was talking about more than the Marines.

"Take this exit to the Mall," she directed him.

She wished she could give them more time. It was obvious the
Westin brothers had a lot to talk about. And she'd like to learn more
about Chase herself. She was finally beginning to understand why
his life had taken such a downward spiral.

Sunrise, Christmas morning found the Logan Valley Mall
deserted, perfect to spot anyone waiting in ambush. KC told Chase
to drive through the empty parking lot to the rear of the building. A
silver Taurus waited at the loading dock outside of Sears.

"Say your goodbyes now," she told them. "Jay, just do what the
Marshals tell you, and you'll be fine."

Jay reached over the back seat to grab her shoulder. "Thanks

KC, for everything," he said with an earnestness that made her blush.

"Just my job." She started to leave them in privacy for the few minutes left to them, but Chase stopped her.

"You're not going with him?"

KC shook her head. "No, the Marshals will take good care of him."

"I want you to go. You know Jay, I can trust him to you." He jerked his head at the two men in the Taurus. "I don't know these guys."

Words of trust coming from Chase Westin? She was surprised a thunderbolt didn't come down and strike him. Trust was a foreign concept to this man.

"I do," she assured him. "That's the way it's going to be—unless you want to take Jay back to Coalton, protect him yourself. In which case, I'm out of here, and all deals are off." She slid her hand under her jacket in a motion Chase could not misinterpret. He said nothing, merely knifed a glare at her.

"Of course, it'll be hard to protect him when you're back in jail." Her fingers curled around the grip of her Glock.

"Cut it out, both of you," Jay said. "Chase, don't screw this up, I know what I'm doing. And KC, I know you think Chase should be behind bars, but I promise you, you can trust him. Please don't arrest him after I'm gone."

KC kept her eyes focused on Chase, daring him to move his hands from their position on the steering wheel, if he even twitched—

Jay squeezed her shoulder once more, his voice dropping into a plea. "I'm trusting you with my life, KC," he said. "Can't you trust me on this one thing? Please?"

She sighed. The kid had no idea what he was asking. "Let me

have the HK," she ordered Chase.

He shrugged and leaned forward, allowing her to slide the semi from its holster. She glanced to see that the safety was on and placed it in her pocket. He was certain to have a back-up somewhere, but with his hands occupied by driving, she was safe enough for the time being.

"Jay, go around to your brother's side of the car and say good bye. Then I want you to take your bags over to the Marshals' car. I'm going to be right here," she addressed the last to Chase, opening her door and easing from the car, her Glock drawn and by her side as she stood with the car door open. Jay pushed the seat forward and clambered past her.

One Marshal approached, Jared Wright, an old friend. His hand was on his weapon, ready to draw while his partner covered him from the car. "Everything all right, KC?"

"Nothing I can't handle," she answered. "Sorry about the sudden change of plans."

"It's all right, we're on the clock the whole day anyway. Always tough when it's a kid," Jared said kindly. "We'll take good care of him."

"Thanks, Jared. He's a special one."

She watched through the windshield as Jay and Chase embraced, her gaze fixed on Chase's hands. She tried to ignore the tears that gleamed on Jay's face or the shaking in his hands as he picked up his bags and trudged toward the Marshals' car like a man facing a firing squad.

CHAPTER 26

CHASE WATCHED IN SILENCE as Jay drove off with his new protectors. He felt a curious sense of relief and disappointment. He should have been able to keep his little brother safe. Instead, all he'd done was make life more dangerous for both of them. But he couldn't help a sense of overwhelming pride at Jay's decision to do the right thing, to step forward and testify against Bruno. That was one bad guy Chase wouldn't have to worry about. Now all he had to do was convince KC to let him go so he could nail Deacon and stop The Crusade.

The Taurus faded from sight. The clink of the chains on KC's jacket cut through the silence as she slipped back into her seat.

"Start the engine," she ordered. Was that a tear he saw in the corner of her eye? She really did care for Jay.

"You plan to be there for him when he's really gonna need you?" he asked, ignoring her command. "During the trial?"

"Of course. I take care of the people I work with. My operations usually go much smoother than this. Everything was going great until you showed up."

He threw a grin at her. "I'm kind of known for that."

"Yeah, I've heard the stories from Old Man Sinderson. You're infamous around these parts."

"Don't believe everything you hear. I'm not all bad."

"Doesn't matter to me one way or the other. Your brother's safe, in protection, now it's time to get you taken care of so I can finish my job."

"I don't like the sound of that. What about your promise to Jay? Didn't you hear what he said?"

"He's a kid who desperately wants to believe his big brother is a hero, one of the good guys. You and I," she met his gaze, "both know that isn't so. Now drive."

He leaned back in the seat, arms folded akimbo, the right hand sneaking under the sleeve of his jacket. "No. You're gonna have to either trust me or kill me. Up to you, KC."

She flinched at the choice he'd given her. He was taking a gamble on her, but hell, he'd already trusted her with Jay's life. He was betting she wasn't about to shoot a presumably unarmed man in cold blood. Her left hand fumbled in her inside jacket pocket for her cell phone, and Chase waited for his chance.

"This is ridiculous," she said as she turned the phone on.

Her gaze flicked down for a split second to check the numbers as she dialed. Chase drew the knife from his sleeve, and in one blinding motion had it at the pale flesh of her neck before she could hit Send.

"Drop it," he said, forcing his voice into a menacing growl. "The phone and the gun."

She hesitated. He saw her calculating her odds of survival if she shot him and come up with a number she didn't like.

"Now," Chase told her.

KC's eyes locked onto his, her pupils wide with adrenalin.

There was little fear in them, though. Cool customer, he thought with approval, calm under fire. He could see her quickly reviewing all her options even as her hands dropped both the cell phone and her weapon into her lap.

He felt for them with his free hand, accidentally stroking her inner thigh as he reached for the phone, which had fallen between her legs. His breath caught, and he hoped she didn't notice. Chase tossed the phone into the back seat, exchanged the knife for the Glock-22 and held it on her as he replaced his HK back in its holster.

"The backup piece, too," he told her.

"That's it." She nodded to her Glock in his hand. "There's no place else for me to carry when I'm undercover." He hesitated, his gaze flicking down her tight leather vest and tighter jeans. "If I had a backup, don't you think I would have used it last night when you broke into my room?"

"You had other weapons to use last night," he reminded her. He was surprised to see a faint blush creep onto her cheeks. "Come on, KC, don't make me strip search you and throw you in the trunk."

He felt sorry for her—the only reason he'd been able to get the drop on her was that she was too decent to fire on a supposedly unarmed man. That and her feelings for Jay, for how Jay would feel if she was the one to kill his brother.

Chase steeled himself not to allow his feelings for her to cause him to make the same mistake she had. The job came first, he reminded himself. He gestured toward her boots with the gun.

"Try the left boot, KC," he said. "Slowly now, don't make me do something you'll regret."

She stalled for time, same thing he would have done if their circumstances were reversed.

"I'm worth more to you alive than dead, Westin. Think about it. How long you gonna last on every federal agency's hot sheet? Do you really want to risk being shot on sight? We could work a deal. You give me Deacon and Gianotti, and I'll get you into the program just like I did your brother. It could be your chance for a new beginning."

He hesitated, not because he was considering her offer, but because he couldn't decide whether to stay in character or to trust her with the truth.

"The backup piece, KC," he said. There wouldn't be any trust until she was disarmed.

She sighed and leaned forward, her hand reaching under her jeans, into the top of her boot.

"Slow, grab it by the barrel and hand it to me."

She eased the Baby Glock from its holster and handed it to him, grip first.

"Good girl."

She cringed at his familiarity. Damn, he hated seeing that look in her eyes. It was worse than the look Jay had given him last night when he thought Chase was one of the bad guys.

Reap what you sow, one of Deacon's favorite scriptures. Chase couldn't wait until this job was done. He thought of Lucky and realized that no matter what, he couldn't trust KC with the truth.

If anything went wrong during the exchange this afternoon, Lucky was a dead man for certain. He couldn't leave her walking around free to call for backup. He needed someplace quiet, someplace where she'd be safe but out of his way.

"Your turn to play chauffeur," he told her as the perfect place came to mind.

CHASE WATCHED KC MANEUVER the low slung, rear wheel drive car with ease over the icy mountain roads. She avoided the brakes whenever possible, using the clutch and gears to slow the car around curves, easing the gas so she had enough power going to the wheels to keep from spinning out.

He regretted not being able to tell her the truth. Where was he going to find a woman as talented, beautiful, sexy and smart as her?

And he didn't even know her real name.

"You carry credentials?" he asked after he directed them onto a dirt road rutted with old tire imprints. A little warmer and the Mustang would have been hopelessly mired in mud.

"They're back at the house," she told him after a long pause, as if she planned to ignore him at first. "Why? You don't believe I'm who I say I am? You think Jay wouldn't check who he was trusting his life with?"

"I think Jay has a blind spot when it comes to you." He allowed his free hand to rustle her spiky hair, trying to see the real color in the roots. Dark, whatever it was. Despite the gel or hairspray or whatever was holding it in place, it still felt like gossamer sliding through his hands. She jerked her head away and shot him a glare.

"I think you knew how to play him and everyone else in this town just right," he said, lowering his hand to rest on her forearm. Even through the leather of her jacket, he could feel her muscles bunch beneath his touch. He fought the temptation to slide his hand down to touch hers, to feel her flesh against his once again.

"Obnoxious enough to have the right people ignore you to your face but talk about you behind your back, giving you street credibility. Sexy enough that no one would think twice about a boy like Jay falling under your spell, not even his best friend."

194 | CJ LYONS

"Look," she surprised him by not taking offense at his words, "whatever you do to me, promise that you won't let Neil get caught in the crossfire. He's just a kid—and he doesn't have Jay's brains to see him safe out of trouble."

He held two guns on her and here she was, playing him again. Damn, she was good. "I suppose you want me to let you go so that you can protect Jay's best friend, is that it?"

"Thought had crossed my mind." She turned a half smile on him.

Chase let that pass. They pulled up in front of a log cabin, snow on its tin roof gleaming pink in the early morning sun.

"This is it, end of the road."

CHAPTER 27

CHASE KEPT HIS GAZE on KC, watching her reaction to his ominous words. She kept it cool, only a slight tightening of her eyes revealed any fear on her behalf. He could see why Jay had fallen for her, Chase was more than halfway there himself, and she wasn't even trying.

"What now?" she asked, her hands flat on the steering wheel.

"Relax," he told her, regretting his earlier testing of her and his need to continue to lie to her. "I just want to talk. Honest. This is my dad's old hunting camp, no one will hurt us here."

She looked at him in frank disbelief, her gaze moving from his eyes to the gun in his hand. "Don't kid a kidder, Westin."

"It's freezing out here, let's go inside."

He gave her credit for not trying anything stupid as he followed her inside the small, one room cabin. She lit the fire when he told her to, not needing instructions in building it or opening the flue. Under different circumstances, he could imagine them here, cozy in front of the fire, making love.

Hard to have love without trust or the truth, he told himself, gesturing to her to sit. She perched on the platform bunk suspended by chains from the wall at waist height. He straddled a straight-backed wooden chair, resting the hand holding the gun along its top slat. As the fire crackled, the small space quickly heated up.

"Jacket off," he told her. "Throw it in the corner."

"Why?" she challenged him.

"Because I said so." She merely stared at him. He rolled his eyes. "How about because I don't trust you not to have another weapon? Or because I'm the one with the gun?"

She frowned, but finally did as he instructed, sliding off the bunk to stand before him. She moved slowly, with exaggerated motions designed to reveal her lack of threat. But to Chase, watching her peel her way out of the form-fitting leather was sexier than any striptease.

Finally she held the jacket at arm's length, its chains glinting in the firelight. Her breath was coming hard and fast as if she too had been aroused by her motions while the lizard on her belly danced in time with her breathing.

"Toss it," he ordered. The jacket landed with a clink and rattle in the corner of the bunk. He shrugged free of his own jacket and let it fall to the floor behind him.

"What do you want, Westin?" she asked. He only wished he knew the answer.

"What can I do to make you trust me?" he countered. Besides telling her the truth.

"Gee, I dunno. Maybe give me back my gun?"

"Here." He emptied the round from the chamber, ejected the magazine and handed the Glock to her. "Pax?"

Anger flared in her eyes as she threw the useless weapon to the floor where it skidded across the rough-hewn planks. "You think I can't take you?"

He shrugged. "You've read my record. What do you think? I've got the reach, outweigh you by eighty pounds or more, I've been in combat—real combat where my life depended on it, not just simulations at Quantico. You tell me."

She swallowed hard, but her gaze never wavered. "I'd like to try. Even money that I make it out the door before you can take me down."

She shifted her weight to the balls of her feet. Jeezit, she was serious. He needed to put a stop to this before someone got hurt. Maybe even him, he thought, remembering KC hefting the fireplace poker, ready to brain him last night.

"Making it out the door and making it back to Coalton alive are two separate propositions," he reminded her in a quiet voice, his right hand reaching behind him to where the HK rested at the small of his back.

"I know," she admitted, looking down as if in resignation. "But I'd still like to try."

"I'll bet you would." He wouldn't expect anything less from her.

Silence as she regarded the floorboards, searching for potential weapons with her peripheral vision. If Chase hadn't been as experienced as he was, there was a good chance that she could have taken him. He took the HK and its holster and, without taking his eyes off her, placed them on the mantle. Then he moved to sit beside her on the bed.

Tension coiled through her body. Damn, did she think he was about to rape her? This had to end. Now. He didn't have time to keep sparring with her. She was much too dangerous.

"I told you, I just want to talk."

"That's what all you guys say," she muttered.

"KC, stop the act. This isn't a game. It's just you and me, right here and now. I need you to trust me or people will get hurt, good people, maybe even your team if things don't go well."

That got her attention. "Are you threatening my team? What are you going to do, call Gianotti, have them killed?"

For the first time, Chase saw true fear on her face. Her people, her team, they were her weakness.

"I don't work for Gianotti. I don't care if you arrest him and throw him in prison for the rest of his life, in fact I would applaud it. But it can't happen today."

"Why? What's so important about today?"

"Consider it a Christmas present. You know, peace on earth, good will to men."

She met his gaze with a frown. "What's your deal, Westin? You going to double cross Gianotti at the exchange today? Or Dinkum? Maybe both? Were you worried one of them might get word of your plans and use Jay as a hostage?"

He was silent for a moment, considering the angles. Her theory fit with all the facts as she knew them. Might as well run with it, see where it led. It was safer than the truth.

"What if I am?" he asked. "Would you trust me to see that no one, including Neil, got hurt? Would you let me go through with it?"

"No," she said in a flat tone. "I can't, even if you were someone—" her voice trailed off and her gaze dropped to his lips.

"Even if I were someone you cared about?" he finished for her, one hand tracing the curve of her jaw line, his thumb skimming over her lips. Their bodies were close enough that he could smell the enticing mix of leather and sensual feminine musk surrounding her. God help him, he wanted her, right here, right now, consequences be damned.

"Even if you were someone I trusted," she corrected him, but her voice had dropped into a husky whisper.

He tangled his fingers in her hair, pulled her face up to meet his and lowered his lips onto hers. She froze. Chase didn't push the issue. Instead he hovered there, awaiting her decision. Whatever she thought of him, he would never take advantage of a woman.

Then her arms flew around him, pulling him fully into her embrace, and he had his answer.

Her mouth opened beneath his, inviting him in as her fingers ranged through his hair, then teased their way down his spine. The kiss deepened, going far beyond the forbidden sexuality of their first embrace, into a world of intimate sharing. His hands slid beneath her vest, found her skin shivering with delight at his touch.

He allowed her to pull his flannel shirt away from his arms, broke contact with her lips for a precious instant as she tugged his T-shirt over his head. She placed a mouth against one of his nipples, teasing him with her tongue as her fingers traced the cluster of scars along his left side. Then she raised her face back to his, and he looked into her eyes, dark as coal in the dim light.

For the first time since he'd returned to Coalton, Chase felt as if he had come home at last.

CHAPTER 28

FOR ONE BRIEF SECOND, KC thought about using her knife.
He was vulnerable, his guard down, within range. She could take
him by surprise, she was certain. But she was equally certain that it
would have to be a killing blow, nothing less would keep him from
overwhelming her.

She looked into Chase's eyes and couldn't do it. She knew
it was the best way to end this quickly, the safest way to protect
herself and her team, to finish her mission. But she could not bring
herself to end his life, to kill the light in those eyes.

She remembered the few minutes they shared in his kitchen,
discussing the merits of old time Westerns. How could that man be
the same one who had brought her here at gunpoint?

Sentimental fool, she cursed herself as she placed a hand flat
against his chest. "I can't do this," she told him. "This is crazy. I
don't even know you."

He sucked in his breath, hard, and pulled away from her. He
gave his head a small shake as if waking from a dream. Rising to his
feet, he stood over her for one taut moment, then turned his back on

her.

Light from the fire gleamed from the sweat between his shoulder blades. Small, irregular scars continued from his side around to his back, white patches aligned against the well-defined muscles and tanned skin of his torso. Another scar, this one straight, surgical in its precision, could be seen below his hairline, ran down several inches over top his spine.

"You've read my file," he said, his voice distant, his back still to her as he threw more wood on the fire. "You know everything there is to know about me."

She heard regret in his voice and wondered if what he said was true. Was the man depicted in the dry legalese of the court-martial proceedings the same man who stood before her? He could have killed her, could have turned her over to either Gianotti or Dinkum, could have betrayed her entire team with a single phone call—but he hadn't. Her instincts told her there was more going on here, that she shouldn't be fooled by appearances. After all, she of all people knew appearances were often deceiving.

She moved to stand behind him, felt him tense as she reached a hand out and touched one of his scars. Everything had changed for Chase Westin, Staff Sergeant of the Marine Force Recon, after a raid outside of Deh Rawood, Afghanistan eleven months ago.

"Tell me about Deh Rawood," she said.

His breath shuddered through him as if even hearing the name spoken aloud caused him pain.

"Not much to tell," he began after a long moment of silence. "I won the lottery—was granted leave for Christmas. Just in time to get my parents killed. They gave me a two-week hardship furlough to get things squared away with Jay. Then I went back to my unit."

"You were working with a tribal chieftain, Rahman. Stabilizing his territory, helping to rebuild, right?"

His gaze was locked on the fire. "Recon doesn't rebuild. We were there to provide security to Rahman, his family, his village. That area has historically been under the influence of warlords who control the opium trade routes. Rahman was running for Parliament, there'd been threats against his life. It was a Green side op—boring duty, we were all itching to get back into action. There were some Army Engineers stationed there as well as some civilian contractors and NGO's."

"NGO's?"

"Non-government organizations. Doctors without Borders, some long-haired, hippy types from Potters for Peace, and a few reps from the UN. We cleared away minefields, escorted aid workers bringing in medical supplies, grain, animals. Between the drought and the war and the tribal fighting afterward these people had nothing—nothing but their pride." He took another breath and finally turned to face her.

"We knew we had to earn their trust, but hell, they were the reason we were there, right? The best way to protect the US and our homes was to bring them democracy, help them rebuild their home. At least that's how the mission briefing went. Me and my men, we risked our lives to protect them, not just Rahman and his family although he was our primary assignment, but the entire village. By the time I left at Christmas, I thought we were making real progress, that they accepted us."

"What happened when you went back in January?"

His eyes grew distant. "Some hotshot from State decided Rahman's village would be the perfect poster child for democracy. Had this idea that the more we got to know each other, the more that trust would grow and eventually the villagers would betray the opium dealers who were causing most of the violence in that area. My men were encouraged to visit the village—they even had

204 | CJ LYONS

weekly soccer games with them.

"Security had gone to hell in a basket, so when I got back the first thing I did was get the NCO's back in line and tighten things up. Too little, too late."

His voice dropped, his face changed in the firelight as memories flooded over him. Haunted shadows darkened his eyes, made his cheekbones look gaunt. This would be a good time to make a move. But she couldn't betray the part of her that was desperate to hear more, to learn the truth about this man.

It was only curiosity, she told herself. It wasn't anything more serious, like love. How could she love a man she was going to have to arrest, maybe even hurt if he resisted? Impossible.

She ran a hand through her hair, clearing her thoughts. The man was a devil, the way he'd wormed his way under her skin.

"Two nights later," he went on, "we were escorting Rahman and some relief workers with a load of medical supplies to a neighboring tribe up in the mountains. He led us right into an ambush. Turns out the opium dealers made him a better deal than we had. All he had to do was betray us.

"My men were out-numbered forty to one by the drug runners. It wasn't just a skirmish, it was a massacre." His voice trailed off.

"Five men under my command died in the fight. It took most of the night before they finished off the aid workers—well, the women, anyway. The men got the easy way out, a bullet to the head."

KC looked away, appalled by the nonchalant tone of his voice. She knew what that meant—that the truth was far more horrific than even his awful words revealed. She imagined him trapped, forced to listen to the cries of women being raped and tortured, of men dying, unable to do anything.

All because he had once trusted the wrong man. No wonder he was so screwed up.

"You were hit by shrapnel after a RPG destroyed your Humvee," she reminded him, quoting the information she'd read in his Silver Star citation. "Thrown thirty feet in the air, had a concussion, four broken ribs, two vertebra and herniated a disk in your cervical spine. Moving could have left you paralyzed for life, but you managed to make it back to Deh Rawood in time to warn the rest of your unit and save the other civilians."

She remembered reading the dry recitation of facts in his record. How he'd been pinned under the remnants of the armored vehicle, floating in and out of consciousness, no chance to reach any weapons and unable to move.

How he had played dead, then waited until the rebels had moved off, before painstakingly digging, scraping away at the hard packed lifeless soil to dig his way out. He'd dragged himself to cover near where the rebels had taken the civilians, then as soon as night fell, he had ambushed the men left to guard the prisoners, killing five men with a knife and his bare hands, shooting the final two, then stealing their Jeep.

Too late to save the male civilian workers but he had rescued three women and arrived back at Deh Rawood in time to warn the rest of his unit about the rebel attack force.

"You were a hero, Chase."

He shook his head as if her words were meaningless. "Tell that to my men, to those dead civilians I was supposed to protect."

The fire crackled in the silence that fell between them. She ached with the urge to reach out and touch him, to let him know she understood his pain, but the way his shoulders were hunched and his eyes tightened, she knew it would do no good.

"That has nothing to do with now, with us," he finally said, turning to face her, placing his hands on her shoulders, his eyes boring down into hers.

"Can't we," he searched for words, "just take a time out, you and me? An hour, just one hour, for us—leave the rest of the world behind?"

She looked up into his face, so earnest in the flickering light of the fire, and she desperately wanted to believe him, to trust him, to give him what he asked for.

"Come on, KC. You can spare an hour, can't you? Or is it the thought of spending it with me that's so awful? Are you that good of an actress? Because I thought, I think, we have something here, something powerful, bigger than you or me—"

She placed a finger to his lips to interrupt him. His hands on her shoulders were gripping her hard as he waited for her answer.

She believed Chase was a good man. She wanted to trust him, but as she looked into his face, she still saw deception. He was telling her only part of the truth. How could she trust him when he wouldn't trust her?

KC pulled away from the distraction of his touch, steeled herself to make her move. There was too much at risk: her team, Neil Gianotti, her own life.

CHAPTER 29

CHASE FELT KC WITHDRAW from him. It was as if they were on opposite sides of the globe when only a few feet separated them. He shivered, turned away and poked at the fire a few times. Before turning to face her, he replaced the HK and its holster back on his waistband.

When he looked back at her, she was leaning against the bunk, her head down so that he couldn't read her expression.

"Damn it, Westin. I need to get out of here." She aimed a hard stare at him.

"KC, you're not going anywhere." He stepped closer to her, within striking distance in case she tried anything stupid.

"I was afraid you'd say something like that." She pivoted into a fighting stance and swept a knife toward him, barely giving him the chance to avoid the sharp edge.

Damn, where'd she get that? The words rushed through his mind even as he feinted with a heel strike to her knife arm. She blocked his first move easily. He countered by pivoting inside her guard and using both hands to twist her wrist backward. She gasped in pain, the sound stabbing through the otherwise silent cabin.

"Drop it, KC," he urged her, hating that it had gone this far. "Don't make me hurt you."

Her body relaxed and her hand opened, the blade falling to the floor. Before Chase could take another breath, he felt a weight lifted from the small of his back. The cold steel muzzle of his HK touched the sensitive skin behind his ear.

"On your knees, Westin," KC commanded. She stepped back, out of range, as Chase slowly dropped to his knees.

"You won't kill me," he said, raising his arms to rest on top of his head in the universal position of surrender, praying like hell that he hadn't misjudged her.

He deserved it if she did. How had she gotten under his guard so easily? Dammit, he'd broken every rule, and now there'd be hell to pay.

"Kill you, no," she said, reaching for her jacket, her eyes never leaving his. "But shoot you? Hell, yeah."

She was serious. Of course, she thought it was the only way to protect her team, just like she'd been ready to bash his head in last night to protect Jay.

"Don't do this, KC," he said as she pulled a pair of plastic flex cuffs from her jacket. Real cuffs, not fashion statements like the ones dangling from her belt. "There's more at stake here than you know. That meet has to go through. Trust me, please. That's all I'm asking, just trust me."

She hesitated for a split second then gave a small shake of her head. "I can't. I'm sorry, Chase, but I just can't."

Finally, she called him Chase. Too bad it was too late. She deftly applied the cuffs with his wrists pinned behind his back. Very professional and almost impossible to escape from.

She grabbed her knife from the floor and returned it to its

hidden sheath at the back of her vest. Then she shrugged into her jacket.

"Look at me." He tried one last time. "Listen to your heart, your instincts. KC, I'm not the man you think I am."

She ignored him as she gathered the two Glocks and opened the door. He was ready to tell her everything, to risk everything and trust her. But it was too late; she was out the door before he had a chance.

Chase hurled himself forward, shouting curses he knew would never make it past the heavy logs of the cabin walls.

Dammit, she'd just condemned Lucky to death, not to mention whatever innocent population Deacon and The Crusade were buying those weapons to slaughter.

He forced himself to calm down. She'd be back, she only went to the car to get the cell phone, he told himself. After all, she'd left him his own knife, the fireplace poker as well as a wealth of other tools to escape from the flex cuffs with. She was too professional to leave him alone for long, she'd call for backup and return to guard him.

Then he'd have his chance to talk her out of this, to explain everything to her.

He heard the growl of the Mustang's engine and swore once more.

Damn KC and her soft-heart, did she think by leaving him, giving him a chance to escape before the cops arrived, that she was doing him a favor?

It was his own fault, he'd told her to listen to her heart, and she'd compromised by stranding him without means to make it to the meet on time or interfere with her operation, while also giving him a chance for a new life.

She'd done exactly the wrong thing for all the right reasons and innocent people were going to pay the price.

Chase squirmed his way over to his jacket, awkwardly sliding his knife from its sheath. He wedged the blade between his feet and arched as far backwards as he could. His spine screamed in pain, he considered it just punishment for his lapse of reason as he began to saw through the cuffs.

If only he'd trusted her sooner, had the courage to listen to his own heart, then none of this would be happening.

CHAPTER 30

KC SAT IN THE Mustang, her vision clouded by tears as she
fumbled with her cell phone. Damn it, she was on the job here, this
was not the time to get emotional.

It hurt so bad, though, she couldn't stop crying. She'd never felt
this way before. Not even after Manny died. No man had ever made
her feel the way Chase Westin had.

Was this what it was like for her grandfather, Konstantine, when
he was forced to choose between his captured lover and the welfare
of the rest of his resistance group?

In the end, her grandfather had chosen to sacrifice himself,
gambled on a brother's honor. What would he tell her to do now?
Risk betrayal as he had? Or walk away and do her job, protect her
team and an innocent civilian?

KC rested her head against the steering wheel. God, she was so
very tired. All she wanted was for this day to be over.

Chase's face invaded her mind, the pain in it as he had
recounted the loss of his men, the way he looked this morning when
he argued with her about Jay's safety.

He was lying about something, that was a certainty. But he couldn't lie about the kind of man he was—loyal, brave, willing to sacrifice anything for his people. KC swiped a hand over her eyes and threw the phone to the empty seat beside her. If she didn't show up, Glenn and Carson had their orders. With or without her, the operation would go forward.

She turned off the Mustang's engine. It might get her killed, but she was going to trust Chase Westin long enough to give him a chance to explain.

When she opened the cabin door, he was almost free of the cuffs. He looked up at her, his expression speeding from anger and frustration to shock, then relief, and finally joy. His knife dropped to the floor with a thunk.

KC drew the HK and held it on him. "You've got five minutes to tell me the truth," she said. It was an effort to keep her voice from shaking. "If you aren't working for Gianotti, who are you working for?"

He rolled back into a kneeling position, his eyes never leaving her face. "When I finished my rehab down at Lejeune, I was in the best shape of my life," he started. "Running half marathons, re-certified on the range, could go through the obstacle course in better time than before we were deployed. None of that mattered to the doctors, though. They won't let you do the things Recon has to do after a back injury—HALO jumps or roping out of a helo. I was through.

"I was drowning my sorrows at a bar in Jacksonville when I spotted Bruno. Overheard enough to realize he'd given up his father's numbers racket to move into arms deals and that he was big time. I contacted a friend at NCIS, and we set up a sting operation."

"So your arrest, almost killing that MP, those were all faked?" If what he said was the truth, it explained a lot. Not everything, though. She watched him closely.

"Not faked—I did put a choke hold on that guy, mainly to keep him safely out of the line of fire if things went wrong. I did sell out the rest of the gang, and the court martial was for real. As well as the time in Leavenworth." He frowned as if the extent of all that he'd lost had finally become apparent. "Maybe someday I can get the record straightened."

He shrugged. "Doesn't matter. Jay knows the truth. I guess that's all that counts. Anyway, Bruno recruited me to help with some deals he was putting together with Deacon and The Crusade."

"And you were reborn as Chase Westin, arms broker." She looked down at him, could find no trace of deception. "Why not just tell me the truth after you knew who I really was? Why all this?" She gestured to the cabin.

"I'm working with a partner, Ed Cavanaugh, he's ATF. Last night Deacon's men took him. If he's still alive and that meet doesn't go down, they'll kill him for certain. I need those weapons to get to The Crusade. I'm supposed to deliver them in person, it'll be our only chance to find out what they're planning and stop them."

"Bottom line, you didn't trust me," she said, anger creeping into her voice. "All those little speeches about how important it was for me to trust you, despite the fact that as far as I knew, you were a convicted felon who could get my team killed. When all along the real problem was that you couldn't trust me."

He rocked back, stood up. She raised the HK out of reflex then let it fall to her side. Never point a gun at anything you wouldn't want to shoot, her first weapons training lesson rang through her mind.

"I'm sorry, KC," he said after a moment of silence. "I couldn't. There was too much at stake. If anything goes wrong at that meet

214 | CJ LYONS

today, they'll kill Lucky."

"And you," she reminded him. "They'll shoot you first. What makes you so certain your friend is still alive?"

He shook his head, his hair falling in his face. She had to stop herself from reaching out to push it away from his eyes.

"Nothing. But I have to give him every chance I can. There's nothing else I can do for him."

KC sighed and holstered the HK. She drew her knife.

"Turn around, let me get you out of those." She sliced the cuffs from his wrists. He massaged the red lines where they had bit into his skin.

"Sorry about that," she told him. "You didn't leave me much choice. So, what do we do now?"

"How about my previous offer?" he said, his fingers hooking in the waistband of her jeans, pulling her close. "An hour for us? Forget about the rest of the world? We have time before the meeting. Then we can figure out how to fix everything else."

She framed his face in her hands, pulling him down to meet her. "One hour, Chase," she whispered, her lips skimming over his as she formed the words. "Consider it a Christmas present."

As she kissed him, his hands slid down her back and across her jeans. The sound of handcuffs clicking jolted through the room.

"Fear not," he said with a grin. "For the next hour, I'm your prisoner, Special Agent."

KC returned his smile. Then his hands began to move and further thought became impossible as the heat spread through her body.

CHASE SQUIRMED WITHIN THE confines of his voluntary restraints. This was kind of fun. He could understand the allure.

The cuffs forced him to be patient, to find new, interesting ways to negotiate simple matters like stripping her clothes from her. She cooperated by shrugging out of the jacket. KC laughed as he tried and failed to open the vest's buttons with his teeth.

"Allow me," she said.

He leaned back to watch her fingers tease each button free until the vest hung open. An involuntary groan escaped his lips as she ever so slowly slid it off her shoulders, then reached her arms behind her, allowing it to drop to the floor.

Chase could resist no longer. He buried his face between her breasts, tasting the sweat that had pooled there. She laughed, and he stretched to take one ripe nipple into his mouth. He rolled his tongue over it, feeling a gasp of pleasure run through her.

She fisted her hands in his hair, pulling him closer. He opened his mouth wider, her heartbeat echoing through him as he quenched his thirst for her. He felt her stiffen once more, a moan echoing through her, and he released her.

"Don't stop," she said, her voice raspy.

"Take your jeans off," he commanded, turning his head so his breath rippled over the wet flesh of her breast. She shuddered once more, and her fingers fumbled for her chain link belt.

Once the belt was unsnapped, Chase yanked it backwards, free of the loops that held it in place. He had more freedom now but was still trapped by her—just as she was trapped between his arms.

She unzipped the jeans, and he pushed the denim and her panties down, the lengths of chain dancing against the back of her thighs, catching the light of the fire. He knelt before her as she kicked free of first one pants leg then the other and he was finally able to appreciate her body art in its full glory.

And art it was. Inked over the flesh of her abdomen was an astonishingly lifelike lizard, its scales rippling as her muscles moved, lying on its back, head and four legs juggling balls with the yin/yang symbol within them. Chase traced the lizard's tail over KC's left hip where it wound down behind her thigh and back around to end just above her knee.

His tongue flicked out to tickle the tail's end. He watched in fascination, it wiggled as her skin quivered. He stroked his tongue higher, each time the effect was slightly different, more intense. He halfway expected the tail to separate from her skin and curl around his neck.

He slid his fingers between her legs, felt her heat, she was wet, ready for him, her hips arching as his fingers stroked her. He rocked back on his heels, watching the chameleon juggle the yin/yang balls as waves of pleasure washed over her, rippling the muscles of her belly. Her hands gripped his shoulders, her body writhed under his attentions, and her knees began to buckle.

He gave her one last climax. The chameleon seemed to wink at him in return as her body shuddered with her release.

"You must be very close to the tattoo artist," he said, surprised to hear jealousy in his voice.

Her head was bent down, touching his as she caught her breath. "Friend of mine, used to be a counterfeiter, served three years at Lomloc. He works for us now. Loves doing my art before I go on assignment, says it lets him use his creativity."

Chase stroked a finger along the back of her thigh, finding a ticklish area that made the lizard jump as she laughed.

"It's temporary of course," she went on, "it'll be totally faded away in a month or so."

Too bad—he liked this karma-juggling lizard. Then he thought about the idea of another man staring at KC naked, painstakingly inking his creation onto her flesh.

"Is that what you do, Special Agent? Get involved with ex-cons? You like dangerous men, don't you?"

His vision darkened with anger and jealousy. He might be the one restrained here, but she was his, belonged to him and him alone.

Chase could not bear the thought of any other man touching her, looking at her with passion in his eyes.

"Raymond's not dangerous," she laughed, missing the edge in his voice. "He just likes to use me as his canvas. He calls this one Karma Chameleon, if that gives you any hint as to where his preferences lie."

Karma Chameleon? KC—it suited her, the way she went so deep undercover that she fell into her characters, juggling fate and circumstances to suit her needs of the moment.

Then the reference hit him, and Chase felt foolish for the irrational wave of jealousy that had overcome him. "Like the old song by Boy George?"

"Yeah, he's Raymond's hero. Believe me, you're more his type than I am."

She wriggled within his grasp, delighting him as the chameleon began to tempt fate once more. "Once I was under as a Catholic school girl, goody two-shoes fallen for the wrong guy, the school drug dealer. He called his heroin 'Crouching Tiger', was really into Kung Fu and stuff, so Raymond inked a tiger around my arm as a sign of my devotion. Really turned the kid on. He wouldn't stop talking, gave up everything, trying to show off. Raymond said it was because of the second, secret tattoo he drew—a small, hidden dragon, right here."

Chase listened to her speech, her words came in a quick rush.

218 | CJ LYONS

He looked up and saw that she was blushing. Was KC nervous? He grinned, rather liking the idea that he could fluster the unflappable Special Agent.

Her finger traced a small circle just below her left breast, directly over her heart. He raised his head, followed her hand with his mouth. Her heart thumped beneath his touch.

"Dragonheart," he murmured, liking how the words fit her. Hot, fierce, fiery. He craved her touch, barely cared that he might get burned.

KC had done more than earn his trust, Chase realized. She had earned his respect. And he was coming perilously close to losing his heart to her as well.

"All right, my turn," she said in a voice of command, pulling him to his feet. "Show me yours."

CHAPTER 31

KC KNEW SHE WAS being cruel as she teased him with her hands, unsnapping his jeans and slowly pushing them down his long, muscled legs. She didn't care. If all they had was an hour, she was going to make it the most unforgettable hour of either of their lives.

She'd never wanted a man the way she wanted Chase Westin. No, this was more than want or desire. This was primal need.

She hiked her hips onto the thin mattress of the bunk. Perfect height, she thought, inching her bare feet up Chase's chest, watching the expression on his face as she opened herself up to him, hiding nothing.

His hands were trapped by her weight and the handcuffs, so she was free to take control. She reached between her legs, her fingers stroking the length of him as he moved his hips forward. He made an animal sound, his fingers clenching her buttocks, tugging her nearer to him.

She traced her fingers back up to his belly button, watching as his chiseled muscles rippled with pleasure.

"Condoms," she reminded him, reaching past him to her jacket.

She grabbed the foil pouch from one of the pockets and tore it open. One good thing about "bad girl" KC—she was always prepared.

After he was covered, KC leaned back, her hand guiding Chase. Chains jangling like Christmas bells, he lifted her hips and thrust into her. She grabbed onto the edge of the cot, holding onto her sanity as another wave of pleasure overtook her.

His eyes locked onto hers. She was drowning in those indigo depths, all time and space collapsing with her as a roar of ecstasy overwhelmed her. His cry mixed with hers, and she felt him break the chains that bound him.

LUCKY DECIDED THAT WITH his one arm still out of commission—temporarily, it wasn't like he'd had a stroke or something—his best move was to play possum.

He heard a car pull up in front of the shed, the sound of one door slamming shut, and lay on the floor, his arms behind him, the shiv hidden out of sight. He kept his eyes slit shut as the door was unlocked and pushed open.

Fergus entered, carrying a chain rattling with thick links. Ballast, Lucky realized, the taste of bile etching his throat. Enough to weight a body as it fell into a mineshaft.

Fergus didn't even glance in his direction, left the door wide open and dropped the chain to the floor with a clatter. Lucky didn't see any weapons on the man. He held his breath, feigned unconsciousness as Fergus finally approached.

The bowlegged caricature of a man squatted down, reached to roll Lucky over onto his stomach.

Lucky kept his body a dead weight until Fergus had him halfway rolled over, exposing the side of Fergus' neck. Then he aimed a knee into Fergus's abdomen and shoved his weight on top of him, the jagged edge of the shiv at the other man's jugular.

Fergus went white, and he shouted a curse. "You were dead!"

"Think again," Lucky whispered as he leveraged his arm against the man's windpipe to shut him up before any of his partners heard his cries. "Where's the Preacher? Who else is here?"

The little man just kept shaking his head, muttering gibberish. Typical bully. Give them any show of resistance and they crumble. Of course, seeming to return from the dead wasn't hurting his street cred any.

"Tell me, Fergus!" He held the shiv in front of the man's face, one tip aiming at Fergus' eye.

"Go to hell!" Fergus crashed his beefy fist into Lucky's throat.

Lucky's vision darkened with pain as he gasped for breath. He swiped his blade down, ripping through the flesh of Fergus' cheek, but Fergus deflected it before it could do any serious damage. Fergus pushed Lucky off him and scrambled to retrieve the chain he'd dropped by the door.

Lucky caught his breath and rolled to his feet. Fergus was swinging the chain before him, aiming to snag Lucky's knife hand with it. Lucky feinted with his knife then stepped forward, extending his left arm to take the blow from the chain.

The heavy chain wrapped around Lucky's forearm like a python strangling its prey. Fergus howled with victory as he wrenched the chain tighter, pulling Lucky forward onto his knees.

"You're gonna stay dead this time!" he roared as he circled a length of chain around Lucky's neck and used both hands to tighten it.

Lucky leaned his weight back, forcing Fergus to step closer. Just a little bit more, he thought as his vision darkened. Fergus obliged, leaning forward to watch Lucky's suffering.

Giving Lucky the opening he had been hoping for. Lucky

rammed the homemade blade up, burying it into Fergus's groin. Fergus jerked back in astonishment and Lucky yanked the knife out. A spray of blood spurted from Fergus's femoral artery. Fergus dropped the chain, clasped both hands over the wound and staggered backward. Lucky uncoiled the chain from his neck and stumbled to his feet, aimed another stabbing blow under Fergus' ribcage.

This time Fergus dropped to the ground, one hand flailing for the shiv stuck in his chest, the other slipping in the blood streaming from his thigh. Lucky dropped the chain onto the floor and crouched beside the dying man.

"Last chance, Fergus," he said. "Where's the Preacher? Who is he? What does he have planned?"

The little man's color had grown ashen. He twisted his lips into a grimace, and his hand tightened on the blade in his chest.

"The death of all of you." Fergus's words were slurred by hatred and effort. "I'll see you in hell, Cavanaugh."

Before Lucky could stop him, Fergus wrenched the shiv free. A fresh blossom of blood streamed over his shirt. Lucky put pressure on the wound, but knew that without the blade slowing the blood loss, it was a useless gesture. He felt for a pulse. There was none.

Lucky sat back on his heels, his body splattered with blood. He dragged in a breath, let it out, his eyes never leaving the body of the man he had killed. When he finally raised his gaze, he spotted a pickup truck waiting outside. Lucky climbed to his feet, wavered for a moment, then staggered toward the door.

Time to blow this joint.

CHAPTER 32

CHASE HELD HER AFTERWARD as they lay together on the scratchy wool blanket that covered the cot. KC played with the remnants of her belt, making the chains jangle and chime as she stroked his wrist. He loved the feel of her hands on his body, anywhere on his body. Her touch shot an electrical tingling straight to his heart. She dropped the chain and ran her fingers up his arm to twirl his hair.

"My Samson," she said with a grin.

"Does that make you my Deliah?" he asked, kissing the side of her neck. "Are you going to betray me, KC?"

A dark look crossed her face for a brief instant, then she returned her gaze to the broken length of chain. "Too bad," she said with the same mischievous grin that she'd given him back in her bedroom—was that only a few hours ago? It felt like a lifetime ago. "I had plans for those handcuffs."

He laughed and wrapped his arms around her, his fingers tracing the yin/yang symbols inked onto her belly. "Karma, that's like fate, right?"

"Hmmm, something like that," she murmured as she stretched, her hands stroking his arms, her body relaxed, totally at ease with him. He looked down at her, past the wild purple hair to those dark eyes, now heavy lidded and languid, and wished they never had to leave this place, this moment in time.

"If I never got that pass home for Christmas," he continued, "then my folks would still be alive, I would've stayed with my team, and they would still be alive, too?"

She straightened, her eyes opening wide, fixed on his. Her hand slid up his arm to rest against his cheek.

"No. That's not Karma," she told him in a serious voice. "Those were circumstances you couldn't foresee, out of your control.

"Karma is, I think, when you do have a choice and you know one choice is more painful, will cost you more than the other, but you make it anyway because it's the right thing to do. Then sometime down the road, those choices add up to something wonderful happening, something you could never in your wildest dreams predict ever happening to you." She leaned forward so that their foreheads touched and kissed him lightly. "That's Karma."

"You could have chosen to take Jay away last night when you first met me," he persisted. "But you didn't, even though it would have made your job easier."

She squirmed, uncomfortable speaking about her own choices. "I knew how Jay felt about the way you two had left things when he saw you in Leavenworth, knew it would eventually tear him apart, so I made a judgment call. I knew I could keep the operation on track—at least I thought I could. I had no idea exactly how much trouble you'd be, Westin." She said the last with a smile, nipping at his lip with her teeth.

Chase felt his body respond to her, but his mind was busy contemplating the choice he had to make now. His original plan, to leave KC here, still seemed the safest for everyone involved. Now more than ever, he wanted her as far away from Coalton as possible when the meeting with Bruno took place. KC sensed his change of mood. She sat up straight, looked him in the eyes.

"This is how it's gonna work," she started in that no-nonsense way of hers that he was learning to love. "I'll drop you off outside of town so we're not seen together. I get Neil out of the way while you finish setting up the meet. I'll tell my people we're doing surveillance only until after you and Deacon leave, then we pop Gianotti."

She frowned, her brow wrinkled in thought, and Chase took the opportunity to get a word in edgewise.

"Then I'll take care of Deacon and The Crusade and the rest is history," he finished for her.

It wasn't as good as his plan to leave her here, far away from the action, but it was the best compromise. Her frown deepened. He traced a finger along her forehead, trying to ease the tension there. "What's wrong?"

"It's too dangerous. Too many unknowns. What was your original plan? It had to be better than this."

Chase smiled. He and Lucky were pretty much making it up as they went along. "I didn't realize you're a pessimist."

She sat upright, turned so that she straddled him, her weight on his hips. Chase liked this, he had a full view of her chameleon in addition to her many other lovely attributes. He smiled and allowed his hands to roam over her body. She pushed them aside.

"I'm not a pessimist. I just don't like unpleasant surprises, that's all," she said, leaning forward, her gaze drilling into his. "Like something happening to you, Chase. If anything goes wrong either at the meet with Gianotti or afterward with The Crusade, you're the first one they're going to kill.

Chase looked away. He knew that. It was the price of doing business. You couldn't get close to maniacs like Bruno and Deacon without taking risks.

"You're a control freak," he told her, trying to lighten the mood again. "You can't plan for everything."

"I had a pretty good track record until I met you," she reminded him.

He reached a hand up to rustle through her hair. "My point exactly. I just take it one step at a time. Focus on my objective, take care of it, and move on to the next."

She leaned back on her heels, out of range of his hands, and looked at him skeptically.

"I needed to stop the thefts at Lejeune, so I did. Then we had a chance to go after Bruno, nail him. He led us to The Crusade, so I worked on that. I'm not going to stop now that we've almost got everything."

"I'd feel a lot better about things if you'd at least tell me who 'we' is," she said.

"I'd like to, but I can't. All you need to know is that we're on the same side here."

"Why is Deacon letting you drive the van to The Crusade's hide out?"

Chase sat up enough so that he could pull her back into range of his hands and began to stroke his fingers along her thighs. Talking about people who might kill him wasn't the way he intended to spend what little time they had left.

"This deal's too big for Deacon to verify the entire shipment. It's a twenty-four foot moving van, it'd take all day to check everything. The arrangement I negotiated between him and Bruno has The Crusade paying my ten percent commission, but I don't receive it until all the weapons are delivered to them and authenticated."

Her eyes widened, and she shook her head in dismay. "Are you nuts? That leaves you vulnerable to either side. If Gianotti double-crosses The Crusade, it's you they'll kill. And even if Dinkum gets everything he's paid for, what's to stop him from killing you, saving some money, and silencing a potential witness? It's suicide!"

"Ye of little faith," he chided her, a hand moving up her arm to rest on her cheek. He pulled her close, snugged her into a tight embrace. Her heart raced like hummingbird wings, fluttering against his. "I'll be fine. And it's our best chance to shut down The Crusade. Trust me."

She raised her head to his. "You, I trust. It's Gianotti and Dinkum and the other nuts in The Crusade that I'm not so sure about. Maybe we can come up with a better plan, something not so risky."

"No time." He ran a finger up her side, making her squirm once more. "Because there are a few more things I'd like to do before we leave. And none of them involve any planning." She opened her mouth to protest. He silenced her with a kiss.

CHAPTER 33

CHASE EASED BACK THE passenger seat of the Mustang,
content to allow KC navigate them back to Coalton and the real
world. The winter landscape flickered by, hypnotic as bright
sunshine interrupted the shadows of the trees.

He let his mind drift, not quite dosing although sleep was a
tempting idea. More tempting was the thought of a future with a
woman like KC in his life.

For the first time in a long time, he allowed himself to fully
relax. No. What he felt was more than relaxation. Contentment, that
was the right word. At peace.

The feeling was almost foreign. He hadn't felt like this since
before his parents died. After that there'd always been something to
worry about: Jay, his squad, recuperating from his own injuries, the
constant stress of undercover work.

Now Jay was in safe hands, his mission was headed in the right
direction, and he actually had something to look forward to once he
completed it.

Chase closed his eyes, the memory of KC's body nestled

alongside his filling his mind. Their time had been so short. He craved more. Day after day of exploring each other, growing together—Chase could imagine a future spent with KC.

It was the first time in years that he'd thought of a future past the next hour or day or mission.

He opened his eyes, rested his hand on her thigh, felt her muscles clench as she adjusted the gas pedal. She geared down for a curve, took the opportunity to grasp his hand in hers, her eyes darting over to his face.

"You're feeling pretty good about this," she said.

She didn't have to clarify, Chase knew she meant all of it: them, his mission, life in general.

"Yeah, I am," he replied with a slow smile that lingered.

KC rolled her eyes. "Men. You always think good sex solves everything."

He straightened at that. "Good? Excuse me, think you might want to change your adjective? You know us men and our fragile egos."

Her laughter rang through the small car. "Sorry. Great sex, superlative sex, sex that will go down in history—"

"All right, now you're making me blush."

"Seriously, Chase. I can't let you go after The Crusade alone. Maybe I could get into Gianotti's warehouse, sneak a GPS onto the moving van?"

"Too risky. I'll be fine. After six months working this job, I'm not letting anything jeopardize it now."

"So you'll drive off into the sunset with a van full of weapons and explosives—"

"Me and Deacon."

"Right, that makes me feel better. You and Lester Dinkum, stone cold killer, heading into The Crusade's top-secret compound, well guarded by freaky nut cases no doubt. And no one will know where you are or if you're in trouble?"

She frowned and shook her head. "I don't like it. Not one bit. In fact, as someone who until now has had a stellar track record for planning operations, I'd have to say that in my expert opinion, this plan pretty much sucks."

He fingered the lapel of his jacket, where the hidden panic button lay. As soon as he triggered it, the cavalry would be on their way. Of course, no guarantees he'd live to see them arrive. "KC—"

"Don't you dare," she snapped. "I know what you're going to say: Trust me, I know what I'm doing, I can handle this. Any macho clichés I've forgotten?"

He looked over at her, surprised to see a single tear slip from her eye. She swiped it away and blinked hard.

"I've heard them all before, Westin, so don't try to soft soap me. Look at your friend, Lucky, what happened to him. We both know there's a good chance you're not coming back from this one."

They were silent as she turned onto Hill Avenue. Chase motioned for her to drive into the cemetery. The trees and bushes would hide them from sight. He got out of the car, still not knowing what to say to her. He'd been content to fantasize about a future, but that wasn't enough for KC. She appeared to want something more concrete. Something Chase was powerless to give her.

KC remained in the car, her gaze locked onto the steering wheel. Chase walked around and opened her door.

"Come on. There's someone I want you to meet," he said, taking her hand and coaxing her from the car. He led her down a blacktop path to a small statue of a man and a woman sitting together on a bench, holding hands, facing west.

"Mom, Dad, this is KC." Chase squeezed her hand as KC stopped beside him. "I don't know if Jay ever brought you here."

Her free hand swiped her face again before she replied. "Yeah. Me and him and Neil used to come up here. Just to talk, to think."

"It's the first time that I've been here since—well, too long." He bent forward, surprised to find the inscription scraped clean of snow already. Jay must have stopped by, left the flowers. Then he noticed the fresh boot prints around Diana's smaller grave to his left. Much too big to be Jay's.

KC recited the words carved on his parents' headstone. "I shall but love thee better after death."

"Thoreau was always Dad's favorite, but Mom loved Browning, so she won. Just like when they were married. Most of their fights were over in moments, without them ever saying a word. It was like they knew each other so well, they could read each other's minds."

She traced the letters as if she were imprinting them onto her heart.

"Jay and I added what is below."

"Forever together, however long the journey," she read. She stood up straight, tilted her head up to meet his eyes. "You're trying to tell me not to worry about the future."

Chase nodded at the grave. "They never did. Somehow they always had this quiet certainty that whatever happened, even if one of them died before the other, they would never truly be parted."

She sniffed hard as if holding back more tears. He wrapped her in his arms, cradled her against his chest, savoring her warmth. Her arms squeezed him tight, and he leaned his head forward, resting it on her riotous purple hair.

After a long moment, KC pushed back, looked up at him. "I'll say one thing, Westin. That was a helluva lot better than the macho crap I have to put up with from most men."

He tousled her hair with his fingers before he reluctantly released her. "I'm not most men, and don't you forget it."

She snapped to attention and gave him a passable salute. "Aye, Staff Sergeant Westin." Then her expression turned serious once more. "Promise me, you'll watch your back, all right?"

"Ma'am, yes ma'am," he said returning her salute. He was desperate to have her in his arms once again. Watching her walk away was one of the hardest things he'd ever done, but Chase held his ground, waited until she and the Mustang were long out of sight before leaving.

"I'll be back," he promised his parents and sister.

CHAPTER 34

KC CRADLED THE CELL phone between her shoulder and chin as she used both hands to control the Mustang. Main Street was eerily silent, except for a black Lincoln Town Car that glided to a stop in front of the life-sized Nativity scene across the street from the school. Probably one of the ministers setting up for services. In her rearview mirror she spied a white man with brown hair, wearing a conservative black suit emerge from the car. Guy looked like a mortician, someone should tell him it was Christmas, time to lighten up. He was going to scare all the kids.

Come noon most of the town would be in one of the two churches, celebrating the holiday, while across the street, Chase would be risking his life. She shook her head at the irony, tried to ignore the knot of anxiety that tightened her stomach.

"The Emergency Response Team leader says his men are in position," Glenn's voice broke into her thoughts. "Dinkum knew what he was doing when he chose the school as the meet site. Nearest cover is the trees behind it, about one hundred fifty yards away. And did you know that at noon Main Street is going to be crawling with people and kids—some kind of Christmas procession."

"Another reason not to go tactical unless we're forced. We'll keep it strictly surveillance, document everything and pick up Gianotti and his men once they're away from any civilians."

"No problem. Carson and I are on the roof of the drugstore. You need anything, just holler. Any problems, give us the high sign."

She rolled her eyes. They'd worked out all the radio codes and contingency plans days before.

"Yes, Father," she said, dropping into her teenager persona.

"Seriously, I was worried about you. Thought we'd hear from you hours ago."

His tone implied that she should have informed him about the change of plans and Chase's true allegiance before this. KC realized that she should be more grateful to Glenn and Carson for their loyalty. They hadn't questioned her inclusion of Chase as one of the good guys when she told them he was undercover with another agency.

"Just a few loose ends to tie up," she said with a smile, remembering Chase and those ridiculous toy handcuffs. The guy was an idiot, but a charming idiot who could make her laugh. And romantic too—those things he said about his parents. It'd been a long time since she'd met a guy like that.

"Carson said to tell you that there were some problems with the audio on the bug in Gianotti's garage last night," Glenn went on in a voice that told KC he and Carson were in on it together. "About ten minutes were lost. Just wanted to let you know."

"Thanks." She owed them both, big time. Once this was over, she'd find a way to make it up to them.

"Anytime, KC. Everything is all right, isn't it?"

"It will be as soon as this deal goes down."

"See you soon."

"I'm on my way to pick up Neil now." She hung up and let the phone drop into her lap.

Strangely, she wasn't worried at all. She knew she should be, she was jeopardizing her career by allowing Chase to drive away with those weapons. Weapons she was responsible for.

He'd offered no proof that he was who he said he was, that they were indeed on the same side, but KC felt certain he had finally told her the truth. It was there in his face, in his body language— she could find no more deception in any of his actions since he'd confided in her.

Was that enough to risk her entire operation and future with the Bureau on? KC cranked up the radio and grinned. Yes, yes it was. Chase Westin was one of the good guys, she was certain of it, could feel in it in every fiber of her being. He would never betray her.

LUCKY BUMPED THE TRUCK over a rutted dirt road, praying that it led somewhere, anywhere near civilization.

Pennsylvania was worse than being on the moon as far as finding any discernible signs of life or better yet, a telephone. The only thing he'd spotted since escaping from the office in the mineshaft was a bunch of trees, tons of snow, and a few deer.

The road came to a fork, and he took the one that seemed to head downhill. Anything to get off this godforsaken mountain.

Of course the last three roads had looked promising as well until they led him into dead ends. Did these people ever hear of the quaint idea of using signs? At least in DC, you might be mired in traffic but you knew where you were.

He squirmed, uncomfortable in his burnt orange Nomex jumpsuit. Damn thing itched like hell, but it was better than running around in the snow in his boxers. He'd found a few of the coveralls wadded up and stiff with mildew outside the office, this was the smallest of the bunch and it seemed designed for Paul Bunyan rather than Lucky's lanky frame.

At least the jumpsuit was better than the boots he wore. He pushed aside the memory of returning to Fergus' body and peeling the boots from the dead man.

Who cared about the inconvenient details? He was alive and kicking, ready to rock 'n roll, nail the Preacher's ass.

He held the steering wheel between his knees as he shifted down, his left hand still wasn't working, just twitched with pins and needles every time Lucky tried to use it. And even when he didn't.

Focus, Cavanaugh. Got to find a phone, a telegraph, hell, a smoke signal would do at this point.

First, he needed to call Rose Prospero, have her get a team up here to go after The Crusade and the power behind the throne. Then, he needed to get to Chase, make sure he was safe.

After that he could dwell on luxuries like comfortable clothing, getting warm, and maybe getting his arm checked out by a doctor.

Once he found a way out of this damned wilderness.

Bright sunshine beckoned in front of him as the road opened into a clearing. Lucky stopped the truck. Wow, an actual paved road, would wonders never cease?

It was two lanes, unmarked with no guardrails. Could lead back to the mine for all he knew, but what the hell, it was a semblance of civilization. He tossed a coin mentally and turned right, bumping the truck onto the uneven pavement.

A huge black-winged bird screeched and dove from the blue sky, heading directly toward Lucky. He hit the brakes and the bird skidded past the truck, shooting into the woods where it was lost from sight.

Lucky cursed under his breath, reversed the truck and laboriously turned around. He wasn't superstitious, not really, but he decided that a bird that big didn't come from anywhere near civilization. Better to head in the opposite direction—it was only logical.

He looked in the rearview mirror, saw the enormous bird spread its wings wide as it flapped down onto the road. The bird strutted in the middle of the pavement as if daring Lucky to change his mind. Lucky gave the bird the middle-fingered salute and hit the gas.

Man, he wished he were back home. This was no place for a city boy.

CHAPTER 35

CHASE JOGGED DOWN MAIN Street to the only outside payphone surviving in Coalton since the cellular revolution. The glass walled box stood in front of Coalton Drugs where Old Man Sinderson could keep an eye on any would-be vandals. He called Deacon first.

"Westin, where the hell are you?"

"Main Street. My brother and I had a fight, I took a walk, lost track of time." The last part was true, at least. "Can you send one of the guys to pick me up?"

"I'll come myself," Deacon told him. "I thought you promised me your brother wouldn't be a problem."

"He won't, not anymore." Chase hung up.

His next call was to Rose. It took Teresa a few moments to patch him through and when she did, there was the background noise of a helicopter. "Any word on Lucky?"

"Chase, where the hell have you been?" Rose asked, mirroring Deacon's words. "No trace of Lucky, but we've been checking on your brother's cell phone."

"Don't worry. Jay witnessed Bruno killing someone and the Feds were here to shepherd him into the witness protection program. They picked him up this morning, he's safely out of it."

There was a pause. "Chase, Jay's phone came from a RICO investigation that has nothing to do with Gianotti. No one from the FBI who was associated with it is anywhere near you. And the agent in charge of the operation was killed after his cover was blown."

Chase thought at first he heard her wrong. He certainly could not have heard her correctly. "That's impossible. I just left the agent—"

"Do you have a name? Did you see the credentials of any of the agents or marshals?"

Chase felt the muscles between his shoulder blades spasm, pain lancing down his spine. This was impossible. It couldn't be true. KC wouldn't do that to him—

Unless she was a better actress than even he had given her credit for. An icy splinter of doubt twisted its way into his heart.

She knew everything about Chase, what did he know about her? He didn't even know KC's real name, had never checked the credentials of the men he'd handed Jay over to.

Good God, had he just sat by and watched his brother walk into a trap?

"You must be mistaken," he finally said, although he knew Rose didn't make mistakes like that. He slumped against the side of the phone booth, ignoring the cold sweat that enveloped his body. Was Jay dead?

No, whoever had him would keep him alive until Chase gave them what they wanted. If he only knew what the hell that was.

"We found no active investigations in your area and no mention of Jay's name in the files we accessed. I didn't want to risk blowing your cover by making official inquiries."

"Why would anyone work so hard to take Jay?" he asked.

"I have no idea, but we'll keep working on it. Billy and I are in the air, on our way there now."

Chase came to his senses and gave her KC's cell phone number. Maybe Teresa could work more of her magic.

"If you can," he told her, "block that number entirely. I'll deal with her myself."

He also described for Rose the two "marshals" and their car, cursing himself when he couldn't even remember the full license plate number. He'd been so preoccupied with dealing with KC. It didn't matter that she'd been holding a gun on him at the time, he should have looked out for Jay.

Chase hung up and buried his head in his hands. Why? Why would KC take Jay? She couldn't be working for either Bruno or The Crusade—they would come after Chase directly. It didn't make sense.

Unless there was some third party involved, someone intent on taking the weapons and who knew it would be Chase driving the truck away from the meeting.

He slammed a hand against the back of the phone booth, shaking the entire structure. It did little to reduce his desire to howl in frustration, to reach out and throttle whoever was responsible for placing Jay's life in danger.

KC had been the perfect distraction—too sexy to ignore, too smart to doubt. She told him to watch his back, just hadn't bothered to mention that she was the one busy plunging the knife into it.

The honk of a car horn interrupted his thoughts, and he jerked his head up, put his game face on as Deacon pulled up to the curb.

Chase hoped KC did show up at the meet. He'd show her exactly how messed up her karma could get when she jeopardized Chase's family.

CHAPTER 36

KC CALLED NEIL FROM her house as she crammed bites of cold pizza into her mouth. After everything that had happened during the night, she was starving.

"Can you come over to my place?" she asked. "We need to talk."

"I can't right now. I've got to go somewhere with my dad in a few minutes."

"Please," she dropped her voice, made it sound low and husky. Wasn't hard since her throat was currently clogged with mozzarella. "You're the only one who can help me."

"What's wrong? Is it Jay's brother again?" Neil's voice sounded worried. "He's mad about last night, isn't he?"

"I'm scared, Neil."

"I'm on my way."

KC finished gulping her pizza and unlocked the kitchen door for Neil. This wasn't going to be easy, but she had to keep him away from the meeting. She would show him the evidence against his father and if that didn't convince him, she'd lock him in the basement.

Hell, her career was already heading down the garbage chute,
what was one more busted rule?

There wasn't any time to come up with something more
conventional, the meeting with Gianotti and Dinkum was in an hour.
She still had to change, grab her body armor and gear, and get into
position.

Her phone rang and she grabbed it on the fly. "KC, it's Jared—"
Then it went dead. She turned it over in her hand, puzzled. The
battery was low but should still have had some juice left. Jared had
sounded excited and there had been a lot of noise in the background.
Had something gone wrong?

She plugged the phone into its charger and tried again. Still
dead.

Neil rushed in, no coat, wearing only a Steelers sweatshirt and
jeans for the quick sprint between their houses. "What happened?"
he asked breathlessly. "Where's Jay?"

"He's gone," she told him, hoping that the flip-flops her
stomach was doing were only nerves. But she was getting a bad
feeling about all this. A real bad feeling.

She had to get Neil to safety, fast. Then she could check on Jay
and the Marshals. "I need to show you something."

Before she could say anything more, the kitchen door burst
open and two men ran in, guns drawn. One immediately tackled
Neil while the other came for KC.

She aimed a swift side kick to his groin, and he went down. She
pivoted, one hand in the process of drawing her Glock when she
froze.

The second man had Neil in a chokehold, a semi-automatic
aimed at his head. "Relax, sister, or Junior here's gonna regret it."

KC feigned fear and raised both hands, backing away until she came up against the counter. Damn it, who were these guys? Had Gianotti somehow found out, sent them after her? No, they wouldn't threaten Neil if they were his father's men. Maybe they were with Dinkum.

"Who are you?" she asked, making her voice sound shrill and frightened. She couldn't let them find the guns on her—they would be impossible to explain. "What do you want?"

If she could reach her cell phone, she could hit the panic button and turn the microphone on. But it was on the counter behind Neil.

Neil's face was turning a dusky purple as he gasped for breath. The man on the floor groaned and struggled to his feet.

KC backed away from them both. Her only exit was blocked. If she could get the basement door open, she could barricade herself downstairs, but by the time she got through the door, Neil would be dead.

Neil began flailing his arms, one last desperate struggle that knocked the cell phone and its cradle to the floor.

"Don't damage the merchandise," the man she'd kicked said, his words coming in quick breaths.

The bigger man dropped Neil, who fell to the floor like a sack of potatoes. KC rushed to his side, deciding that the safest thing would be for her to stay in character.

As she pretended to comfort Neil, she pressed the panic button on the phone. Then she almost panicked herself as she realized that if Dinkum suspected her, Chase was as good as dead.

Damn it, she'd warned him his plan wouldn't work. She only wished she had a better one.

"You almost killed him," she cried, cradling Neil's head in her lap.

"I oughta kill you, bitch!" The man she kicked her and yanked her to her feet. He shook her so hard her teeth rattled, then looked at her. "Hey, you're Westin's girl, aren't you?"

KC smelled sour whiskey on his breath as he leered down at her.

"Yeah, he was bragging how he did his kid brother's girl. Said you were a fine piece of ass."

She turned her head as he leaned forward and kissed her, his tongue brushing over her clamped lips and onto her cheek. His fingers dug into her arm as his other hand roamed down her side, then traced along the waistband of her jeans.

Neil tried to get up, but the other man held the gun on him at point blank range. KC had to fight the urge to reach for her Glock or to spit in the goon's face as he fondled her. No. She had to find out who they were and what they wanted. And she couldn't risk Neil.

"Leave her alone, you creep!" Neil shouted. KC was touched by his show of courage.

"Who are you?" she asked again, this time in a whisper.

"Call me Redman, sweetie. You and I are going to have a long time to get acquainted later." He gestured at the second man. "C'mon Freddie, time's a wasting."

The second man hauled Neil to his feet, twisted his arm behind his back and marched him out the door.

Redman yanked on KC's hair, pulling her head back until she met his gaze.

"Thanks for calling Junior out of his house so we didn't have to deal with all that security," he told her. "But I owe you big time for that kick to the balls."

He planted his lips on hers, thrusting his tongue past her teeth, making her gag. "Just remember," he said when he pulled away, his face mere inches from hers, "we need him alive. You're only alive as long as you make it worth my while to keep you that way. Understand?"

Her scalp was screaming with pain as he twisted her hair. KC didn't have to fake the tears streaming from her eyes.

"Yes," she whispered.

"Yes what?" he yelled, yanking on her hair once more.

"Yes, sir."

"That's more like it. You be a good girl, and we'll have some fun later."

KC allowed him to goose-step her out to their Blazer. It was Neil they wanted, not her and Chase. She still had to think of a way to free Neil and herself without blowing her cover or sabotaging the meet. At least Redman hadn't frisked her. And the cavalry was coming.

CHAPTER 37

DEACON KEPT STARING AT Chase as they drove.

"Everything in place for the meet?" Chase asked, trying to break the tension.

"Wasn't it your job to see that it was?" Deacon retorted.

"Yeah, sorry, won't happen again. Cavanaugh meeting us there or what?"

"Not Cavanaugh. Me and Redman are going in with you. The rest will be nearby, just in case."

"In case what? Bruno's not going to screw us. He has more to lose than you do. Besides the deal was me and one other person."

"We'll need Redman to keep watch on the kid."

Kid? Did Deacon have Jay?

"What kid?" he strained to keep his voice normal.

"I was worried that Gianotti might be double crossing us, setting us up. I sent Redman to collect his kid, figured the old man won't try anything with him there."

Deacon meant Neil, not Jay. Chase found himself able to breathe again. If KC was who she said she was, she'd protect Neil.

Which might blow the entire operation. But if KC wasn't FBI,
then—he pounded a fist against his knee. It was all too confusing,
he had no idea who was whom anymore. All he knew for certain
was that he could trust no one except himself.

"Something wrong?" Deacon asked, his gaze narrowed in
suspicion.

"Nah, just thinking about my brother, is all. Kid's a nut job,
wants to quit school, run away with his sleazy girlfriend. And let me
tell you, she's a real piece of work—one cold-hearted bitch."

Chase felt Deacon's attention drift away, bored by his problems.
Fine with him, it hurt too much to talk about Jay, was too painful to
even think about KC and what she'd done to him.

His hand drummed against his thigh as he fought to control his
fury. Trust no one, assume nothing—when was he going to learn?

Deacon pulled the truck into the elementary school parking lot
and raised a pair of binoculars, scouring the back of the high school
that was clearly visible past the playing fields.

"Your brother, he's going to be all right? I mean, he has his girl
to take care of him, right?"

Chase startled. He should be used to it by now, Deacon was
always asking about family. "Yeah, he'll be fine."

"You never told me about your sister. I like the bird on her
headstone."

"Hawk. It's a red-tailed hawk." Chase remembered the fresh
footprints at Diana's grave. It was hard to think of Diana and be
angry at KC at the same time.

"How old were you when she died?"

"Five." Chase knew Deacon wouldn't stop until he had the
entire story.

Damn it, he didn't need this right now, had enough on his mind.
Talking about dead people made him wonder if Jay was going to be

the next Westin buried in the family plot. Which would leave Chase
absolutely alone.

"She was only two months old. Was it SIDS or something?"

"No. She came too early—the doctors were surprised she made
it past the first day. She was a fighter, though." Chase shut his
eyes for a moment. God, he was tired. Hadn't been this tired since
Afghanistan.

"Ahh. That's why the hawk instead of a dove or angel."
Deacon reached across Chase to replace the binoculars in the glove
compartment. "My sister was four when she died. The baby of the
family. There were six of us. I was the oldest. The man of the house,
supposed to watch over everyone. Me and my homies, we did that,
no one messed with our families."

Chase opened his eyes, turned to the older man in surprise.
Deacon never talked about his personal life. Never. "What
happened?"

"Tanesha was born with a heart condition—left side of her heart
was too small. She almost died a bunch of times, the doctors had her
under the knife and in the hospital more than she was home."

Deacon's gaze drifted to the playground equipment beside
them. "My baby girl. I was fourteen when she was born. My mom
was never there for her, so I made it my job to watch over her. But
she just kept getting sicker and sicker. Turns out, she got some
bad blood, had Hep C on top of her heart problems, it was just too
much. The doctors said they could maybe save her with a liver
transplant, but the goons at Medi-Cal, they said no, it cost too much
and she'd never make it anyway, not with her bum heart."

Frustration and anger filled Deacon's voice. To know there was
a chance to save your sister and be told you weren't allowed to try
it—that would have driven Chase over the edge if anyone did that to
his family. Now he understood all those visits to pediatric hospitals,

prowling among the graves of dead children.

"I'm sorry," he said, meaning it.

"She was a beautiful baby. An angel." Deacon took a deep breath, turned the engine back on. "Sometimes, you just gotta take the time to remember why you do what you do, you know?"

They pulled away from the school and he turned to Chase. "You carrying?"

The abrupt change of topic startled Chase. "Yeah, my Heckler Koch. Why? Who you thinking I'm going to need to use it on?"

Deacon shrugged. "Just keep your eyes open. I'm depending on you to make this deal happen. There's others who will be watching as well."

"Others? Who?"

During his time with The Crusade, Lucky had mentioned rumors of powers behind Deacon's public leadership. Men with money and political clout.

If they were here, in Coalton, maybe they could have everything wrapped up today—not just the weapons off the street, but The Crusade demolished, their plans aborted. And Jay back home, safe and sound. "What others?"

Deacon gave him an indulgent smile as if Chase were a child asking for an extra helping of Christmas turkey. "After the deal is over, if everything goes as planned, you may get a chance to meet them."

Yesterday, before he met KC, Chase would have sworn that nothing could possibly go wrong with the setup, not after six months of planning and establishing his cover. Now, one day of KC running around loose, and for the first time he felt afraid, as if events were conspiring against him, hurtling out of his control.

For an instant he felt KC's touch on his arm as she explained to him about karma and its consequences. He could almost smell her

scent fill the truck cab, and his stomach tightened in anticipation
of seeing her again, of her body gliding over his, teasing, exciting,
leading him to the heights of passion.

He rolled the window down, cleared his head with a deep breath
of fresh air. Next time he saw KC, he might be forced to kill her.
Or at least hurt her. Whatever it took to find out where Jay was and
ensure his safety.

Bad karma, he thought, an image of KC's playful chameleon
blazing through his mind.

CHAPTER 38

REDMAN BACKED THE BLAZER into Chase's driveway and came around to the rear doors. He yanked Neil out first. Freddie and a man who came from the house escorted the teenager inside. Then he grabbed KC's arm and twisted it behind her as he marched her through the carport and inside the house to where the others waited.

"Where's Deacon?" he asked the third man.

"Went to pick up Westin. Who's the girl?"

In answer, Redman wrenched her arm up, pulling KC to her tiptoes as she tried to keep from dislocating her shoulder. Pain lasered down her arm. It took everything she had to keep from breaking free, grabbing her gun, and shooting the bastard.

Not yet. Only if it became absolutely necessary. Glenn or Carson would be here soon, just had to keep these guys playing a little while longer.

"Man asked you a question," Redman yelled in her ear as he yanked her arm again. "Answer him, little girl. Tell him how you slept with your boyfriend's big brother—I heard you were really something."

Neil came to her rescue. "Stop it! You're hurting her." He flailed uselessly at the two men holding him. "Tell them KC, tell them you never slept with Chase."

Neil's captors shoved him down onto the sofa, one of them holding a gun on him. Redman loosened his hold on KC enough so that she could spin free of his grip. She stood and glared at the men, hands on her hips.

"Keep your filthy hands off me!"

The men exchanged glances and laughed. KC thought furiously. It was obvious Chase had told Redman that he'd slept with her— Lord only knew why—but now it was up to her to protect his cover story.

"Looks like we've got a live one here, boys." Redman said, taking a step toward her.

"Hey," Freddie called out from his position at Neil's side, pointing to KC's tattoo, "show us your picture, there, little girl."

"Yeah, make her do a belly dance for us," the third man joined in.

KC had to get her jacket off before they found the Glock. She narrowed her eyes at Redman who feinted to one side as if he were playing tag with her.

"Boo!" he shouted.

KC held her ground and with the finesse of a stripper, slowly slid her jacket off, taking care to fold it so that the Glock remained concealed. She pivoted and draped it over one of the dining room chairs, then moved around the large table, keeping it between her and Redman.

"C'mon girlie, we just want to look, that's all."

"Yeah, we're not going to hurt you any."

Stall, she had to keep stalling. What was keeping Glenn so long? Even though she'd been forced to leave her phone at the house, he should have figured out where they were by now.

She completed her circuit of the table, ending up across from Neil's spot on the sofa. The two men on either side of him were focused on her. The one with the gun, Freddie, held it limply in his hand, ignoring Neil entirely.

KC stared at Neil, trying to telegraph her intentions, to tell him to stay put, do nothing, that she had everything under control. Redman crossed over from the dining room and lunged for her. KC saw his movement, could have easily blocked it if she had wanted to, but before she could do anything, Neil reached for Freddie's gun.

The nine millimeter went off, the bullet plowing into the Barcalounger. KC rushed to haul Freddie off Neil before anyone got hurt.

She shot an elbow into his gut as he raised the gun and aimed at Neil. Freddie stumbled back from KC's blow. His partner tackled Neil, wrestled him face down onto the sofa.

She was about to send a snap kick into Freddie's crotch when Redman stepped into the fray. He grabbed a handful of KC's hair and hauled her back, wrenching her head so that all she could see was the ceiling and his leering face. And the Smith and Wesson semi-automatic he lowered to rest against her cheekbone.

"How many guys does it take to babysit two kids?" he asked his comrades. They both looked up sheepishly and stood at attention. "You," he yanked at KC's hair to punctuate his message, "baby girl, are beginning to get on my nerves. You're a trouble maker, ain't you?"

KC squirmed in his grasp, desperate to take the pressure off her scalp. Maybe she shouldn't wait for backup, she thought as she saw the gleam in Redman's eyes. This creep was getting entirely too much enjoyment from causing her pain. She'd love to return the favor.

260 | CJ Lyons

He hauled her back to the dining room and forced her to lean over the table, his elbow in the middle of her back, leveraging her head back. He pressed his hips against hers. His arousal told her exactly how much he enjoyed her struggles.

KC let her body slump in surrender, her right hand dropping below the table. She was getting ready to draw her Glock from her boot when the kitchen door slammed open.

"Let her go!" Chase shouted, his gun raised at Redman.

Thank God. The Marines had landed.

Chase's eyes were bright with fury and his face flushed. She looked at him, hoped he didn't take things too far. All he had to do was calm these idiots down, maybe take Redman to the meet with him while she handled the rest.

He didn't look in the mood to calm anyone down. She swallowed hard as she saw his finger tighten against the trigger guard. Redman must have seen it as well, because he released KC and stepped back.

"Sorry man, thought you were done with her."

KC sidled out from between the table and Redman so that she stood beside him, near to his gun hand. She cut her eyes across the room; the other men were staring at Chase, waiting to see what he did next. Neil was slumped on the couch, all fight drained from him.

Redman laughed and holstered his nine millimeter. He opened his hands wide. "No hard feelings, right?"

To KC's surprise, Chase's fury didn't diminish. Only now, instead of Redman, he turned his glare onto her. He raised his HK so that it was aimed at her chest.

"Into the bedroom, KC," he said, his voice tight with rage. "Now!"

KC froze. What the hell was going on?

Redman grabbed her by the wrist and spun her out into the

living room where she collided with the Barcalounger.

"Guess he's not done with you yet, honey," he said, one hand slipping down her back to caress her buttocks. He gave her a squeeze. "I'll be waiting when he is."

Chase was silent as he stalked through the dining room, his gun still aimed at her. He did nothing to come to her defense, didn't even seem to notice Neil cowering on the couch. Redman grinned and planted a boot on her rear that sent her sprawling across the room, into the hallway.

"Sure you don't need any help in there?" Redman asked Chase.

"Wait for me out here," Chase ordered them in that same tight voice that frightened her so.

He reached for her arm and dragged her across the hall into Jay's bedroom, then kicked the door shut behind him. KC looked up, hoping that what she'd see would still the fear racing through her veins.

Chase's face was the face of a stranger. A stranger intent on murder.

CHAPTER 39

IT TOOK ALL OF Chase's resolve not to squeeze the trigger. Because of that, he holstered the HK and took a deep breath before he did anything.

He couldn't kill her. Not until she told him where Jay was. Not until Jay was safe.

He grabbed her by her shoulders, hauled her to her feet, her back to the door. Just like when they had met in her bedroom—was that only last night?

This time she looked at him with true fear in her eyes. He almost had second thoughts. Almost.

Until he remembered how good an actress she was. Chase shoved her up against the wall, rattling the glass in the photos hanging beside her head.

"Chase, what's wrong? Why are you—"

"Cut the act, KC," he growled, one hand on her throat, ready to squeeze the truth out of her if need be. "Where's Jay? What have you done with him?"

A frown creased her forehead. "Jay? What happened?"

"I said, quit the act!"

He pressed the flat of his hand against her throat. Her pulse skittered beneath his fingers.

"My people found no record of Jay being placed in protective custody. Tell. Me. Where. He. Is."

Her eyes widened as she processed his words. He waited for the next lie to escape her lips, ready to pounce on it.

Instead, her knee connected with his groin, and she broke his grip on her throat, sending an elbow into his solar plexus, knocking him back a step.

He almost hauled off and hit her, desperately wanted to hit something, have some avenue to channel his fury and fear into, but the look on her face stopped him.

It was the same look of concern and worry she had when he'd threatened her people back at the hunting camp.

He lowered his hand. No one could be that good of actress. Could they?

"Your people?" she whispered, her words coming in a furious rush. "Who the hell are you, anyway? Don't you know security at Justice has been compromised? My God, what have you done!"

Chase could see no deception on her face. He raised both hands in surrender.

"Please," he said, "just tell me the truth about Jay." His voice took on a tone of pleading, but he no longer cared. He needed to know Jay was safe.

"You really think I could do anything to hurt Jay?" A single tear slipped from her eye, and she swiped it away with the back of her hand. "He's safe with the Marshals, just like I promised."

Chase stepped toward her, and she backed up until the doorjamb stopped her. He lowered both hands to her shoulders, surprised to feel her tremble at his touch. She really was frightened.

This was no act.

"He's safe?" he persisted. "Are you certain?"

"You don't believe me?" Her dark eyes looked at him with disappointment. "All right, I'll prove it."

She opened the door, nodded toward the living room where Redman and the others waited. "Deacon has someone feeding him info on undercover operatives. Go ahead, tell them who I am. Shouldn't take them long to verify it for you." She shrugged. "If your people have been raising a stink at Justice, my cover's most likely already blown."

"I can't do that, KC," he said, pulling her back from the doorway and lowering his voice. "They'll kill you."

"But you'll know Jay's safe, and that I was telling the truth." She gave her head a small shake of resignation. "I don't know any other way to prove it to you, Chase. Go ahead. Do it. I can take care of myself."

"Cut the macho crap, KC." Nothing made sense—the FBI had no record of Jay, the cell phone didn't match, Lucky was missing— how could he dare believe her?

She made no move to resist or defend herself, merely looked up, met his eyes. "I promise you, Chase," she whispered, "I would never do anything to hurt Jay. Trust me."

Trust no one—it seemed like such an easy code to live by.

Only sooner or later he had to make a choice, had to put his trust in someone. He couldn't go any further on his own. He searched her face for an answer.

Her gaze was clear, her voice calm. She was offering her life to answer his doubts.

Then he realized that he had his answer—had been looking right at it all along. KC had all the answers he needed. Chase only needed to listen, to believe.

It was time to stop living one day at a time and start living as if he had a future. A future with a woman who'd earned both his respect and his trust.

Chase exhaled the breath he'd been holding and squeezed his eyes shut against the flood of relief that poured over him. He believed KC. She was telling him the truth.

He opened his eyes. "Thank you."

Footsteps echoed down the hall, and he pressed KC up against the wall, forcing his mouth on hers. Her eyes widened, then she glanced to one side as Redman approached. She made a choking sound and struggled, finally pushing him away and giving him an open handed slap across the face.

"Get off me, you animal!"

Chase saw Redman's grin out of the corner of his eye. He tightened his grip on KC's shoulders, shoved her back against the wall once more.

"You liked it well enough last night," he said in a loud voice.

"You said you'd hurt Jay if I didn't—" She broke down, sobbing. "If I didn't let you—"

Chase eased up on his grip, and she crumbled to the ground, drawing her knees up to her chest in a fetal position.

"Go away," she cried. "Leave me alone."

It was an Oscar caliber performance. Chase felt himself drawing back as if he were actually guilty of raping her.

Redman bought it as well. He looked down on KC's broken form with a predator grin that Chase wanted to permanently erase from his face.

"Hate to interrupt you, now that you've got her softened up," Redman said, clapping Chase on the shoulder, "but we've got to get moving. Don't worry about her." He nudged KC with the toe of his boot. She whimpered like a wounded animal. "Freddie will keep an eye on her until we get back."

Chase hated leaving KC like this. Then he realized that, thanks to her acting abilities, she still had access to her knife and both Glocks. It was Freddie he should be worried about. The guy didn't stand a chance.

He squatted down, placed a hand under her chin and forced her head back. Her eyes darted about like a cornered animal and wouldn't meet his. Redman chuckled and returned to the living room.

"I'll be back," Chase told her in a menacing voice loud enough to carry down the hallway.

He turned so that his back blocked the view from the living room and bent down to kiss her thoroughly, trying to express in the few seconds of their embrace everything he didn't have time to say aloud.

"I promise," he added in a whisper.

"Take care of Neil," she murmured back, her hand squeezing his.

Chase couldn't contain his smile. All hell breaking loose, and she was worried about keeping one kid safe. He ruffled his fingers through her hair.

"I will."

"Watch your back," she said as he left to join the others.

CHAPTER 40

THE CLOSEST PARKING SPACE Lucky could find near the school was down at the drugstore. Streams of children were pouring out of both churches, lining up for some kind of procession. Their attendant parents contributed to the chaos until it looked like a colorful herd stampeding the pristine snow of the church lawns.

He shook his head as a clock struck noon. No wonder Deacon wasn't upset with the timing or location of the meet. All these people would keep the attention away from the exchange.

And make excellent cannon fodder if things went wrong. There was no time to get help from Rose Prospero and he knew the local force was compromised.

Redman's Blazer pulled into the maintenance drive that ran behind the school. Lucky followed on foot. No gun, no weapons of any kind and marked by Deacon's men as a Fed—but still he went.

Chase was his partner, Lucky had to watch his back. There was no one else to do it.

CHASE FELT THAT ITCH between his shoulder blades—the same one he'd felt in Afghanistan right before all hell broke loose, the same one he'd felt when he rode into Coalton yesterday.

He had a bad feeling about this. Should've listened to Lucky in the first place. He unholstered his HK. If he was going to go down, at least it would be fighting.

He looked across the backseat at Neil. The kid looked like he was going to puke at any second. "Don't worry," he told him, "everything will be all right."

Neil looked at him with disbelief in his eyes. "My dad is going to kick your ass."

Chase gave the kid a mental thumbs-up for his show of bravado. Neil was an okay kid, even if his father was a scumbag.

"Whatever happens," he said in a low voice, "just stay calm and do what I say, all right?"

Neil swallowed hard and nodded as the SUV came to a halt.

"End of the road," Redman shouted gleefully from his position in the front seat.

Chase hoped not.

KC HUDDLED AGAINST THE wall, trying to calm her nerves. She had a bad feeling about this, a very bad feeling. Nothing was going as planned. All her preparations and still the operation was going south—thanks to Chase Westin. Whoever he worked for, they had connections good enough to trace the cell phones and paper trail she'd left at the Bureau.

She could understand why Chase would be furious if he thought she'd placed Jay in danger. She almost regretted her misdirection at the Bureau. She'd thought she was protecting her team, but it seemed as if her plan had backfired.

Freddie skulked into the room. He crouched down in front of
her, reached out a hand, testing to see if she'd bite it. She pulled
away, hugging the wall, as if she'd go through it if possible, and
made a small, feral sound.

"Now, now, little girl," he crooned.

She heard the sound of the Blazer leaving. Other than Freddie
and her, the house was empty. Freddie patted her head, and she
curled further into herself, edging one hand behind her to the boot
with her Glock.

"Freddie won't hurt you," he said as he drew closer, on his
knees, both hands reaching out to stroke her body. "You'll see, we'll
be great friends. You should be thanking me. Because of me, you
won't have to worry about Chase Westin no more. One way or the
other, he'll never hurt you again."

What the hell did that mean? She angled her head up, barely
meeting his gaze. "Really?" she asked in a small voice.

Freddie took this as encouragement. He nodded vigorously and
moved closer. She could smell pickled beets and sauerkraut on his
breath.

"Westin is the only connection between Deacon and Gianotti.
Deacon figured Gianotti mainly deals with drug dealers, scum like
that, so why should we give him any of our hard-earned money?
So we're gonna take him down and Westin gets to play fall guy."
He smiled encouragingly at her as she sat up straighter, hands still
behind her back.

"When the shooting starts Westin will be firing blanks, same as
he did with you, I'll bet," he finished with a sly grin. "I know how
to make a pretty thing like you happy," he continued, his mouth
moving to caress her with sloppy kisses over her forehead and
cheeks as his hands fumbled with the buttons of her vest. "You let
me open my Christmas present, then I'll have a present for you."

KC had enough of sweaty men with fetid breath pawing her. She raised the Glock and held it to Freddie's temple. He froze.

"Back off, hands where I can see them," she ordered. The look of astonishment on his face would have been priceless if she wasn't in a hurry to get to Chase and warn him. She saw a roll of strapping tape on Jay's desk, thanked God for the kid's anal organization, and quickly had Freddie restrained.

"What's the plan?" she asked him. The would-be rapist was about to wet himself, but she had no sympathy. She chambered a round, the resulting click echoing throughout the small room like a cell door slamming shut.

"Look, all I know is Deacon had me switch out Westin's ammo last time we were out shooting targets. Maybe it's just a joke—can't arrest me for a joke, now can you?"

"How about attempted rape, false imprisonment, kidnapping—" She cocked her head and smiled at him. "Or maybe I should just save the taxpayers all the money of a trial. Self-defense, right?" She gestured with the Glock. "When is Deacon going to start shooting?"

"After the exchange, as soon as he gives Gianotti the kid back," Freddie stammered, his face florid with fear.

KC shoved a pair of Jay's socks in his mouth as a gag and raced to the door. She only hoped she wasn't too late to save Chase and Neil.

CHAPTER 41

KC TRIED THE LANDLINE. The phone was dead. She grabbed
her coat and the second Glock then spotted Jay's phone shoved
down into the Barcalounger. She tugged the phone from its position
wedged between the seat cushion and arm, dialing Glenn's number
as she ran out to the carport.

Her transportation options were limited: Jay's mountain bike or
Chase's motorcycle. She straddled the Harley and saw that he'd left
the keys in the ignition. Of course he had—this was Coalton. No
crime here—at least none not sanctioned by Gianotti.

"Glenn, it's KC," her words came with a rush as soon as he
answered the phone, "tell everyone to standby, I repeat standby."

"KC, what's wrong? Where are you? The party's getting
started."

"Just listen to me. They're going to double cross Gianotti and
take everything. Gianotti's kid is also there—Dinkum has him as a
hostage."

"Damn, it. We're not set up for that kind of deal. Someone's
gonna get hurt out there."

"Not if I have anything to do with it. Pass the word, no action until I say so. We've got to get Westin and the kid clear."

"I hear you, KC, but we can't let The Crusade get their hands on those weapons."

"I know, I know, I'm working on it."

She started the motorcycle and roared down the street, praying she wouldn't be too late. And that she could come up with a plan in the few minutes it would take her to get to the school.

"WHAT'S THE MEANING OF this?" Bruno Gianotti demanded when he saw Neil in the SUV. His baleful gaze fell on Chase, who stood beside the open doorway.

"You'll pay for this, Westin."

"Wasn't my idea," Chase told him.

"I don't care whose idea it was," Bruno snapped, gesturing at his driver to start the moving van. Deacon pulled up in his truck with two more men, sauntered around to the front of the Blazer, but Bruno ignored him, still focusing on Chase. "You watch out for family—doesn't matter who you're working for or how much money is at stake."

He strode over to where Deacon lounged against the hood of the SUV. "Deal's off, keep your money. Neil, get out of there, we're going home."

Chase herded Neil from the Blazer, kept one hand on the kid's shoulder so that he could shove him out of the line of fire if things went bad. If? When was more like it.

Who was he fooling? Things had pretty much already gone to hell in a hand grenade. This was merely the countdown before the detonation.

Then he heard the familiar sound of a Harley speeding down

the road toward them.

"I don't think so," Deacon drawled. He nodded to Redman who drew his gun and leveled it at Neil. The rest of the men also raised their weapons, aiming at Bruno.

Bruno smiled. "If that's how you want to play it, fine by me." The side door of the moving van opened and four men armed with AK-47's jumped out, facing Deacon.

Before anyone could say anything more, KC and the Harley screamed into the cluster of heavily armed men.

Everyone jumped back as she spun the bike in a tight circle and laid it down, jumping off it like a pro. Chase used the distraction to nudge Neil away from Redman, to the rear of the SUV where he had more options for cover.

KC spun around, a Glock in each hand, her hair windblown, her face blazing with that fierce, defiant look Chase had first fallen in love with.

"Stay here," he told Neil. He edged toward KC, his HK in his hand.

"I don't care who you are," KC told the men in a voice that was colder than the snow they stood in, "or what you're doing here. All I want is him."

She aimed her guns at Chase, one at his heart and one pointed at his groin. The other men gaped at her, weapons forgotten as they watched her performance.

"You're not going to get away with it, Chase Westin," she yelled, fearlessly parting the Red Sea of armed men, focused totally on Chase as she strode toward him. Chase played his role.

"You're crazy!" he shouted back as he stepped forward to meet her challenge. "I didn't give you anything you didn't ask for!"

They were almost together, where they could make a stand. Chase saw no fear in KC's eyes, just determination and a tinge of regret.

He understood—if only they had more time, time enough for him to explain everything, how he felt, the life he wanted with her, how much he regretted not trusting her sooner. But time, it seemed, was the one thing they'd run out of.

Before he could reach her side, a man appeared at the edge of the basketball court. Chase did a double take as he saw Lucky, a pair of oversized orange overalls flapping around his body, running through the gates.

Dammit, what else could go wrong?

CHAPTER 42

LUCKY HAD PLANNED ON a more stealthy approach, but when the purple-haired girl drew her weapons on Chase and he saw the look in her eye that said she wasn't afraid to shoot, he knew he had to do something, even if it was only to provide a distraction so Chase could take her down.

Then, together, they could deal with Deacon and Gianotti's men.

"Chase!" he shouted, drawing all eyes his way.

To his surprise, Chase didn't take the opportunity to tackle the girl. Instead he pivoted so he and the girl stood back-to-back, facing the other men. Suddenly Lucky was standing alone, in front of nine men with guns—all pointing at him.

"Take them all," Deacon said, shooting Gianotti at point blank range.

Lucky ran toward the SUV, the nearest cover, as the bullets began to fly.

"KC," he heard Chase shout, "he's one of ours."

The girl hesitated for a split second then she turned away from

Chase, fired at one of Gianotti's men drawing a bead on Lucky.

To his amazement, she hit the gunman twice in the ten ring.

She yelled something at Chase, but it was lost in the roar of gunfire. Then she pivoted and plowed into Lucky, knocking him to the ground as bullets whizzed overhead.

"Neil, are you all right?" she asked the kid cowering beside Lucky.

She didn't look back, her gaze glued to potential targets. By now everyone had taken cover under or behind one vehicle or the other, except for two unlucky men who lay motionless on the ground between. No man's land.

"He's fine," Lucky answered after making a quick check to see if the kid was shot. "Just scared. That was nice shooting."

"That's what they pay me for."

One of Gianotti's men leaned his head forward just a little too far, and she fired off two shots, the second one hitting home. His body slumped forward, gun skidding across the icy pavement. "Where the hell's Chase?"

"He ran inside, after Deacon."

She took a second to look over her shoulder at Lucky. "You must be Cavanaugh. ATF, right?" He opened his mouth to answer, but she shook her head. "Never mind. Can you shoot?"

"Yes."

"Good. Your job—your one and only job," she stressed, "is to take this gun and get this kid safely out of here."

She handed Lucky a short-barreled Glock-27 and leaned forward so close he could see the menace in her eyes. "You understand?"

"Yes, ma'am."

"Go, I'll cover you."

"What about Chase?"

"I'll take care of Chase. Now, go."

She rolled out from behind the van, drawing fire from both camps as Lucky grabbed Neil's wrist, and they sprinted across the blacktop to the relative safety of a large dumpster. They dove behind the smelly refuge, and he watched from beneath it as the girl zigzagged in a low crouch, taking Gianotti's last man down and ending up at the moving van filled with explosives.

She jumped inside the truck, ducking low as Redman took a potshot through the windshield, and started the engine, revving it loudly. Lucky watched as she gunned the truck, aiming it like a juggernaut through the double doors leading into the gymnasium.

"Who is she?" he asked Neil as the doors exploded open in a crash and Deacon's remaining men swarmed inside after her.

"That's KC," the kid said in a stunned voice, his eyes fixed on one of the bodies in the basketball court, tears flowing freely. Then he turned and looked at Lucky. "Why?"

"I think I'm going to ask her to marry me," Lucky said.

CHASE SAW DEACON TURN tail and run into the gym as soon as he gave the order for the others to start shooting. He ran after him.

It wasn't what he'd originally planned, but it would work well enough. Chase would bring Deacon in for questioning and by the time Rose Prospero was done with him, they'd know everything about The Crusade's plans.

He fired twice at Deacon's legs, couldn't believe his aim was off that badly, he didn't even hear the bullets hit the pavement. He looked down at the HK.

Blanks—someone had replaced his load with blanks. He skidded into the gymnasium and heard the click of Deacon chambering a round. Chase threw the useless gun to the ground in disgust and turned to face Deacon.

"What's the game?" he asked. "You were going to use me as a fall guy."

Deacon nodded. "Your town, your connection—keep any of Gianotti's friends off our back. That was the plan."

Chase's shoulders tightened with fury. Deacon clicked his tongue and shook his head in a silent warning as Chase took a step closer.

"It's your own damn fault. Messing with your brother's girl. Fornicating. That's not right. Family comes first, Westin. I tried to teach you, hell, even Gianotti tried to warn you, but you wouldn't listen."

Before Chase could make his move, the doors exploded, and a truck roared toward them.

CHAPTER 43

CHASE DOVE SIDEWAYS AS the van plowed through the doors, skidding to a halt with its front passenger tire mere inches away from his body. Deacon seemed unperturbed, merely strolled to the front of the truck as KC emerged, Glock raised.

"Drop it," she shouted.

To Chase's amazement, Deacon smiled. He pulled a small remote control car starter from his pocket. "I don't think so, Sister. Not unless you want hellfire and damnation to rain down on those innocent lambs across the street."

Chase rolled to his feet as Redman and the other two ran inside.

KC yelled down from her perch on the truck's running board, her gun never wavering, "Chase, is he bluffing?"

He thought before answering her question. The Nativity scene—perfect place to hide a bomb. Deacon knew bombs, had worked with Lucky on a few designs, designs Chase and Lucky thought they could stop from ever being built.

He looked over at Deacon. There was true regret on the man's face. He'd played poker with the man, Deacon never bluffed.

"No," he told her, raising his hands over his head and marching forward, escorted by two of his former comrades.

"Now be a good girl and give Brother Redman your gun," Deacon called to KC in a condescending tone of voice that Chase knew would have her temper sparking.

He craned his head to give her a warning look. Deacon would kill her if he had to, so no stupid heroics if she wanted to stay alive. To his relief, KC frowned, then slowly handed her weapon to Redman.

Chase had to keep from rushing into a vainglorious suicide himself as Redman twisted KC's arm cruelly behind her, forcing her to her knees. All eyes were on her and Redman.

"Bitch shot me!" Redman yelled, displaying a bloody upper arm to the others.

He leveled his gun at her forehead. KC looked over at Chase, her hands at the back of her neck just as his were, and in her eyes was a question.

Deacon stood at the edge of the small gathering, clearly enjoying himself. He pocketed the remote but held onto his Beretta.

"Do her now, if you want," he told Redman. "But make it fast, time's 'a-wasting."

Redman's laugh echoed through the cavernous space. "Yeah, I'm going to do her, right here, right now."

LUCKY WATCHED AS REDMAN and the others rushed inside, following the truck.

"You stay here," he told Neil, then edged closer so that he could see and hear what was going on in the gymnasium.

Where was the backup? Surely Rose Prospero had sent the girl to help him and Chase—why wasn't Rose or any of the others here?

Hell, he'd settle for a local yokel cop.

Then he heard Deacon's announcement about the bomb. Maybe cops weren't a good idea right now. He ran back to grab the kid.

"Come on," he told Neil. "We've got work to do."

They raced down the drive and across the street to the churches where the Baby Jesus procession was now in full swing.

"Who's in charge here?"

"Reverend Holloway." Neil pointed to a fat old man dressed in red and gold vestments.

"Go get him, tell him to clear the area, there's a bomb. Tell everyone!" Lucky shouted as he plowed through the crowd to the life-sized manger with its many possible hiding places for enough C4 to blow both churches to hell and back.

People began to screech and scatter as word of the bomb spread. Adults ran forward to grab their children, children ran every way in confusion, some still singing "Away in a Manger".

Lucky was fortunate he wasn't trampled in the melee. He stumbled into the manger, overturning the paper-Mache and plastic figures with his good arm. Nothing.

Where'd you hide it, Deacon? Where it would do the most harm, of course. It would be portable, easy to maneuver.

Lucky's gaze darted around, ignoring the chaos before him, then zeroed in on a black Lincoln Town Car parked at the curb. Shiny like it was just out of the carwash—or someone had buffed all the prints off it. Exactly the kind of car no one would expect to house a bomb.

He sprinted to the car, crouched below it. Damn, he hated it when he was right. Wires to the ignition—if he started the car, it would blow.

Lucky opened the door, thankful Deacon hadn't bothered to lock it behind him, and shifted the car into neutral, releasing the parking brake. He hoped there weren't any motion sensitive mercury switches. If so, this was going to be the shortest trip on record.

"Someone help me move this," he shouted.

He struggled against the weight of the car, unable to use his left arm to push. Several people raised their faces to him, but ran in the other direction. Including a man wearing a police uniform, Lucky noted.

Refusing to give up, he kept pushing and straining and abruptly the car began to move. He looked across the hood and saw Neil there, pushing in tandem with him.

"Thanks, kid," he said. "Let's get this thing away from people."

He didn't have to mention that it could blow at any second, the look of terror on Neil's face told him that the kid already figured that one out for himself.

CHAPTER 44

KC MET CHASE'S EYES, hoped he understood her unspoken message. She tapped a finger against her collar, watched as he responded by tapping his sleeve.

God, she could look into those eyes of his for a lifetime. She jerked her head to Deacon, and he nodded in reply. Too bad that lifetime was going to end in a few seconds, but as long as one of them got to Deacon before he triggered the bomb, it was worth it.

If only one of them made it out alive, she prayed it would be Chase.

Then she focused on Redman's drooling countenance. "What's wrong, Redman? Scared you won't be able to get it up when it counts? Have to resort to a bullet in the head—kind of cliché, don't you think?"

Redman twitched, his eyes narrowing with fury. "Bitch, you're going get everything you deserve."

He slammed the gun across her face. KC saw the blow coming and was able to roll with it, deflecting most of the force. Still her vision blurred for a moment, and her nose began to bleed.

The diversion had the effect she was aiming for, Chase's guards had pretty much forgotten about him and were focused on her, and most importantly, she was able to slide her knife hilt into her fingers, ready to use.

Redman returned the gun to her forehead, his finger caressing the trigger.

"Now!" she called out as she drew her knife and thrust it deep within Redman's throat, burying it in his windpipe.

He pulled the trigger on the Glock. The shot went wild as he crumbled to the ground, still holding the gun in a death grip.

She saw the flash of a knife fly past her, heard Deacon cry out and looked over.

Deacon was holding his arm, blood seeping between his fingers, but was still standing. She glanced at Chase who'd grabbed one guard's gun and turned it on its previous owner.

The second guard was sprawled on the floor, she hadn't seen how he'd gotten there, probably a kick from Chase, but he aiming his gun at Chase.

"Look out!" Chase called out a warning to her, but she was already raising the Glock, still wrapped in Redman's dead hand, targeting the man aiming at Chase.

The sound of gunfire screamed and echoed through the room, and the man beside Redman fell on her.

KC pushed the corpse away, thankful for Chase's quick shooting. Her own aim had been true, the man trying to kill Chase lay gasping, blood staining his shirt on the floor.

Chase was running across the gymnasium, pistol clutched in his hand, following Deacon.

LUCKY HUFFED AND PUFFED as he and Neil struggled with the

heavy car. Finally they got it going fast enough that all he needed to
do was steer.

"Get out of here," he said.

The kid ran back to the churches. As Lucky passed the school,
he saw a familiar figure slipping into the gymnasium. What the hell?
It was the Preacher.

He could catch him, put an end to it all. But he couldn't leave
the car—it was a juggernaut now, heading down Main Street,
crowds of people streaming the opposite direction. Several burly
looking SWAT guys appeared, trying to block his way.

Were they nuts? Did they think he wanted to stay with this
Death Star on wheels?

"I'm ATF," he shouted at them, wrestling with the steering
wheel with his one good hand. "There's a bomb in this car, we need
to get it out of here."

They looked doubtful at first, disarmed by his brilliant disguise,
no doubt, but then two of them took up positions on either side, one
of them replacing Lucky at the steering wheel.

"The football field!" one of the cops shouted, and the two men
began aiming the car toward the empty expanse of snow beside the
school.

"HOLD IT!" CHASE SHOUTED to Deacon. The other man
skidded to a stop beneath the basketball hoop. "Give it up," he
continued.

Deacon's eyes cut over to the back doors of the gymnasium
which now stood open. Chase could have sworn they'd been closed
a few moments ago, but he didn't see anyone nearby and had more
important things to concentrate on.

"Looks like we have a stand-off," Deacon said. He reached into his coat pocket and pulled out the remote. "Don't make me call all those babies home to Jesus, Chase. Don't you make me do that."

Chase stared at the other man. Shoot him and he might still be able to activate the remote—all it would take is the wrong twitch of a muscle, one nerve ending firing. He lowered his weapon.

"Deacon, think of Tanesha. What would she want you to do?" He furiously thought, trying to remember a bible verse that might sway the other man. The Psalm on Diana's tombstone was the only one that he could think of. "For He will save the children, and precious shall their blood be in His sight."

Deacon jerked his head up at Chase's words.

"You know that's true, Deacon. You believe. Just give me the remote—" Chase stepped forward.

Deacon raised the remote, held his thumb over it. "Don't think so, Westin. The Lord has more work for me to do. He will bring justice to the poor and break in pieces the oppressor."

His eyes narrowed as he gave Chase an appraising look. "You too, maybe. Drop the gun, kick it over."

Chase had no choice. He had to end this now, before KC's back up arrived and came in guns blazing and Deacon pressed that button. He placed the semi-automatic onto the floor and kicked it away from Deacon into the bleachers.

"Heard you were a wide out in high school," Deacon said, the same smile on his face he wore right before he won a round of poker. "I'll give you a chance. It's all up to you, Westin."

He cocked his arm back and aimed the remote in a high spiral across the gym.

Chase swore, pivoting. He sprinted as if it was his life that depended on the outcome.

His body remembered the old moves, he could almost hear Nicky Gianotti cheering him on with their old war cry, "Gianotti to

Westin, the one-two punch!", as he dove into the air.

Bullets flew around Chase, but he paid them no heed, his entire being focused on one small black square of plastic. If it hit too hard, would the bomb go off? Chase had no idea, was taking no chances.

As he leapt for the remote, putting all his strength into the last ditch effort, he saw a dark suited figure silhouetted in the open gymnasium doors and heard a gunshot.

He didn't feel anything except gratitude as the remote landed in his hand. He hit the floor, crashed against the bleachers and everything went black for a moment.

"Are you hit?" KC collapsed to the ground beside Chase, her hands flying over his body, checking for injuries.

Chase pushed himself upright. He opened his hand and revealed the remote cradled within his palm.

KC couldn't stop the small, choking laugh that emerged from her. She stared at the carnage around her, the coppery acrid stench of cordite and blood filling her nostrils. She shook her head, her ears were still ringing from the concussive weapons discharge.

They were alive. They were both alive. The words echoed through her mind, shutting out everything else.

Chase sat back on his heels, his hands tugging at hers, squeezing so hard her fingers went white. She was surprised to see silent tears slip from his eyes.

"Chase, are you hurt?" KC pulled one of her hands from his, brushed a tear away from his face.

He laughed. "It's the adrenalin, gets me every time, once the bullets stop flying. Some guys barf, some get the shakes—I cry like a baby."

Chase put an arm around her, pulled her tight as the rest of her team crashed through the door, weapons drawn.

"Stand down," KC ordered, her voice more steady now. She stood up, caught herself as she wobbled a bit. "Glenn, clear the weapons and tag them, Carson, check for survivors. This is a crime scene now, people. Let's do it by the book."

Chase held her hand, standing beside her as her people moved to do their jobs.

"You shot Deacon?" Chase asked.

KC looked past him, saw that a single bullet had torn through the center of Deacon's forehead. Great shot, but it wasn't hers.

"That wasn't you?" she asked. He shook his head. "It wasn't me, either."

"One of your men? I saw a guy come to the doorway," he nodded to the rear door.

Before he could say anything more his friend with the goofy overalls appeared there.

"Chase, why'd you let him go?" Lucky called out.

"It's okay guys," KC called when one of the Staties challenged the newcomer. "Let him through."

Chase held her hand as he made formal introductions. Lucky looked like he'd had a rough time of it, his left arm dragged at his side and his face was bruised and swollen. Of course she didn't look her best at the moment either.

"You let him go," Lucky repeated, collapsing onto the bleachers, tugging at his hair in frustration. "All that work for nothing."

"What are you talking about?" Chase asked. "We tried to take Deacon alive."

"Not Deacon. The other guy, the one in the suit. He shot Deacon, cool as you please. Then walked out again. He's the real Crusade leader. They call him Preacher."

Chase looked at the door. "Someone get out there, see if you can find anything," he ordered.

"I really blew it," KC said, echoes of gunfire still ringing in her head. "We lost Gianotti, we lost Deacon, I'm out of leads and these guys are planning something big."

She turned to Chase, her mind spinning with recriminations. "You going to fill me in now? Who are you really working for? What was The Crusade going to use those weapons for?"

Chase looked down at her, and she realized she was shaking uncontrollably.

"It's the adrenalin," he repeated. "Are you going to be sick? Best not to compromise any evidence."

Damn him, how could he be so calm? She'd just killed four men, of course she felt sick.

"Before today I never even fired my weapon in the line. Never. My ops don't go south like this. I plan for every contingency—except you. You owe me an explanation, Westin."

He frowned at her, ignored her glare. "It's on a need to know basis."

"Bull. If people are shooting at me, then I'd say I need to know, wouldn't you?" Her voice was trembling.

Adrenalin, he'd said. Did that explain the nausea and the sweat pouring down her back? She felt like she might faint.

KC put a hand out to steady herself and Chase caught her, his arm circling around her waist as he helped her to a seat on the bleachers beside his friend.

"Just put your head between your knees and breathe, it will pass," he coached her.

She slumped forward, but the dizziness only grew worse.

"Chase—" she didn't have the energy to say more.

All she could do was look up to see him staring at his hand that had rested on her back.

Blood dripped from his fingers onto the gym floor. Then everything went black.

CHAPTER 45

GOD, SHE LOOKED SO vulnerable lying on the gurney, naked from the waist up. The doctor had her lying on her stomach, and Chase couldn't take his eyes from the bloody furrow plowed through her flesh from her left shoulder blade angling toward her spine.

His hand tightened on the leather jacket KC had worn. Damn thing saved her life. The bullet had ricocheted off one of the metal rings so it only grazed her. If she'd been wearing ordinary clothes instead of her Hollywood hype costume she would be dead now.

Chase clenched his teeth against the sucker punch of fear that came with that thought. The doctor adjusted KC's IV then began flushing the angry looking wound.

"Can't stitch it. It'll heal like a partial thickness burn. She'll have a scar of course, but she's lucky, a slightly different trajectory and—"

Chase closed his eyes, blocking out the doctor's words, remembering the muzzle flare of Redman's gun firing as KC stabbed him.

God Almighty, if she'd been a second slower or moved an inch the wrong way, that bullet would have torn through her neck.

He opened his eyes, forcing the vision of KC's lifeless body from his mind. KC moaned, and he squatted down so that he was at her eye level.

"What's wrong? Something's wrong," he shouted to the doctor.

"Let the man do his job." Her voice sounded muffled, distant. "Sooner he finishes, sooner I can kick your butt for getting me into this mess."

"She'll be fine," the doctor said with a smile. "A little woozy from the blood loss and the morphine, but once I'm finished and we get more fluids into her, she'll be good to go."

"Go where? You're keeping her here, aren't you?"

"No need, a few more hours, some antibiotics and she can go home."

Chase was relieved KC would be all right but the last thing he wanted was for her chasing after The Crusade on her own. And he had a good idea that was exactly what she would do.

"There," the doctor said. "I'm all done, I'll give you folks some privacy."

Chase began to follow the doctor, hoping to convince him to keep KC overnight at least. The door to the treatment room opened and Hollywood entered.

"Heyya champ, Rose is looking for you. Lucky's stuck here overnight, they want to monitor his heart." He glanced over at KC's wound and pursed his lips in admiration. "Nice one."

Hollywood met the glare KC sent his way without flinching. "Hi, I'm Hollywood, I'm with him. You must be Special Agent Zd— Zdzieba."

He stuttered out KC's last name, and Chase realized Hollywood knew more about KC than he did. She'd never told him her real name.

Hollywood's gaze traveled down to glimpse KC's naked breasts. Jealousy flared through Chase.

KC raised an eyebrow at Hollywood. "This isn't a free show," she said in an ominous voice that made both men jump.

Chase grabbed Hollywood by the shoulders and propelled him toward the door.

"Pleased to meet you, ma'am," Hollywood said as Chase shoved him out of the room.

KC rested her head on her arms. "If you're not going to help me, then just get out," she told Chase. "Go away, leave me alone, I'll take the heat for everything. It was my op, it's my fault."

"I beg to differ, Special Agent Zdzieba."

Chase looked up to see Rose Prospero striding through the door, somehow looking starched and pressed in faded jeans and a Ravens' sweatshirt.

Thank God, someone who could talk some sense into KC. Go away? She couldn't mean that. He wasn't leaving her, not after everything they'd been through. How could she even think that?

"Who are you?" KC asked, raising her head and looking at Rose with a gleam of interest.

"Rose Prospero. I'm his boss." She nodded at Chase.

"You in charge of the Brad Pitt look-alike as well?"

"So you've met Hollywood. Yes, he's one of mine."

"What part of the alphabet soup are you people from? CIA, NSA, ATF? What's the story? Maybe if you tell me what's going on I can help."

Rose smiled. "Nice try. You know it doesn't work that way. I am curious why the FBI was in charge of an arms smuggling investigation. And why your superiors have the mistaken impression that you're collecting evidence on a RICO case in Reading."

KC groaned and dropped her head once more. Chase moved to her side, uncertain where to touch her without hurting her more, only knowing that he had to touch her. He patted her head then eased one of her hands out for him to hold.

"Rose, she's been through a lot. Can't this wait?"

He almost wished he hadn't said anything when Rose cut a glare his way. She seemed angry and surprised by his words.

"You of all people know it can't. One of my people is lying in a bed next door and both of you could have been killed. And, thanks to this debacle, we have no idea what The Crusade is planning."

He winced at the truth behind her words. KC jerked her head up at the mention of The Crusade.

"The Crusade? I'm in." KC swung her legs around and pushed herself to a sitting position. She didn't seem to care that she was naked from the waist up.

Chase grabbed a hospital gown and draped it around her. Her face had gone pale once more and a sheen of sweat showed on her upper lip.

"Lie back down, KC. The doctor said—"

"The doctor said I'll be fine. Get me my clothes."

"You're not going anywhere."

"Like hell I'm not. Who are you to tell me what I can or can't do? You don't know anything about me—"

"You're right, at least you know my name." Chase heard the anger in his voice and tried to force it back.

"Hers is Konstantina Christabel Zdzieba," Rose said in a soft voice. Damn, Chase had forgotten she was there. "Chase, why don't you find Agent Zdzieba something to wear under her coat?" She indicated the leather jacket that Chase still clung to. "Give us a minute."

Chase hesitated, but Rose had moved to stand beside KC,

effectively cutting him out.

"How much do you know?" Rose asked KC. Chase paused at the door, hoping to be invited to stay.

"Nothing. He," KC jerked her head at Chase, "wouldn't tell me anything. I thought he was working for Gianotti at first. Imagine my surprise when I get dragged into things, and he's on the other side holding a gun on me."

"I told you to trust me. It was need to know," Chase protested.

"I'll handle this," Rose said in her voice of command. "Now, go."

Chase absorbed the icy glare KC threw at him and decided to exercise the better part of valor. He retreated into the neutral territory of the hallway.

BILLY PRICE LOOKED UP from his conversation with the two State Troopers who were trying to pump him for information about the corpse they'd found in the Westin house. The one with the bullet hole in the middle of his forehead, his arms and legs bound by strapping tape. Chase Westin stampeded down the hall toward him, a leather jacket clutched in his hand like it was the flag at Iwo Jima.

"I'm out, as of now. Want it in writing?" Chase demanded as he came to a halt.

The two troopers looked up, eyebrows raised, but Billy just chuckled and took Chase by the arm.

"Let's talk this over like reasonable men," he said, guiding Chase into an empty exam room.

"I almost lost everything today, so excuse me if I don't feel very reasonable. Tell Rose I'm out, I quit, I'm done."

"You selfish bastard." Billy didn't hold back. "You know what's at stake, you know Rose isn't asking anything of you that she wouldn't do herself."

"I can't do it anymore. I can't lie to the people I love. I almost lost my brother and KC because I couldn't tell them the truth. It's not going to happen again."

"You're choosing a woman over the needs of your country? That doesn't sound like you, Westin."

Chase faltered, took a step back and Billy thought maybe he had him. Then a look of wonder crossed the ex-Marine's face, like a kid opening the best Christmas present ever.

"Yeah," Chase blew out the syllable, nodding as if liking the sound of it. "Yes, that's exactly what I'm doing."

"C'mon, Westin. Think it over, you don't have to quit The Team."

"You know as well as I do that Rose doesn't like her people to have any attachments. And I planned to be attached for hopefully a long, long time."

Billy looked up at that. Chase Westin taking the plunge? Walking away from the job for the love of a woman?

Unbelievable, the man was a walking Marine recruitment poster—sacrifice all for Corps and Country.

The blissful look on Chase's face told him everything he needed to know. The guy had fallen, hard. Looked like he might keep on falling for a long time to come.

"Let me talk to Rose," he told Chase.

"Talk to her all you want, I'm not changing my mind."

ROSE SCRUTINIZED THE YOUNG FBI agent, noting how she handled the pain and the emotions of the day's events. She'd read Zdzieba's file on the way here, knew the official story. It was the unofficial story she was most interested in.

For an agent so young, Zdzieba had an impressive record. Rose understood her frustration over how this operation imploded, up until now every one of her assignments had ended in an arrest with no bloodshed.

"Why not the ATF?" she repeated her previous question, the one Zdzieba had so neatly dodged.

"Jay Westin didn't trust the local PD, he came to us. We were after Gianotti for murder and racketeering, not arms dealing, so why complicate things?" the younger woman said nonchalantly, more relaxed now that Chase was gone.

Rose looked more closely. Oh, this girl was good, very good—Chase definitely found himself a winner in Zdzieba. She almost had Rose fooled.

"Try again. The truth this time. Why did no one in your office know what you were working on?"

Zdzieba met Rose's gaze with a look of innocence, but Rose didn't back down. Finally Zdzieba shrugged, conceding the point.

"A lot of undercover agents have been burned in the past year, not just FBI either. There must be a leak somewhere. I knew I could trust my team but that was all, so I switched the case numbers so no one would ask questions or insist on calling the ATF."

"By no one, you mean your superior, Special Agent in Charge Halstrom?"

Zdzieba rolled her eyes and clucked her tongue. For a moment she looked exactly like the teenager she'd been playing in her undercover role.

"Yeah, the guy's a weasel. Look, I can give you a list of Gianotti's activities and contacts. The Crusade might try one of them if they still want those weapons."

"They do." The one thing Rose was certain of was that The Crusade wouldn't back down. They might be more careful in the future, but they weren't going away anytime soon. Not after being forced to sacrifice one of their own. They had to be planning something big. And she had the feeling that the clock was definitely ticking.

"Let me in on the action," Zdzieba continued. "I know Gianotti's organization like the back of my hand. I can help. I'm good, my cover's solid. Everyone who saw me at the meet is dead except Chase—" her voice trailed off, a frown furrowing her forehead.

"You can't send Chase back," Zdzieba said, her eyes meeting Rose's, pleading.

"Why not? Everyone who knows he's not kosher is dead, just like you said."

Chase was her sole remaining asset connected to The Crusade. Rose couldn't bench him, not if she was going to stop The Crusade before they acted.

"They suspected Chase before the meet," Zdzieba told her. "They swapped his ammo for blanks. His cover is blown. But no one connected with them ever saw me."

Rose considered that. She would have Billy go over the ballistic reports. But she couldn't risk The Crusade getting their hands on enough weapons to blow up Staten Island, not if there was the slightest chance of Chase stopping them. "I'll take it under consideration."

Zdzieba shook her head. "You can't risk it, it's too dangerous. I know who you guys are, well, I can guess anyway. There have been rumors of a covert group that gets called in when other counter-terrorist teams fail. We call you guys the Justice League over at the Hoover Building. You're like superheroes to the rest of us grunts."

Rose had to smile at the enthusiasm in Zdzieba's voice. Did the girl really think Rose didn't know a con job when she heard one?

Still, she rated an A for effort. The kid was good.

"Point is, I'd like to join you guys. Sign me up. I'll take Chase's place. I'm tight with Gianotti's son, know his contacts, I can use that as my in with The Crusade."

Rose almost took her up on her offer. The kid had talent, under other circumstances she might have invited her to join The Team. But not now, when she was wounded, barely functional, and it was all too obvious she and Chase were involved. Rose couldn't risk anything distracting her people from the job.

Chase returned before she could answer Zdzieba. He handed Zdzieba a surgical scrub top and helped her on with it. He winced when he looked upon Zdzieba's bullet wound, anguish crossing his face when a small painful noise escaped from the FBI agent.

Damn it, had Chase picked now, in the middle of the biggest red flag op they had going, to fall in love?

Her most steady operative. She couldn't lose him, not now when they needed him the most.

"Did you check on Jay?" Zdzieba asked him as he hovered over her.

"Yeah, he's fine. The Marshals are bringing him here."

"Chase, we have a lot of work to do." Rose ignored the look of fury Zdzieba sent her way at her interruption. "It was nice meeting you, Agent Zdzieba." She shook Zdzieba's free hand and started to the door, then paused. "I once knew a Konstantine Zdzieba, years ago in Razgravia."

The FBI agent straightened at that. "My grandfather. He went back to help the freedom fighters. He died there."

Rose nodded. She knew. She had cradled Konstantine's head in her lap as he took his last breath.

"Same man. He knew my grandmother back in the old days. Maybe when this is all over we can sit down, I'll tell you about it."

She left them alone for their farewells. "Five minutes, Chase."

CHASE REACHED FOR KC'S hand, drew close to her as he searched for the right words. The sound of running footsteps echoed down the hall and the door burst open before he could find them.

"KC, Chase said you'd been shot!" Jay said as he rushed into the exam room.

Chase reluctantly pulled back from KC. Damn, the kid had bad timing. Jared Wright, one of the Marshals, followed close on Jay's heels.

"Sorry, he got away from me," he said, his eyes cutting from KC to Chase, an eyebrow arched in question.

"S'all right, Jared," KC said. "Thanks for bringing him."

"Are you okay, KC?" Jay asked in a strained voice once the Marshal left. Then he whirled on Chase. "You let her get hurt! How could you?"

"It looks worse than it is," KC told him. "You and your brother saved my life."

"After she saved mine first," Chase put in, squeezing her hand in his.

The door opened, and Lucky walked in, tugging an IV pole and wearing a hospital gown that revealed more of his scrawny legs than Chase ever wanted to see.

Jeez, this place was busier than Grand Central. Couldn't anyone give them a few minutes alone? He needed to talk with KC, needed to know how she felt about everything, about him.

"Can't treat me like I'm some kind of invalid," Lucky was saying to someone over his shoulder. He grinned at KC. "Hi again, remember me? I just wanted to stop by, see what you're doing for the holidays—"

Chase threw Lucky a glare. "She's busy."

Lucky looked to KC for confirmation, "Really?"

KC gave Chase a full wattage smile. Chase decided his new mission in life was to make her smile like that more often.

"I guess so," she told Lucky, her gaze never leaving Chase. Her talk with Rose seemed to have calmed her down. That had to be a good thing, right?

Lucky turned to Jay. "You must be Jay. I'm Lucky, I work with your brother."

Jay looked over at the IV. "Were you shot, too?" he asked with wonder in his voice.

A shadow passed over Lucky's usually amiable face. Hollywood had told Chase what the man called the Preacher did to Lucky.

"Nah, but I was almost blown up. Your friend Neil helped, I'll bet he'd love to tell you about it."

"Great idea," Chase said, tugging at Lucky's IV pole so the ATF man had no choice but to follow. "Why don't you tell Jay all about it—somewhere else. Like the cafeteria."

Jay looked confused, but Lucky grinned and gave Chase a wink. "Sure thing, partner," he said, ushering Jay out into the hallway.

Chase turned back to KC, his fingers rubbing the small box in his pocket. He took a deep breath. Going into battle was a hell of a lot easier than this.

KC LOOKED UP AT Chase. He had a mournful expression on his face as if he'd just lost something vital to him. His hand kept stroking her arm, her hair, and she wondered if he was trying to find the words to say goodbye.

"Guess we really screwed things up," she said.

He grimaced, his gaze still on the door Lucky and Jay had exited through.

"Guess so." He sighed, then a half-smile crossed his face. "What were you thinking, crashing in there on my Harley?"

"Wasn't really thinking anything except that you were in danger. Freddie told me your gun was loaded with blanks."

"Crazy thing is, your stunt almost worked."

He ruffled her hair with his fingers, tilted her face back and looked appraisingly at her swollen eye. The doctor said nothing was broken, but she was certain that she had a beauty of a shiner starting.

"Until your friend, Lucky showed up."

"He thought you were going to kill me. Anyway, I owe you one."

"If you're keeping score, I figure it's about even."

She couldn't stop the shudder that crept over her as she remembered the firefight. His arm slipped around her waist, carefully avoiding the wound on her back.

"You were right earlier," he said. "None of this would have happened if I had trusted you. Every decision I made, I kept placing the job ahead of my feelings. And you, you kept doing all the wrong things for all the right reasons."

KC sighed and laid her head on his shoulder. She was so tired. "What can I say? I've never been in love before."

She felt him tense beside her. He slid off the gurney and stepped away from her, head hung low. Oh boy, here it comes. She'd lost everything on this operation. The Bureau would fire her, she'd be lucky to get a job as a meter maid, she'd killed four men—there'd be a price to pay for that, sooner or later—and now the man she'd done it all for was going to leave her.

"I was wrong, KC," he said, his voice barely audible. "Every time I chose the job over you—I was wrong."

He turned to her. "You're the answer to all my questions. I choose you, KC."

KC felt her mouth fall open. "You choose me?" A thrill of hope banished the weariness from her soul. "You mean—"

He pulled a slim box from his pocket and handed it to her. "They didn't have any rings at the gift shop," he said as she opened it.

A metal Medic Alert Bracelet lay on a small sheet of tissue paper. She dangled it from the chain, the red enamel Star of Life glittering in the fluorescent lights.

"Turn it over," he said. "There's this machine, you just type in what—"

"However long the journey," she read, interrupting him, "together, forever."

He shuffled toward her, took her hands in his. "I resigned from The Team," he said, his eyes meeting hers finally. "I'll go anywhere you want, do anything you want—" he faltered.

"Yes," she said in a clear, firm voice that belayed the quivering in her belly. "Whatever you're asking, the answer is yes."

He opened his mouth again, but she had no need for more words. KC covered it with hers, her free hand twisting in his hair, pulling him close.

EPILOGUE

ROSE FOUND BILLY IN the staff lounge, coordinating the search for The Crusade's mysterious hit man via his Blackberry. "Anything?"

"No, but that's no surprise. Lucky's going to work with a sketch artist on a composite."

She blew her breath out, resisted the urge to hit something. Damn it, they were so close. To almost lose both Chase and Lucky and still come up empty—frustration didn't even begin to come close to describing how she felt.

"Did Chase tell you he's leaving us?" Billy asked, adding more fuel to her bonfire of aggravation.

"No. You're kidding me, right?"

He shook his head, a sly grin playing across his features.

"It's that girl, isn't it? Damnation, I knew she was trouble the moment I laid eyes on her."

"I hear she's talented—excellent field skills, natural at undercover work, walking lie detector one of her Quantico instructors called her. She'd be a good addition to The Team."

Rose ignored him, pacing the room, looking for something expensive to break. Damn hospital, everything was made from plastic and Styrofoam.

"He's going to ask her to marry him, Rose," Billy continued as she settled for slamming the vending machine, earning herself a free Milky Way but little else. "Think what that could mean for The Team. Two for the price of one. And," he paused as if delivering a coup de grace, "she knows Razgravia. Her grandfather was Konstantine Zdzieba, Gregor's brother."

The Milky Way did take the edge off the gnawing in Rose's stomach. She pivoted and faced Billy. "You know my rule. No attachments."

"No outside attachments."

Did he not see what he was asking of her? If Chase and KC both worked for her, she might have to send one of them to their death, and face the other.

Or worse, have the other going off on their own instead of completing the mission. Maybe lose them both. Rose shook her head, an image of Victor Krakow, the SEAL murdered last week flashed through her mind. Krakow was about Chase's age.

What good was fighting this fight if she couldn't protect the people in it, give them some small chance at happiness when they found it?

"I can't," she said to Billy.

"Can't or won't? Rose, your job is to put the needs of this country above everything and everyone else. These are two consenting adults. Who are you to make this decision for them? It's your responsibility to the Team to at least ask them."

Rose turned away. The man knew her too well, knew exactly which buttons to push. He was right—she had to do what was best for the Team, even if she didn't think it might be the right thing for KC and Chase.

"Damn you, Billy Price," she muttered, hating the look of triumph that crossed his face. "You win. But you're coming with me to ask them."

"Me? You don't need me—" He trailed off as she grabbed his arm and marched him down the hall to the examination room.

Rose knocked first, but it had no effect. Nor did her throat clearing. Only Billy's ear piercing whistle seemed able to break the spell that embraced the couple.

Slowly, as if waking from a deep slumber, KC and Chase parted from a kiss that was X-rated in sensuality.

"I've a question to put to both of you," Rose said once she had their attention.

They turned and stood before her, holding hands like school children in crush. She sighed. This wasn't going to be easy. They were obviously mindlessly in love, and she was about to propose something that could ruin their lives.

"Chase," she started with him, thinking that, given his recent experiences, he might decline and make her job easier, "if you stayed on the Team and KC joined, would you be able to take orders from her, give her the freedom she needed to operate independently on missions, and do you think you could work with her, knowing that you may have to order her into dangerous situations?"

His mouth dropped open as he digested her words. Rose waited for his answer, hoping he understood the gravity of what she asked and turned her down. Instead, he straightened and gripped KC's hands tighter, his face breaking out into a wide grin.

"Rose, do you mean it? That would be great!"

She raised a hand to silence him. Should have known better than to start with him. KC was certain to be more levelheaded. Rose

310 | CJ LYONS

hoped. "How about you, KC? If you come on board, you'll have to leave the Bureau—"

"That's all right," KC interrupted her, "no way they're not going to fire my ass after today. Yes, I do, I will—"

"We will," Chase answered for them both, his eyes on KC, holding both her hands.

Rose sent a glare Billy's way. He slouched against the wall, smirking. She threw up her hands in resignation.

"Have it your way. As far as The Team's concerned, you're both on board. I now pronounce you man and wife."

She meant the last as sarcasm, but the man and woman before her took it literally, locking lips like a pair of teenagers.

Rose tried to conceal her grin. She remembered how it felt, once upon a time—a very long time ago.

KC broke away from Chase, reached into her jeans pocket and handed him a set of car keys. A brilliant smile lit his face as if sharing a private joke.

"You're driving, partner," KC said. Chase laughed, then pulled her into a soul-stirring embrace.

Billy sidled up to Rose, nodded to the young couple in love. "See, I told you it would all work out in the end."

"Then why do I have such a bad feeling about this?" Rose asked him. She tugged her second in command's arm and started toward the door. "C'mon, Billy. Give them some privacy. We've still got a madman to stop."

About CJ:

AS A PEDIATRIC ER doctor, New York Times Bestseller CJ Lyons has lived the life she writes about in her cutting edge Thrillers with Heart.

CJ has been called a "master within the genre" (Pittsburgh Magazine) and her work has been praised as "breathtakingly fast- paced" and "riveting" (Publishers Weekly) with "characters with beating hearts and three dimensions" (Newsday).

Learn more about CJ's Thrillers with Heart at www.cjlyons.net

Legacy Books

Made in the USA
Lexington, KY
05 September 2019